A Safe Retreat

By

Jessica Kapp Green

Prologue

1740

 secured the last knot, my mind numb with disbelief. Three lifeless bodies lay wrapped in the tangled weave of a hammock-one woman and two small children, all wearing threadbare, dirty garments; all gaunt and pale. Their cheeks hollowed like empty bowls. Holding them close to my chest one last time, their weight doubled by the canon ball entwined within the ropes, I stepped to the edge of the wooden ship.

"Dear God," the gut wrenching moan escaped from my lips. "Please forgive me." The water was ice to my fingers as I lay my family down on the great expanse of sea that was to have carried us to our dream. The impatient clearing of a throat came from behind.

"Let's get on with it then," the gruff voice of a sailor demanded.

I bowed my head in grief, as the tears finally ran free, coursing down my cheeks. *"Ich bin so leid,"* I sobbed, my arms now empty, "I am so sorry."

Part One

Johannes

Chapter 1

Born to thrive amidst challenge, I always thought of my adventurous spirit as a gift. But it led my family far from the safety of home and at times I reconsidered it to be a curse. Some would say I got what I deserved, that I was too willing to risk it all.

In the year 1715, we were just children; I eleven and she nine. Her melodic and cheerful voice floated down to me like a perfect snowflake and I looked up as the wisp of a girl reached the hilltop first, challenging me to catch up with her. I attempted to gain traction on the icy slope and irritably wiped a mitten across my frozen nose. The cold air burned my lungs as my breathing came fast and hard.

Picking up the pace, I slid my way to the starting point, careless of the dormant grapevines that flanked our sides in orderly rows. Humiliation painted my cheeks crimson at the idea of losing to this feisty girl…again. I glanced at the other boys, who thankfully also lagged behind, but then my gaze refocused on the daring little imp smiling at me and I narrowed my dark eyes in determination. Throwing caution to the wind, as its icy tentacles whipped through her long blond hair, she shot off down the hill.

Petite and pretty, Judith Massmuenster was a pixie-faced, self-proclaimed tomboy. Our culture- and her mother especially- made demands for her to act like a well-behaved Swiss girl, and I witnessed those attempts on special occasions as she begrudgingly plaited her hair into neat braids and donned fine linen gowns precisely stitched with colorful blossoms and blooms. But no one would have mistaken her for a French or Prussian princess and that was a badge she wore with honor. I tried to forgive her gender and grudgingly admitted that whenever she was around, life *was* more fun and interesting. Despite everything, she was my friend and though I liked to tease, I admired her spunk.

Trying to gain ground, but to no avail, I watched as her sled shrank in the distance. *I'll catch her someday,* I decided and my boyish laughter rang out in the crisp, fresh air. A playful smile was companion to the sparkle in my happy brown eyes, but my wry grin was soon erased as my hopes of winning slid further and further away and then ended altogether as Judith crossed the finish line with wild celebration. In the midst of her silly victory dance, she flashed me another smile as I slid to a stop.

Defeat stung, but though I acted like a scamp at times, my parents really had done their best to train me to act like a gentleman. Extending my hand to Judith, I stoically offered congratulations. "Not bad... for a girl," I admitted.

Mother would have approved my gallant gesture and I dared hope that reports of my actions would promptly find her as usual. She often reminded me of father's friends in high places among the bailiffs who acted as judges and lived in Münchenstein Castle. She declared that from their lofty perch in the fortress overlooking the village, they could see everything. An empty threat probably, as the exploits of a vexing boy must have been least among their concerns. But I never knew for sure, and I often cast a wary gaze upward just in case.

Despite its inhabitants I loved the castle, for it represented the history of my village. The once influential Münch family established the dwelling in the thirteenth century upon a foundation of solid rock, or in German, *Stein*. Over many years, bad political decisions and the canton's religious swing toward the Protestant religion eventually ebbed away the Münch family's Catholic clout. Finally, they were forced to sell the estate to the city of Basel and thus, so many years later, I lived in the shadow of Basel's bailiffs.

8

Aware that the town folks had their eyes trained on me too, one afternoon I tried to sneak home from the Birs River with a string of fish. I should have been at school, but the thought of fresh trout made my mouth water and my upcoming lessons paled in comparison to the beckoning spring sunshine and the call of trickling river water as it flowed through the east end of town. Just on the verge of completing a successful hiatus, my scheme was foiled.

A four-storied forge stood close to the river's edge and usually, the repetitive ting-ting-ting of metal banging upon anvil drifted from its tower. But on this day, instead of the normal resonating clangs, I heard the distant call of a bird. This detail alone should have piqued a warning, but I paid it no heed. Oblivious to its implications, I looked over my shoulder in the direction of the chirping melody trying to decipher its origin.

My bird call contemplations ceased when I ran directly into the blacksmith as he stepped from the doorway of the sweltering forge. Sweat leaked from his forehead and flowed down the crags of his severe face. With a rough, calloused hand he wiped at his brow and mopped the salty drippings from his chin with a yellow stained shirt-sleeve. Then drying his hand across the thick leather grain of his apron, he wordlessly reached out to take the fish. Offering them up with reluctant chagrin, I hoped at least to buy his silence, but apparently he was not the bargaining type. I should have kept those trout because he told Mother anyway.

Even the jolly-faced wine maker, who happily pressed grapes in the pink and olive toned *trotte* building at the center of town, managed to catch me involved in one harmless skirmish and felt compelled to inform my father. He might quip with us youngsters, but I found the base of his true allegiance. All of his jokes, good humored winks and thundering belly-laughs amounted to nothing.

Truly, I was a friendly child, but as I have just admitted, I was not above mischief and in the past caused my share of commotion. Yes, some people probably viewed me as a bit of a rascal back then, for my thoughts often took on a life of their own and landed me in a heap of trouble.

"What will become of Johannes Kapp?" I overheard an elderly woman question her companion one afternoon as I slipped down a narrow cobblestone street. Hunched toward each other, their shadows hovering like vultures against the gabled building behind

9

them, the two old women sat side by side on a rough wooden bench. Gossiping loudly and weighing my fate on the scales of their experience, their decrepit voices echoed harshly against the thick walls of the surrounding buildings, bounced off the hipped roofs of the ally-way homes and lodged firmly in my scorching ears.

"Yes, always into something, that one!" The other replied, pursing pale, narrow lips and arching a thinning grey eyebrow, acting as if I was a hopeless cause. Then, trying to make sense of the puzzle, she shook her head back and forth and marveled that such a youngster could belong to the town's *Untervogte*.

As a young child, I wasn't exactly sure what my father did every day at work, but I had heard the words "deputy magistrate" and "mayoral sheriff." All I knew was that he really did speak to those bailiffs up in the castle from time to time and that his children were expected to behave in a manner befitting the honorable *Untervogte*.

Well, I'm not evil, I consoled myself. *I just keep things interesting.*

Throughout that winter my days were spent playing with my brothers and sisters, attending school, doing chores and socializing with my family. Although Münchenstein enjoyed temperate weather compared to the more mountainous areas nearby, during the colder months we spent extra time inside, as did our animals. Sometimes, our conversations competed with the hens cackling as they roamed free in the warmth of the kitchen or with the loud bellows of cows stabled in the space that connected to our living quarters. The barn separated our residence from the livestock, but we were all contained under the same roof. The system did have some drawbacks, but made up for them through sheer convenience by saving us time, space and exposure to the elements.

I looked forward to evenings when my normally stern and busy father, Mathis, softened a bit and gathered my large family in front of the crackling fire at the center of our home to spin tales of days gone by and heroes of the past. A Swiss folk hero named William Tell was one of my father's favorite characters and he fed our greedy childhood imaginations with stories of bravery and valor. Visions of a tall, muscular man with curly hair and a beard jumped into our fantasy world. He could expertly draw an arrow from his leather

10

quiver and skillfully string his crossbow. Father launched into his story with great gusto, impressing upon us the seriousness of the situation.

"Small and frightened, a boy stood in front of William Tell…" he stared straight at me and paused for effect, "It was his very own son!" A collective chill ran through us as the story continued. "The child was forced to stand stock-still with a bright red apple on top of his head. Do you know why?"

"I know, I know!" piped up my sister, Barbara. "It was the hat!"

"Right you are, sweetheart. It was all because of the governor's terrible hat, raised up tall in the middle of the town square." Father scratched at his beard and said thoughtfully, "Always did remind me of that Bible story of Shadrack, Meshack, and Abednego… the way Governor Gessler thought so much of himself that he made people bow down whenever and to whatever he wanted them to, just like the king did in the Bible story."

Getting back on track, father continued. "William Tell would not bow before the Governor's hat." At this, father removed his own hat and held it up high. "The governor was mad as…" Father stopped mid-sentence and cast a quick look at Mamma who shot him a warning glance and frowned at the words that had almost slipped.

"Mathis!" she half-heartedly scowled in exasperation.

Father just smiled. "Well, let's just say, the governor could not let this man mock him in front of the crowd so he ordered a punishment. William Tell must either shoot the apple from his son's head… or be executed." Although we had heard the story countless times before, our eyes were wide and focused on father, expectant of what would happen next.

"In the quiver rested two arrows," he held up two fingers and mimicked the upcoming action, bringing the story to life as he became both actor and narrator. "Smoothly, he pulled out the first arrow. Taking careful aim he slowly inhaled, whispered a prayer, and with great faith…he let the arrow fly!" The arrow whistled through my imagination and I wondered if the little boy cried out in fear or if he trusted his father without doubt, remaining calm and quiet in the face of such grave danger.

Wiping his hand across his forehead in relief, Father continued. "Thankfully, that arrow split the apple in two, right down the middle and Mr. Tell's son walked away without a scratch on his head or a hair out of place!"

We cheered our hero, and pretended to shoot apples from each other's heads. Father quieted us and continued. "Later, the governor asked William Tell why he put two arrows and not just one in the quiver. That brave man looked the governor straight in the eyes and replied that if he had missed the apple and hit his son instead, he would have used the extra arrow to kill the governor!"

Our boisterous appreciation for this bold and courageous response was shushed by my mother, who cast a smile over her large brood and observed her husband with loving regard. I could see that she enjoyed watching him tell the story. We quieted down to hear the conclusion.

"Of course, the governor could not let such a brazen act of defiance go unpunished and swiftly, the guards secured William Tell and threw him aboard a ship bound for prison."

"Boo!" we hissed.

"But never fear! As legend goes, the great William Tell escaped the ship and when the governor got to the castle, who do you think was waiting for him?"

"William Tell! William Tell! William Tell!" I chimed along with everyone else.

"That's right! That old governor got what was coming to him when William Tell looked him straight in the eye and shot him dead with an arrow from his crossbow!"

"Oh!" my older sister Anna squirmed. "I don't like that part!"

"Well, maybe you don't dear one," father said, hugging her close to him and planting a kiss on the top of her head, despite the fact she was no longer a child, but a young woman. "But you know the legend…that in part, it was because of William Tell's bravery that the people rebelled against the government and formed the Swiss confederation."

Yes, we knew, for we had heard the story many times. My father loved history and inspired us with thrilling versions from the viewpoint of his imagination. In our living room, I met Roman Empire soldiers garbed in red tunics and heavy-soled sandals as they settled Basel, or as it was known in Latin at that time, *Basilia*. I witnessed the Catholic bishop collect money from Jews of Basel in 1225 in order to pay for construction of the Bridge over the Rhine.

My sisters openly wept as father told us how over one hundred years later, the Jewish people were kicked out of the city after being tortured and blamed for bringing the plague upon Basel. We struggled along as power shifted back and forth from Catholic to Protestant, and because our family belonged to the Reformed church, in 1536 we rejoiced along with John Calvin when he published his exposition during the Protestant Reformation.

So yes, we knew the legend of William Tell's bravery. One man set into motion such a grand chain of events and it inspired me, even as a young boy. This act of resistance to the governor's order taught me that one must be true to himself and stand firm in conviction. Even as a victim of injustice, William Tell did not give up, but through sheer will and skill he persevered and accomplished great things.

Routines filled up the winter days and Father's grand fireside stories comforted the nights. The cold clung to Switzerland far beyond its welcome, but finally as it always does, the icy drizzle melted into fresh spring rains and warm rays of sunshine fell upon us anew. Judith breezed into my life once again with summertime.

On a faultless June afternoon we took a short walk north through Basel and then settled amicably together on the banks of the Rhine River. Soft, billowy clouds floated above as we sat side by side, fishing poles and sandwiches at the ready. Light twinkled in reflection off the water, and contentedly we waited and hoped for the firm tug of a fish on the other end of the line. Judith, of course, was determined to catch the biggest fish. It was the kind of day to be looked back upon with a nostalgic smile, when one remembers the ease and simplicity of childhood.

The stillness was disturbed only slightly as Judith, momentarily distracted from her fishing quest, took a satisfying bite into her sandwich. I looked over and studied her for a moment before nonchalantly framing my question.

"How's your sandwich taste?" I asked, perhaps sounding a little too interested in the thick slab of cheese stuffed between the soft bread.

"Good," she smiled sweetly.

"I'm glad you're enjoying it," I replied, covering a smirk behind my bait-smeared hands and crusty dirty fingernails.

Suspicion flitting across her gaze, she cautiously took another smaller bite. Her complexion blanched and she drew in a sharp breath as her cheeks puffed in protest. A pale lump of expelled bread and half a wiggling worm sailed into the river. Mouth wide, inhaling deeply, and drawing her eyebrows together in distress…. a high pitched squealing scream rang out that surely scared away any remaining fish and made the squirrels scamper for cover.

'It just doesn't get any better than this,' I thought, regretting the lack of audience. But my laughter was checked by a funny feeling, akin to regret and remorse pulling at my conscience as unexpectedly, a tear drop trickled down Judith's cheek. I reached out with my muddy hand to brush it away, feeling guilty for causing such distress and for breaching the friendship that we had formed. I knew in that instant I would not be sharing my story with the other boys like I had planned.

She let me wipe away the tear. I don't think I have ever felt anything quite as soft as her tender cheek was that day. She sat motionless in the grass, my hand upon her. I did not recognize what it was, but young as we were, something changed for me.

I did not dwell on these new found emotions, for the moment was fleeting. Judith slapped my hand away as if it were a venomous bee and looked at me with wide, hurt eyes that reminded me of a deer staring at a hunter in the forest. Slowly it dawned on me that her eyes were starting to remind me more of a wild cat as they narrowed into a vengeful glow.

"You are going to pay for this, Johannes!" Judith exploded, jumping up from the grass, making a full recovery. The chase was on as I sprinted away from her, down the winding trail. Silver-gray beech tree branches waved me on toward my village home, as Judith followed close behind.

She never really did get over the worm sandwich and I paid for it by baiting her fishing line over the rest of that summer. We avoided taking our trips over lunch-time. It still surprises me that she was willing to be my fishing companion at all.

As we grew, I could not help but continue teasing Judith just a little bit. She did eventually get past that tomboy stage, but then I found it an irresistible challenge to try to make her cheeks blush when I called her name or watch her become tongue-tied trying to defend herself against my attention. At first, she seemed an easy target for my silly jokes and lighthearted jesting, but it did not take me long to find out that I underestimated her.

Though still petite and thin, once she laid claim to the woman within, there was renewed power in the virulent looks she sent my way. She could just as easily shoot searing daggers through my heart with a glance or leave me wondering about the frozen reserve I saw in her icy blue eyes. I was always willing to risk a steely gaze from Judith on the chance that I might get to see one genuine smile. And it usually came. I guess she was helpless to prevent it. In those moments I began to believe that deep within she really did like me. After all, who could resist my charm?

Chapter 2

Eventually I realized that my exasperating childhood tricks and tendency to misbehave were unfair to my mother and father, for they endeavored to raise me right and had seen to it that I received a proper education and attended church regularly. I counted myself fortunate to have parents who appreciated the value of a good education and understood that not all children had the same advantage. A heavy emphasis was placed on religion within the school and much of our learning focused on the Bible. But besides religion, the altruistic school master thoroughly instructed me in reading, writing and arithmetic and later on in secondary school, I excelled in my memorization of Latin and Greek.

While I attempted impulse control for the benefit of my parents, teachers and community at large, it did little to squelch my spirit of adventure. Small village monotony bored me. Now don't misunderstand me, I loved my family, friends and Münchenstein, but I was looking for something new. Come to think of it, I was always looking toward the next thing…anything… hoping it would make life better. Relentlessly, I pursued each next experience, trying to fill an emptiness I could not explain or understand.

When I was nearly fifteen, I made the decision to become an apprentice wagon maker. Like other merchants and tradesmen, such as carpenters, blacksmiths and butchers, I joined a guild which had been organized hundreds of years before to promote standards and fair practice. In my naivety, I supposed that my participation in a guild would eventually afford me at least some small semblance of authority or prestige, or maybe someday a magnificent mansion in Basel, but I would soon learn that only the wealthiest of merchants and tradesmen achieved that kind of power.

Rather a strange juxtaposition I suppose...finding independence by signing an apprentice indenture. Binding myself to a "master" for years sat a bit uneasy with me, but I chose to focus on the relationship between teacher and student, and not subservient slave to owner. Maybe it wouldn't be as glamorous as going off to fight war and maybe I wouldn't be gaining fame or fortune, but the prospect of learning the art from a master and then traveling to neighboring countries sounded interesting. And it met my main goal of getting out of Münchenstein for a while.

On my birthday, father presented me with two gifts. The first, an intricately crafted small wooden box, designed for carrying my guild papers and valuables; the second, a horse. Perhaps both gifts were a bit premature, as most of my traveling would take place in later years after completing my apprenticeship and beginning my time as a journeyman. However, they were appreciated nonetheless.

"A man needs a reliable horse, Johannes" my father had said with authority, leveling his steady gaze at me. "Train him with discipline and patience and in time you will have yourself a dependable companion."

The horse whinnied and my feet kicked up the fresh but dusty straw of the stall as I brushed him. I wanted to make sure he looked his best for our upcoming journey south, where I would begin my apprenticeship. Running my hand over his soft muzzle I crooned to the animal, "What a noble steed you are!" I said the words and then had to laugh, for I could not lie, even to a horse. I toned down the compliment. "Well, 'Noble Steed' might be a bit of an exaggeration. "But you're a solid horse; nothing wrong with you at all," I said, slapping him firmly on the hindquarter.

The horse was not from champion stock, but he was the best my family could afford. I filled his bucket with feed and inhaled the scent of horse, hay and grain. As the animal pushed his mahogany-colored head up against my shoulder, his intelligent ebony eyes reflected the excitement that burned in my own.

Proudly, I straddled my mount and father followed closely beside on his own horse, a Swiss bred Warmblood. I would miss home, but I was eager for the new opportunity. Most of my friends were content to stay closer to town, but I welcomed the change. In my opinion, there would be plenty of time later on in life to settle down. As we traversed the dirt road, the horses remained alert and their energy was only bridled by the reigns in our hands. We planned to reach our destination of a small village, still within Switzerland, the following day.

I would begin my apprenticeship with one of my father's friends, a master wagon maker. Living and eating with the family as I learned the trade, I would earn no money at first. Eventually, after a few years, I would hopefully move up to junior apprentice and might make a small income. Thereafter I would travel as a wandering journeyman, or a so called *Wandergeselle,* learning and working in different workshops throughout the region and in other countries. However, it would not be until I created a worthy model of perfection, that I would be considered a 'Master' and approved to practice my trade and hopefully profit well from it.

After two days on the trail, the sun centered itself high in the early summer sky when my father and I wearily approached a country inn. Our horses' steps remained steady even as their coats glistened with sweat. Father continued to be an active man at fifty-five years of age, but his bones were tired from jouncing across the undulating terrain. I knew that the site of a well-kept inn along with the promise of a cool drink made us both feel refreshed already.

"Glad to finally see this place," father acknowledged, jutting his chin out towards the attractively gabled, four-story building. Cheery red blooms spilled out from window boxes lining the first story windows.

"Me too," I agreed, my voice carrying the husky ring of a boy turning man. The open air was invigorating and served to heighten my already demanding teenage appetite.

We securely tied our horses to a hitching post at the front gate and entered the inn through a heavy wooden front door. The interior was considerably cooler than outside, the sturdy wood beams of the walls insulating the rooms from the summer warmth. Though dim when compared to the radiance of the noon-day sun outside, light spilled through the many windows and reflected off of the polished wood floors, providing the room with a welcoming cheer.

"*Willkommen!*" greeted an attractive, brunette woman whom I judged to be about twenty-five years old. She carried herself with a sense of purpose and dignity, and her charming nature perfectly suited her role as hostess. "My name is Anna Maria," she said warmly. "My husband Hans and I are so happy that you have come to spend time with us! How may I help you gentlemen?"

"Thank you for your kindness," replied father, removing the hat from his head and casting a meaningful look toward me to do the same. "We plan to stay only for a night until we get my son settled with a family who lives quite a bit further down the road. Johannes will be apprenticing as a wagon maker," he said with just the barest hint of pride, which was observed by the perceptive innkeeper's wife.

"How wonderful for you, Johannes. You must be thrilled!" She seemed genuinely pleased for me.

"Yes, Ma'am. I have been looking forward to it for a long time," I responded.

"Now, before we get you situated in your room, have a seat at one of the tables and let me get you a drink. I'll have my oldest son take your horses to a stall."

Only too happy to oblige, we placed our leather satchels on the floor and settled into one of the sturdy, but well-worn chairs and took in our surroundings. Multiple tables and chairs filled the expansive dining area and heavy, dark beams ran the length of the high ceiling above, making the area feel cozy despite its size. Finely woven tablecloths graced each seating area and we could see that the pewter dishes provided to the men at the neighboring table were of good quality. Cleanliness and order prevailed in the space, announcing the owners' ambitions of excellence and commitment to hard work.

Soon, Anna Maria hurried through the kitchen door, carrying one glass. My eyes traveled from that glass downward, where a little girl around the age of three carefully carried the other. Her eyes were glued to the cup and both hands grasped it firmly. Her mother used her free hand to guide her daughter toward us.

"Mr. Kapp. Johannes. This is my daughter, Katharina. She is my helper today." She smiled down lovingly at the girl. Katharina looked up with a confident smile, and offered the cup to me. She had thick dark hair like her mother's, and deep brown eyes that sparkled with intellect.

"Thank you, Katharina." I gently took the drink from her and somehow in this simple act of being served by the small girl, I felt for the first time as if I had finally broken totally free from the ranks of childhood and was being treated as a man.

"Du bist willkommen, Sir, " she replied and curtsied cutely. then retrieved her doll from her mother, cuddled it to her and rocked it in her arms. Pressing up against her mother's skirt, she hugged her leg as they walked back to the kitchen. My feelings of maturity quickly dispelled as I unwillingly felt a pang of homesickness for my own mother. But for better or worse, the decision was made and I was on my own.

Chapter 3

The years passed quickly as I worked alongside my father's friend. He expertly and patiently passed down tricks of the trade and I learned that being a self sufficient master required a combination of skills belonging to blacksmith, carpenter and wheelwright, ultimately culminating in wagon maker. Many men worked side by side on projects with these other skilled laborers, but it was important to be independently capable of each job.

After completing my apprenticeship, I traveled, spending my time as a journeyman in France, Germany and Italy, gleaning additional knowledge from other hardworking and proficient wagon makers. Speaking my native German tongue came most naturally of course, but having lived in such close proximity to our neighboring countries, I had also been well educated in the French and Italian languages so had no trouble communicating.

Oak, ash, beech and elm, I learned to speak their languages too, and I became adept at identifying and choosing the best specimens the woodlands offered. To build a strong and tight wagon, each part required a specific type of wood. Wheel construction was of paramount importance and exact calculation was imperative, for if the wheel was not precisely rounded, a man might as well start over. I preferred using elm for wheels, as it was less likely to split, and ash for the hubs. Besides meticulous attention to this type of detail, the

23

wagon making craft demanded endurance, for once the tree was chosen and felled it must be left to season for five or six additional years until ready to be cut into usable timber. After that, the wagon itself could take up to six months to complete.

Progressing well towards my goals, I was no longer a young boy missing my mother. Though consumed with the work of perfecting my trade, I made time to absorb the culture of each new city as I traveled. Intellectual stimulation, an emphasis on reason, a yearning towards freedom of expression; it was a time of illumination throughout Europe and I did not want to miss out on it. An age of *"Aufklärung,"* as we said in German and in French, *"les Lumières."*

While the sons of European gentry took their *Grand Tour* of Europe, I did the same, albeit in a more round-about nature and without an entourage of personal cooks, valets and guides such as I saw trailing many wealthy young Englishmen. They seemed to think highly of themselves and their ability to absorb cultures around them and many took it as their mission to gather accounts and amass collectibles to take back to those "less fortunate" souls at home who were unable to travel. I happened to read an old book on the topic once, written in 1678, by Jean Gilhard called *The Compleat Gentleman*. He pointed out that *The Tour* only served to "reinforce the old preconceptions and prejudices about national characteristics" and observed each as such: "French courteous. Spanish lordy. Italian amorous. German Clownish."[96]

Gilhard's assessment of the French people may have been mostly true, and to be fair, I met many respectable and kind Frenchmen. But unfortunately, I also had numerous personal experiences among the community which proved counter to his observations. Those in high society may have been known for their superior manners and sophisticated fashion, but I found this was not always the case among the men of more humble origins which I encountered.

As an example, I present my experiences at the French theater. After an exhausting day of complex computations and muscle straining exertion, I desired the reward of rest and relaxation. The public working folks in France, such as local students, laborers, journalists and myself included, enjoyed spending free time in the *"parterre"*, or pit, of the French theater, and so I made my way there one warm summer evening. Along with my crowd, I stood on the floor in front of the stage, while those with more ample means, perhaps those more "courteous French," occupied the box seats which rose from floor to ceiling around us.

The actresses twittered and twirled elegantly upon the stage, the soft folds of their elaborate dresses billowing with the dance. Vibrant pink rose petals and luscious purple iris blooms accented complexly arranged mounds of cascading hair and I wondered in passing just how long it took those ladies to get ready before the show. The actresses surely wore the finest French perfume and my thoughts ruminated in the illusively sweet warm tones of jasmine and the addictively cheerful scent of orange blossom. The actors, I will admit, were of considerably less interest to me than their female counterparts. I did notice however, that they embellished the fashion of the day with dynamic wigs taller and grander than any I had ever seen before.

The acting troupe sang boisterously, competing with the crude laughter, persistent hisses and shrill whistles emanating from the boorish crowd around me. It was common knowledge that pick-pockets abounded and my valuables did not attend the theater with me, but remained tucked away secretly at my residence, locked securely in the wooden box father had given me. Truth be told, being in the *parterre* was almost like being involved in a side show of its own and held a certain excitement completely separate from the actual play.

Over the chaotic atmosphere, I tried to follow the plots unfolding on the stage. I always enjoyed the romantic comedies of Marivaux. Kidnappings and lies, love and lust, fairies and sorcerers…well, it kept my attention. I had also attended some productions by Voltaire and found these to be a bit more my style. Much different than the comedies, these were tragedies with deep political undertones that gave voice to the stirrings of unrest I felt in the working class as I made my way through France.

Gilhard hit the mark closer to where I stood when it came to his ideas of a "romantic Italy." The music of Italy stirred my soul. Sweet concertos of Vivaldi, performed by orphan choirs, enveloped me with melodies beautiful in singularity, but perfected in harmony. I was sad to have missed George Frideric Handel, whose operas had met with great success in Venice a decade earlier, but I determined I would not miss viewing the great masterpieces of artwork on display at a collection in Florence. Though usually only open to the elite, one day I casually made my way to the gallery, along with a large group of other young men my age who were on *Tour*. I spoke to no one, lest it be found out that I did not fit the standard required in being a person "of quality." Of course, this had nothing to do with anyone's true "quality," just the happenstance of their birth. My eyes were just as keen, probably more so than most noblemen's due to my years of deciphering detailed wagon patterns and making difficult calculations and adjustments to my form of artwork. I soaked in the colors, imaginations and emotions left behind hundreds of years earlier in the paintings of Leonardo da Vinci and Michelangelo.

While working in the Lower Palatinate of Germany, just north of Basel, I took in the sites of construction in Manheim where the new palace was being built for the ruling Prince-Elector. Only a few years into the project, and the tax payers already complained of the increased financial burden of the new palace tariff. As a young man now earning my own money, I found a new interest in this type of conversation. I sarcastically speculated that perhaps the drunken dwarfed court jester, known as Perkeo, might be able to cheer the disgruntled working class as he did the Prince-Elector. I guess Gilhard may have been right about some of the Germans too.

But, in contrast to the pomp and grandeur of prince and palace, I also became briefly acquainted with several Mennonite families who lived in the Rhine Palatinate. Their interaction with the broader population was limited, and the people I met lived simple lives in attempt to avoid outside influences that might distract them from Godly devotion. Personally, I did not understand why a person could not enjoy all good things the world had to offer and worship God too, but I admired their commitment.

Like the Jews from my father's stories, this deeply religious community had faced persecution by the government and church leadership. The Reformation of the 1500's sparked the flame of oppression, but a century later the situation was no better. In 1671, a large population fled their homes and relocated to the more welcoming environment of the Palatinate. Their non-conformist ways were better tolerated in no small part because of the industrious farming skills they brought with them. They took to heart the motto, *"no feed, no cattle; no cattle, no manure; no manure, no crop"* and developed mineral fertilizers, used manure to its greatest advantage and introduced "everlasting blue clover." On a Mennonite farm they grew the fields greener and the cattle fatter.

The Lower Palatinate was located just to the north of Basel, so I took a few days to visit my family during the week of Ash Wednesday in 1723. Returning home was a good feeling, but strange. Everything was the same, except for me. At nineteen years of age, I had grown, changed and matured. An invisible threshold crossed, I could not go back to what once was.

While home, I spent many hours of the week in Basel, reveling and participating in the Fasnacht Carnival. It was something that I looked forward to every year. The festival was ancient, said to have begun back in the 1500's. The entire community participated; from the top of society, right down to the poor who lived on the street.

In the black of night, costumed groups paraded in the dark streets, the lantern light casting shadows upon their masks and instruments. The smiling, fixed expressions on the masks, although festive, lent a surreal and eerie tone, lending to the mystery and excitement. Marchers ruled Basel, playing lively music and throwing sugar ball confetti.

"That drum sounds good," said Jacob Künzly. Although he was a few years older than me, he was one of my closest friends. "How did you find time to practice?" he questioned.

Looking at him through the eye-holes in my costume mask, I laughed. "I haven't had time to practice at all! I'm just talented," I smiled with confidence.

Although joking with my friend, most of what I said was true. Extensive travel did not leave much time for practicing music, but I had played the snare-like drum since childhood and was proud of my skillful ability to play it in the clique group as we marched together. We were only one of the many participating groups dressed in costume and parading in meandering routes through the city streets.

Jacob played a high, trilling note on his piccolo flute, the music floating away on the air like the song of a bird. "Not too bad yourself," I also acknowledged the proficiency of my friend. I closed my eyes. With the rhythmic rat- a-tat-tat of the drums and whistling flutes, I could almost imagine that we were marching off to battle instead of enjoying a parade.

As the night progressed, we stopped at one of the old city restaurants. "It feels wonderful to sit down and rest," I admitted, relaxing. "I always forget how tired I get from having all this *gut fun!*"

It was a special treat to eat at the city restaurants during this holiday time. They stayed open during the entire carnival. My friends and I chatted about the local news as we sat around the table.

"Did you notice how the government is cracking down on emigration?" questioned Jacob.

I had only heard bits and pieces of the news lately and asked him to tell me more. Jacob started to explain what he knew about a local Basel man who found himself in jail for telling people about the wonders of the colonies, but was interrupted when a pretty waitress brought a hot bowl of flour soup and some traditional *Zwiebelkuchen.* My mouth watered in anticipation as she set down the steaming hot *Zwiebelkuchen* in front of me. The comforting aroma of steamed onions, diced bacon, cream, caraway seeds and fresh baked dough assailed my senses. Across the table, one of my friends was digging into a creamy quiche-like baked *Käsewähe.*

"Hey Johannes, have you seen Judith since you've been back?" Jacob asked me, raising an eyebrow and giving a nod and wink to one of my other friends at the table.

I gave him a quizzical look and replied, "No. Why?"

"I saw her the other day, and I remembered how you two spent time together as kids, that's all." Jacob said easily, but there was a teasing tone in his voice.

He said no more about it and I thought it best to let the subject drop. I had not thought about Judith Massmuester for a long time. Sure, we had been friends as children, but that was far in the past. If Jacob wanted to talk about girls, I could describe for him the women of Italy and France, both of which I had accumulated some first-hand knowledge.

The serving girl made her way toward us again, offering drinks for all. My sense of magnetism at a peak, I accepted with a wink that I expected to send her blushing back to the kitchen. But evidently not the circumspect type, she returned my flirtation with a look of unexpected brimming intensity. A little more than I bargained for, I feigned distraction and quickly took up another conversation with the men.

We finished our meal with the glass of rich, local wine to quench our thirst. Only one glass for us, since Basel looked down upon any drunkenness involved with the carnival. *Ah, Basel*, I thought. *It's good to be home.*

The carnival ended and the following night, and as was tradition on the Saturday after the festival, I made my way from Münchenstein to a masquerade ball held at the home of a well-to-do family who lived in Basel. Their stately-looking home spoke of a family whose money came from generations of silk ribbon merchants. Having been exposed to large doses or reality during my *Wandergeselle* years, I no longer carried delusions of ever owning a similar home of my own.

In my estimation, the Kapp family sat squarely in the middle class of society, but we did have a few extra privileges because our family was native to the Münchenstein area. My own father's job as *Untervogt* rested upon the fact that our family's roots went deep there. Only families with such a heritage were allowed to hold public office. Still, we were not considered wealthy or noble, or anything of that sort. During carnival however, and especially during a masquerade ball, the lines of social classes became blurred and we intermingled quite freely with each other. Sometimes the beggars dressed as gentlemen and I heard that the kings in England sometimes dressed as paupers. But I doubted there was any need to expect a king that night, for Switzerland had no royalty of her own.

There was nothing like going to a masquerade ball, especially for a young man like me. In fact, a few years before I became so enamored by the excitement and mystery of the costumed women that I found myself dancing in the arms of a very intriguing female.

"Your costume is so beautiful. Such a lovely lady," my adolescent voice whispered in her ear.

Soon after, Jacob walked toward me purposefully. "Don't go falling in love, Johannes. She's a prostitute," he said bluntly and not quietly. Shock, surprise, and embarrassment must have registered on my face and I quickly excused myself to seek better company. I did not think to ask where Jacob obtained his knowledge.

I hoped for a better outcome as I made my way to the ball this year. The moon and stars were shining high in the black sky above. Perhaps this time I would find more suitable company. One never knew if hiding behind the mask was a wealthy heiress, or according to my former misfortune, a bawdy woman of ill repute.

Stepping from the shadowed street into the illuminated doorway of the lord's home, I waited with a group of other flamboyantly costumed guests to enter the party. I imagined that I was difficult to recognize. Gone were my every day workman's clothes, replaced with my mother's homemade rendition of Louis the XV, the ruling king of France. I might not be the most respected figure at the ball, but I did have an interesting outfit. Tall black boots, leather riding gloves, and a long ornately decorated jacket over a white puffed collar clothed my body. Atop my head, which sported a raven-black wig, rested a dark cap accented with an ivory vulture feather. My sister told me I looked "dashing" as I left home that evening and I believed her. My father's comments were less complimentary.

As I passed through the door, a servant cordially received me into the foyer, and invited me to take the narrow steps down to the basement where the party was being held. Noisy laughter wafted up the corridor as I descended. Stopping midway down the stairs, I surveyed the room below. The candlelight glimmered over the crowd, sparkling against ornate masks.

As usual, people had outdone themselves with their beautiful, outrageous, and gaudy costumes. To the right side of the room I could see one such spectacle. An old man, dressed in a white and wiry fur looked like a goat. On a leash beside him prancing, was the real thing. The goat cried loudly and obnoxiously, but the effect was hardly noticed by the excited party goers who were intoxicated with the festive mood.

I fiddled with the collar of my costume, trying to catch a cooler breeze in the stifling overcrowded space, but I stopped my hand in mid-adjustment of the lapel. A delightful vision smiled demurely and laughed with her friends along the back of the room. Something about her lithe, willowy form seemed very familiar. Her eyelashes fluttered enticingly through the openings in the partial mask of frosted feathers, and her full, crimson lips parted in a beguiling smile, but from a distance I was unable to conclude her true identity.

One thing I knew for certain - she was stunning. Dressed as a Greek goddess, the creamy-white fabric of the woman's gown clung alluringly to her body. A wreath rested upon hair arranged loosely and twirled atop her head. Shiny blond locks fell around her

30

delicate face and softly touched her elegant neck. A pristine diamond among the rough and common charcoal, she dazzled brighter than everyone else in the room.

I hurriedly finished my descent to the bottom of the stairs. I had to get a better look at her. Turning sideways, my solid shoulder and the harmless costume scabbard accidently bumped into another guest who blocked my path as I moved toward her. "Beg pardon," I murmured distractedly, intent on getting to my prize. I felt a tug on my costume and realized with annoyance that my sword had caught on the cape of a man dressed in black from head to toe, masquerading as a vampire. His disguise ill concealed his identity, and I immediately recognized him as one of the Bernoulli sons, a Basel family well known and respected for their brilliant scholars and mathematicians.

If rumor could be trusted, this particular son, Daniel, was thought to be among the brightest in his family. That was impressive, considering his father was one of the early developers of calculus and his uncle discovered the "theory of probability." Despite my quest to reach the other side of the room, after freeing my sword from the cape, I took a moment to address the man.

"Mr. Bernoulli," I acknowledged discreetly. "My name is Johannes Kapp. It is an honor to make your acquaintance."

Daniel Bernoulli eyed me sharply, looking down his straight long nose assessing me thoroughly, as he did with everything and everyone he contacted. He exuded a great sense of aplomb for one so young, only four years my senior, but a confidence earned on merit and not mere arrogance. Years of living with a father who feared being overshadowed by his son's accomplishments had taught him that a humble spirit brought much more peace and happiness than any satisfaction he would find in gloating.

"Yes, likewise an honor to meet you, Sir," Mr. Bernoulli replied. "A very good portrayal of King Louis," he complimented and then returned to his conversation with another man about fluid dynamics. Apparently, it was difficult for him to leave his work behind, even on such a festive occasion. It was his passion and if anyone had the misfortune of showing so much as a hint of interest in the topic, they were in for a long night.

Like swimming upstream and fighting the current, I resumed my way through the crowd toward her. She was conversing with friends

31

as I finally made my way to her side. "Excuse me, miss." I politely, but boldly interrupted. She turned slowly and knowingly contemplated me with mesmerizing blue eyes.

"What do you want, Johannes?" She questioned me, her voice tinged with a hint of playful annoyance, as she deliberately brought down the mask she had been holding to her face.

I stumbled back a step. Certainly, it had been a long time since I last saw her. Where was the childish messy fisherman of my memory? She did not look embarrassed about anything now and I do not think I could have found the words to tease her anyway. Fascinated by the beguiling vision before me, I tried to recover from my shock and hoped that she had not noticed my startled reaction. But by the amused upward tilt of her smile, I knew that she had.

"Would you like to dance, Judith?" I asked in the deepest voice I could muster, hoping to sound more dauntless than I felt. She raised an eyebrow skeptically, as if expecting me to steal the mask or pull out the pins in her hair. When she finally realized that I was serious, her face softened and revealed a look I had never seen written there before.

"I'd love to," she admitted softly. "I feel like I've been waiting my whole life for you to ask."

Chapter 4

1728

I ascended through the Wagon Maker Guild ranks and finally achieved the coveted title of master of the trade. Now rather than confining me, Münchenstein comforted instead. I was back in my hometown, anticipating a successful future.

It had been five years since the eventful masquerade ball and on this morning I awoke in my childhood bed to the familiar, jarring noise of mother banging kettles in the kitchen and the heavy scent of breakfast drifting through the crisp, early morning air. Despite all that had changed, these sounds and scents had been one constant in my life for a majority of my twenty-four years and this morning it was no different. The comforting aroma of hashed *rosti* potato cakes, which sizzled in the skillet, and the pungent smell of soft boiled eggs permeated my surroundings.

Yes, the environment was familiar this day, but tomorrow I would wake up as a married man. An untroubled smile further softened the demeanor of my sleepy countenance as I envisioned Judith. Her gentle confidence and unpretentious yet riveting beauty made me the envy of many a man.

Contrary to my usual habit of rushing to start the day, this morning I continued to savor the last few moments in bed before starting with breakfast and chores. I could hear the animals milling about in their stable and the hens clucked loudly from their home under the staircase. The cows and horses had no qualms about getting started with their own day and the urgent moos and nickering indicated their eagerness to be fed. I lingered longer than intended until mother called out for me to come down to the kitchen.

"The food will get cold if you don't hurry!" She admonished with a loving, but firm voice.

Heeding her call, I dressed and then made my way down the stairs from my second floor chambers, ambling over to my seat at the table. "It looks wonderful as always, Mother," I complimented as I sat down and picked up a heaping bowl of potatoes and scooped a hearty helping onto my plate. Freshly baked bread, mellow butter, flavorful jams, and cheese enhanced the meal. Mother's solid pine kitchen table always overflowed with a tempting assortment of fresh foods prepared with love and she kept adequate supplies of additional vegetables, bread and homemade wine in our huge cellar.

She gave me a tight hug and then smoothed down a piece of my dark wayward morning hair one last time. "I'm so proud of you, Johannes. You are going to make a wonderful husband," she smiled. I noticed tears threatening to escape, and she dabbed the edge of her wide blue apron at her eyes, but her voice was filled with confidence. However, soon a worry line appeared and I could sense she was about to broach a subject that we had visited together many times before.

"I do hope that you will now take seriously your commitment to the church. I know it has been difficult to be fully involved in the congregation while apprenticing, but now that you will be a family man you know how important it will be."

"Yes, mother," I agreed with a nod and sidelong glance at my sister. She winked at me and shrugged her shoulders, helpless to stem the tide of this chronic argument and not inclined to try.

But I would not let myself get caught up in it again, especially not on this day. My mother's heart weighed heavy with the knowledge that I prized my independence and exploits over strictly adhering to the tenants of the church doctrine. It pained her to watch her son follow a path of worldly pursuits rather than those of a more spiritual nature. Thankfully, father entered the room and took his

34

usual place at the head of the table, stifling further comment on the subject.

"How are you feeling, son?" my father inquired as he laid a big, firm hand on my shoulder.

"*Très bon!*" I replied in French. I enjoyed speaking other than German sometimes and felt it would be useful in business to maintain my current level of fluency.

Accustomed to this tendency of mine, Father ignored the use of a foreign tongue and said, "I just want you to know how proud I am of you. You have become the mature and responsible man I always hoped you would be."

I heard the short giggle escape from my sister, but chose to overlook it and acknowledged my father and mother. "Thank you both. I know I wouldn't be who I am today without your guidance and love."

Mathis looked at his wife and recalled his own distant memories. "I remember the day I married your mother. One of the best days of my life." He pulled mother to him and squeezed her hand. She kissed the top of his head and then moved to her own seat. He continued, "But I also recall that sliver of doubt. The one that said, 'Will I be a good husband…a good father…will I be able to support my family?' Big questions that of course only time will answer fully."

I nodded in agreement and recognized the same feelings within myself. Father imparted a sense of peace and confidence as he told me, "Fortunately son, it's not all up to us. Took me a while to learn that, but I finally did. It is God who clothes the lilies of the field and cares about the fallen sparrow, and it is the same God that you will stand before today as you pledge your love and honor to Judith. It is God who controls such events of a man's life."

I nodded my thanks for the advice. It was comforting to once again hear lessons learned long ago in Sunday school, but it did little change my feelings. I believed in God, but he seemed very distant and uninvolved with the details of my ordinary life. *Thoughts better left to another day,* I decided and finished with my breakfast I thanked mother again and then hurried off to the stable.

We were to be married at the St. Arbogast Church in Muttenz, the same church in which I was christened in 1704 as an eight-day-old babe, where my parents pledged their vows to each other thirty-seven years ago and where I attended church since the earliest days of my childhood. My father's parents had once lived in Muttenz, but my grandfather died when I was only three and my grandmother's spirit departed before I was born. It was a very short trip to the north-east of us, even closer than Basel, and I knew the homes and streets almost as well as those in Münchenstein.

Situated at a crossroads in the old town, the ancient whitewashed church stood proud with a tall bell tower and fortifying walls. While sitting through many long church services, I had imagined the knights and ladies that respectfully knelt and bowed at the altars as far back as the 12th century. Parts of the building succumbed to earthquake damage in 1356, but I was proud to know that Prefect Münch came to the rescue and rebuilt it. Perhaps not the most humble of men, he placed his family coat of arms up in the choir, giving testament to the Münchenstein-Muttenz bond, and there it remained.

Originally built as a Catholic church, the congregation converted to the Protestant religion during the Reformation. When the church was stripped of all Catholic excess and symbolism, the 16th century wall and ceiling paintings were indiscriminately suffocated under a coat of whitewash. After my journeyman experience, I had often wondered if the paintings were as captivating as the artwork I witnessed in Italy.

On this fair and lovely afternoon, the church would be witness to a great event in my own life. My purposeful steps tread on the rough, cobbled courtyard and up the stairs to enter the arched doorway. I made my way down the familiar aisle towards the beautifully crafted large window recessed within the thick stone wall at the front of the church. Taking my place, standing taller this day than on any other in my life, I was still dwarfed by domed ceiling above me.

Swells of music produced by three trombones resonated against the church walls. The congregation was heartily singing Psalms, since the more popular compositions of the day, such as Pachabel's

36

Canon and the music of Bach, were not allowed to be played or sung in the Reformed church. It was considered too worldly.

I waited for the first glimpse of my bride and time seemed to stand still. Scanning the crowd, I saw Mother and Father sitting in the front pew, their mouths moving in time with the music. I was not the first child they had seen married, as I was sixth out of nine children and the third son. Mother's aging back remained straight, her graying head held high. I was a treasured son, a pride and joy. Only on rare occasion did she express the desire for me to become more involved with the ways of God and the church, and I knew that today she would not approach the subject with me again.

Father's emotions were more difficult to decipher. At age sixty-four he continued to be a practical man, accomplishing necessary work and doing it well. He still took his position as *Untervogt* to the most serious degree. Even now, on this celebratory day, he carefully guarded his dignified reputation and bore not the glimpse of a smile.

Behind my parents, trying to tactfully corral their brood of restless youngsters, my sister Magdalena and her husband sat distracted. As a backdrop to the chaos created by the youngsters in front of them sat my oldest brother Mathias, who was eleven years older than me, and beside him, his wife. Mathias had not felt well lately, and his looks wore the strain of ill health and worry.

My other brothers and sisters, along with their families, were also seated and present, scattered about to the left side of the church. Mathias, Barbara, Anna Margreth, Jannes Bernhard, Magdalena, Anna Marie, Solome, Barbara; that was all of them. But, though not all of my siblings had lived through their childhood, I could feel the presence of all with me today as I prepared to take this momentous step into my future.

At long last, the great door swung open and all else receded into the background. The guests ceased singing and stillness permeated the air. Then, cued by a renewed crescendo of the trombones' melody, the attendants gracefully glided down the long aisle. Heart pounding and mouth dry, my eyes bypassed the slow moving train of women and my focus intently fixed upon the back of the church.

In a moment of transcendence, my heart quieted and my mind relaxed. The morning light streamed in through the high church windows, causing even the dust specks caught in its beams to sparkle and dance as it cast a soft glow upon Judith, accentuating her fair skin and gently kissing her innocent smile. She was my companion of childhood, my beautiful friend, my Greek goddess, the love of my life. I was filled with wonder that she was going to be my wife.

When she reached me, I took her delicate hands in my own and the gleam in her twinkling eyes told me that she too greeted this day with joy. She gave me a quick wink and whispered, "I love you Johannes." We were young and life was full of promise.

Chapter 5

1737

Sometimes, I think of time as a river, passing rapidly and sweeping life along in a swift current. To the unobserving eye, its course seems unchanging and it would appear that the water's current flow will be its set course forever. Only upon careful scrutiny, and often in hindsight, can the subtle changes it makes in the landscape be clearly detected.

Such it had been in our lives. Nine years passed by with lightning-quick speed. On that idyllic day in St. Arbogast Church, even I, familiar with risk and adventure, could not have imagined that years later I would find myself many hours east of Münchenstein, in Benken, Switzerland, meeting secretly at the home of a man named Lienert Heyer. Candlelight flickered and cast suspicious shadows on peeling white walls. Four of us sat in the darkened space, farmers and artisans by trade. Our cautious and soft-spoken manners masked our deeper feelings of discontent. Carefully pushing my chair back, I rose to speak.

"Gentlemen," my deep voice was calm and quiet, but full of conviction, "thank you for coming to this meeting. Jacob, you know me well, but for the sake of Antoni and Mr. Heyer, let me formally introduce myself."

Before proceeding, I quickly ducked to glance out the window into the darkness. Had the wind picked up, or was there an unusual movement in the hedge? "I'm just nervous," I thought to myself, "...just being overly cautious."

I continued the speech, "My name is Johannes Kapp. I spent my youth roaming the rolling fields and woodlands around Münchenstein and Basel. I've spent my share of time exploring the curves of the Rhine." I pictured myself fishing for salmon or catfish along the muddy banks of the river. I could almost feel the cool water lap at my ankles and the gooey mud squeeze between my toes. I called my mind back from those perfect days wrapped in dappled sunshine and focused once more on the matter at hand.

"You've perhaps heard of my father, Mathis Kapp. And mother, she will probably feed you at some point." Mother took pride in her family's tradition of culinary skill and she was intent that the process would not end with her. Just yesterday Judith visited her house to make cheese. Of course, my mother sent home cookies and *Leckerli*, traditional honey cakes, as well for her grandchildren to enjoy.

"I am a husband and father," I continued. "Judith and I have three living children. I have buried the other four in this land." Thinking of leaving those tiny gravesites behind caused me to pause for a moment, and then I looked up at the men. "Gentlemen, this is my home." Affection for family and country, laced with nostalgia saturated my words. I swallowed a lump in my throat but endured with the speech. "I strive to be a man of strong character and resolute purpose."

"Here! Here!" The men lent their support, their enthusiastic cheering somewhat tempered only by our need for secrecy. We knew the authorities would disapprove of the meeting, but had decided to gather anyway.

"So, while I respect the Swiss government," I said, my voice taking on a harder edge, "I do not rely on her to meet my needs. I must take responsibility to provide for myself and my family."

"Heaven helps them who help themselves!" Jacob, now the town carpenter, intoned.

"I enjoy my business and I work long, hard hours. Hopefully, I have earned the respect of the members in this community. But, competition has been increasing, and it has been more than difficult to pay my bills."

"Likewise," interrupted Jacob. "My business has been suffering too."

"I do not want to drown in debt," I continued, "leaving a failing business, if any business at all, as a legacy to my children." The men nodded their heads in agreement. "I feel it is unjust that the Swiss government has put us in the situation where we must choose between supporting our family and living in our homeland. It should not be. It is not as I would wish it to be. But, alas, it is so." The more I talked, the angrier I became. "We work hard, pay our bills; and this is what we receive in return? The government takes more and more, never to be satisfied. They will not stop until they have all my land and crops and wine!" I exhaled in disgust as I quickly sat down on the wooden chair.

Picking up the conversation, Antoni Reiger, a resident himself of Benken, spoke up. "We have all read the letter from that settler of the British Colonies. Said land is plentiful and affordable there. I don't expect the government will let us go easy, but I have a plan. If they won't grant me traveling privileges to cross the ocean, I'm going to claim I've got friends up in Manheim, in the Palatinate. I'll tell them that if I don't find my fortune there, I will seek it in another country. They might figure they can keep a closer eye on me if I'm only up north a bit," he concluded. He then added, "Now this settler from Charleston, he was writing from South Carolina, but I've got my heart set on Pennsylvania."

"I agree," I said, still trying to settle down a bit. "I could pay the debts that I owe here in Switzerland and have enough left to buy a substantial amount of farmland in the Pennsylvania colony. I fear that if I remain here, my finances will eventually dwindle away, leaving us with little on which to live." That was my biggest fear and greatest motivation. I could not abide the thought of my children facing a future of poverty when there might be a better opportunity. I could already picture them prospering on the new land, gathering an overflowing harvest from flourishing fields. And what an adventure it would be!

41

It was Sunday morning and the cherry trees dressed in pink ruffled glory to greet springtime. Twice the trees had blossomed since the late night meeting to discuss the merits of traveling to Pennsylvania. As I took in the early morning light, my thoughts were distracted by the more pressing matter at hand.

Like the other times I found myself in this situation, I took stock of the pine tree in our yard. Years ago, as young newlyweds, Judith and I playfully planted the little tree in front of our home, for it was a tradition said to bring luck and fertility. I remember that day, now long past, when Judith stood back from the house. Hands on her hips, she sized up the location of where she wanted me to dig the hole. It seemed to me it should have been a simple process, but she evaluated as if it was a monumental decision. She wanted to know if it lined up just right with the window boxes. Did it complement the geraniums? Would it grow too tall for that spot in the yard? And so on and so forth.

Back then, I had been more than a little impatient. But years later, as I looked at the maturing tree and awaited Judith's labor to bring forth another child, I just chuckled to think about the three holes I produced before the scrawny pine found its perfect home. I welcomed the distracting thoughts of the "good-fortune" tree. Not that I really believed in luck, but we were certainly blessed with the coming addition of this, our fourth child.

I paced outside the door of my home for most of the morning, my thoughts churning with anxiety, excitement and hope. Not all of my sojourns in this yard had ended happily. There were times I re-entered our home to Judith's sobbing grief, her normally bright and snapping blue eyes dulled with sorrow and flooded with tears as she held a tiny, perfectly formed, but still baby. There had been times when I arrived to the faint, weak whimpers of an infant, and again to my wife's cries, and I knew that soon our baby would find his everlasting peace on the hillside, forever resting beside his siblings in their tiny graves. People always suggested remaining unattached to a baby since they were as likely to live as to die, but after burying my own children, I had not yet learned how to do that.

With each passing of a child, the Judith I once knew slowly faded. Harsh reality replaced optimism. The invincible spirit she once possessed was substituted with painful knowledge that, try as she might, pray as she did, she had no control to save her own children. I grieved the loss of what could have been, but I would not dwell on it. I would look to my future, the one that played in the side yard by the grapes in the vineyard. Bundled in a warm sweater to ward off the chilly morning air, Johan Jacob, my eldest of nine years old, had organized the two younger children to play a game.

Little Jonny, just turned four, tried his best to follow the rules set by his big brother, but he got confused and I could see frustration shadowing his eyes. He was so eager to please, to do it the right way and I knew that Jonny would stick with it. As the morning wore on, I continued to watch the children have fun. I laughed at sixteen-month-old Leo as he toddled about with an innocent grin on his sweet face, enjoying the outdoors and the presence of his brothers.

At long last I heard the loud and lusty cries of a newborn. I took this as a good sign and ran to the house. Though a very short jog, it seemed to take forever as I traveled through the kitchen and living area and into the bedroom at the back of the house.

Judith rested against her bed pillow and looked up at me, her eyelids heavy with exhaustion. Relief was evident when she told me, "He's healthy. Say hello to our new little boy, Ben."

I did not count myself among the poorest of men quite yet, but I was by no means viewed a rich or powerful man. To the world, I was just a wagon maker. But the world was so wrong. As I drank in the sight of my newborn son and his happy mother and heard the giggles of my other three children playing outside, I felt like a mighty warrior with a quiver full of arrows. I would take aim at Pennsylvania and strike a target of hope and bounty.

Despite our caution during the meeting in 1737, efforts to maintain secrecy failed and a full investigation was conducted regarding our plans. Some of the men pushed against the government mandates forbidding emigration to the colonies and succeeded in leaving anyway. I decided to follow the course of the law. Our plans were delayed for three years, but at last, permission was granted.

"I can't believe we have to pay fifty-eight pounds in taxes just to leave. A tenth of everything we have, which is practically nothing to begin with!" I muttered as my family prepared to depart for Basel for the first leg of our journey. "But anyway, the more we have, the more they take!" I shook my head in disgust.

I hated to start the journey in bad spirits, but the knowledge that the bureaucracy felt entitled to my personal belongings and wealth made me cringe with bitterness. But despite my exasperation, I knew I would miss Switzerland. No matter where I landed in life, the ground I now stood upon would always be recalled as "home."

"Don't forget where you came from," reminded my father. He and mother came to see us off on our journey. The likelihood of reuniting with them once we left was improbable. His usually calm and composed voice was breaking with emotion. "You will represent our family in a new land. Make us proud." Deep wrinkles on his face told of seventy-six years of discipline, love and laughter. How I would miss him.

At seventy-three years old, Mother leaned heavily on father's arm. "I love you, Johannes," she wept softly. She appeared so sad and elderly. I did not remember her looking so old before. My heart ached with guilt, knowing I caused her pain.

The colonies had claimed two of my sisters and their families as well. Anna Catherina, my older sister, went with her husband Hans Jacob Banga. Their twenty-two-year-old daughter, Catharina, accompanied them and they were living in Lancaster County, Pennsylvania. Anxious to see them again, we planned to settle close by once we arrived.

"Now Anna, *meine Liebe*," father consoled my mother, attempting to shine light on a very dark day. "My Love," he repeated. "Don't make this any harder than it has to be. This is exciting! To be a young man again! To explore a virgin land! I wish I could come with you, Johannes."

Not to be placated in these, the final moments spent with her family, mother continued with urgency, "Write me a letter when you arrive so I know you have crossed safely." She paused, "No," she rescinded her request with force, "No, write me *numerous* letters. I want to be sure of your safe passage. Little Ben and Leo are so young. And if you hear word of Barbara, please, please let us know!" She said with every ounce of her reserved hope.

44

My sister, Barbara, was among those who took leave of Switzerland in 1737. We received bits of information from other passengers who arrived safely at their destination, but we never received any news of her arrival. Still after three years, my family held out hope that a letter had been lost or destroyed. After all, a mere paper could easily vanish when crossing such a great distance.

Opposition to emigration had been very strong during the time Barbara left, so it was also possible that any letters may have been held or kept by the authorities. Our "caring government" supposedly only wanted what was best for her citizens. Perhaps they thought us too simple or foolish to realize they were manipulating the truth. But I saw the letters and read the illegal printed pamphlets about people who braved the unknown and reaped the benefits.

The reality, as I saw it, was that the government feared a mass departure of tradesmen and artisans from Switzerland. Would they miss our skill and craftsmanship? No, but they would miss the incredibly high taxes we paid that in turn lined the official's pockets with silver. More emigration requests had been granted recently and fortunately for us, Basel seemed to be one of the easiest places from which to leave. I was unsure how long the sentiment would last and thought it good timing that we were able to leave when we did.

All of that aside, however, I still feared for the fate of my sister. Perhaps messages from Barbara were lost or stolen, but deep in my heart resided dread that we had lost more than correspondence. Though unspoken, I thought my mother and father must also sense it.

Despite misgivings and unease, the horses were hitched to the carriage, my family loaded, and I took my seat. Casting a final glance back, I captured images to cherish as portraits in my mind and stored them to view at some distant time in a foreign land.

Soft, golden rays of sunshine illuminated the early morning skyline of Basel's ancient cathedrals, university, and government buildings. Cloudy river mist covered the lower part of the city like a comforting gray blanket. The city was the hub for trade in the Northeastern region of Switzerland. This was where our journey would really begin.

Basel was often described as "hugging the knee" of the Rhine River. Germany and France, the Black Forest and Vosges Mountains were nearby. Basel's architecture was secured in stone. One historical building that I greatly admired was the University, the oldest in the Swiss Confederation, built in 1460.

In Basel, we sold many of our belongings, lightening our load considerably and giving us needed extra money for the trip. Two trunks remained which contained some clothing, my wagon making tools, the family Bible, a doll, a few books, special pieces of lace made by Judith's mother and a few other necessities for the trip. It seemed like such a small amount considering we would have nothing else when we got there, but space was premium on the ship.

While in the city, I bought each of the children a traditional Basel honey cake at the market. Their eyes brightened at the treat; a luxury for them. Although we made honey cakes at home, to buy one was unusual, as over the past few years every extra penny was saved for this trip.

The morning sun brightened as we stood in line waiting for our physicals and eye screenings. After successfully completing those, we were allowed to pay the fare and load our luggage. At long last, we boarded the barge and set course from Basel down the Rhine River. Passing grand castles, we floated four very long weeks on the river. We had to stop quite often at custom houses along the way, where our belongings were examined at the convenience of the officials. Each stop took a considerable amount of time and we ended up spending a lot of money while we waited. It was hard to imagine that so much of the journey was yet to come.

Finally we arrived in England, and our family plus thirty-nine other men and their families boarded the "Friendship," a vessel bustling with activity and captained by William Vettery. At the time we arrived on the ship, it was already filled with forty-nine men and their families who had previously boarded in the Netherlands. With everyone accounted for, the total was estimated to be nearly one-hundred-twenty passengers aboard.

Judith blanched when we were shown our new living quarters, but then squared her shoulders in self-determination as she surveyed our small space below deck. The dim, close quarters would provide no privacy.

"No matter, the trip will be over before we know it," I said, trying to cheer the family. "It might be uncomfortable, but when we get to Pennsylvania, someday we'll sit around our supper table and tell 'remember when' stories about the voyage."

We moved up to the ship's deck for fresh air and to wave goodbye to the shoreline. "Look at me, Mamma! I'm Captain Blackbeard," Johan Jacob squinted in the glaring sunshine and danced a jig on deck.

Laughing at his antics, Judith and I smiled at each other as we stood hand-in-hand, inhaling the sprays of tangy sea air. Judith, understandably, had voiced many misgivings about the trip, her main concerns being the safety of the children and the pain of leaving loved ones behind, but I noticed a renewed vitality in her spirit as we stood ready to embark on the grandest enterprise of our lives.

Later that night, dancing under the starry sky with the rest of the passengers, we celebrated the commencement of our journey in an atmosphere charged with optimism. Moonlight bathed the lips of the woman I loved, and unconcerned of public scrutiny, I kissed her and breathed promises in her ear.

It did not take long for the dance to end and the optimism to crumble. The voyage was horrendous. I had not expected leisurely sailing across a sea of glass, but what we experienced week after week was akin to a nightmare.

"Throw me a piece of meat," the dirty, toothless sailor called out. I almost gagged as I watched him place the salty, wormy meat on top of the pile of newly opened hardtack, drawing out the maggots before distributing the food to the many immigrants for supper. He threw away the first piece of meat, and then continued the process a few times until only a few maggots were drawn out.

"Oh Johannes," swallowed Judith, bringing her hand to her mouth, bidding the bile to stay down. "I don't think I can eat that!"

But, we did. As she balanced baby Ben on one hip, and toddling Leo pulled at her skirt, Judith pounded the hardtack to a pulp. Then she added it to the thick, brown water to make soup.

We used our trunk as a table, which was often a difficulty in itself. When the ship moved, so did the table. We were actually lucky that day, as the Atlantic had been unusually calm.

Salted pork, mutton, and a small amount of horse meat were part of our diet, but now in the midst of the journey the food was covered with mold and bugs. The drinking water had by now also turned into a brown sludge teeming with worms and disease due to prolonged storage in the dark barrels.

My discontent with the poor food was distracted as I heard the ship's white canvas sails billowing in the breeze. I went above deck and saw that the wind had started to pick up and dark clouds gathered on the horizon. The air was cooling and lightning streaked in the distance followed by the rumble of thunder. We had weathered other storms, but I had a very uneasy feeling about this one. It was late summer and I had overheard a sailor mention that in this part of the Atlantic "conditions are ripe for a hurricane." I turned to see Judith and the children standing next to me.

"Take the children below deck. A storm is coming," I warned.

Judith's hair was tied back, but long strands of blond escaped and whipped against her frightened face. Raindrops stung against the children's skin as they all stood facing me, hands interlocked. She hesitated, "Please come down with us. You know how scared the children become during a storm. The ship rolls so violently they cannot even stay in their beds. They slide across the floor!"

I turned to answer, but having overtaken us remarkably fast, the storm was now almost upon us. The thunder cracked and the waves splashed up over the side of the boat, making the deck slick under our feet. The clouds darkened in ominous hues of green, gray, and black.

"All hands on deck!" Captain Vettery bellowed as lightning forked across the sky. "Secure the supplies! Protect the drinking water!" he shouted.

"Take the children *now*! I will be down after I help take care of the supplies," I yelled above the deafening screams of howling wind and the mighty roar of the pounding sea. This time she did not question, but ran down the stairs to the bottom of the ship, the children closely surrounding and following her.

We gathered what we could. Some of the rations were saved, but much food and water and many cooking pots were lost as they washed over the rails and out to the sea. I barely kept myself on board, let alone anything else. The storm was relentless. The ship tossed side to side as the giant waves crashed all around it.

We are going to die! I thought frantically, echoing the cries of the sailors around me.

After saving what we could, everyone scrambled to the pitch-black hulls of the ship to wait out the storm. Some sailors tried to drink away their fear of drowning while most passengers tried prayer instead. The storm raged on for hours. The violent pitching of the ship made many passengers sick and the air was thick with the smell of vomit. It was almost unbearable, but preferable to the likelihood of death waiting for anyone on the ship's deck. We doubted that the violent storm would ever end, or if we would live to see it end, but finally the howling wind and rough seas abated. The sky cleared and precious rays of sunshine snuck through the open hatches, shining light on the aftermath below deck.

Soaking wet and chilled to the bone, I surveyed my family as we huddled close together. The children's wide and innocent eyes stared up at me in fright. To the youngsters, I was sure that Judith appeared calm, but when I looked closely I could see her shivering, if from cold or terror, I did not know.

We had weathered a horrific storm. It was difficult to assess the extent of the damage, for the crew, though they were quite a sorry lot of men, still seemed to think themselves above immigrants and they did not give us much information about anything. Besides, many were still drunk. It was almost certain that the captain would not speak with us. Already it had taken us far longer than I had supposed it would to reach our destination, but there was no alternative but to trust the captain. He had made this voyage before, and I consoled myself that surely he must be prepared for such an event.

I was very wrong. The captain was not equipped to handle such an emergency. Alarmingly, weeks passed following the storm and we did not reach land. Unbelievably, almost half of our fellow passengers had died, mostly from starvation as well as from disease, as we lacked adequate food and water. I assumed we had been thrown off course, the only reason I could think why it was taking us so long to reach Pennsylvania.

Judith and my two youngest sons Ben and Leo were among those who took sick, and I attempted to maintained hope that we would reach land soon. I told myself they would recover, but anyone could see it would take a miracle. Hunger, thirst and disease waged war against their depleted bodies and they had few resources with which to mount a defense.

Aboard was a Moravian missionary, Andrew Eschenbach. Formerly a shoemaker, this humble man represented true Christian love to me and my family. He was traveling to Pennsylvania in response to a request from a Methodist preacher named George Whitefield, who desired to minister to the German people in the colony. Unfortunately, Mr. Whitefield could not speak their language. Reverend A.G. Spangenberg had interpreted previously, but returned to Europe. Mr. Eschenbach planned to do his best in replacing him. The missionary spent much time praying with us, but it seemed that our prayers continued to go unanswered.

"We must reach land!" I cried in desperation. But each new sunrise dawned upon an infinite sea and I watched helplessly, unable to hasten the journey or provide sustenance.

"I'll be waiting for you ...with the children." Judith whispered in a fading voice. She understood her fate as she witnessed the demise of those around her. "You must press on." Her passionate spark, which I had so recently thought renewed, was now replaced with aching melancholy.

There was no doctor; no medicine; no food. I sat beside them, hoping that somehow my presence might bring a sense of peace. If only I could have borne their agony and taken the suffering upon myself instead. As they became too weak to whimper or cry, silence ensued.

Oh that we had never boarded the ship! I replayed the early days of our journey. What an inspiring time it had been. The children imagined they were commanders and whalers and mercenaries. Every boy's fantasy coming true! But it had been only an illusion, and my sons' childhoods were slowly and rudely being stripped away as they watched their friends and family die.

She was my beloved Judith, my best friend, my loving wife. Forever in my memory as the celestial vision of the ball. She was only thirty years old. She was too young. She was mother of my children. She *was*... she *was*. I wanted her to *be*. I could not imagine a world without her.

Judith…gone. My curious, adorable Leo, only three years old, was dead…gone. And Ben…my innocent six month old infant…gone. I would never have the chance to walk with him, to talk to him. It was incomprehensible.

I secured the last knot, my mind numb with disbelief. Three lifeless bodies lay wrapped in the tangled weave of a hammock-one woman and two small children, all wearing threadbare, dirty garments; all gaunt and pale. Their cheeks hollowed like empty bowls. Holding them close to my chest one last time, their weight doubled by the canon ball entwined within the ropes, I stepped to the edge of the wooden ship. "Dear God," the gut wrenching moan escaped from my lips. "Please forgive me."

The water was ice on my fingers as I lay my family down on the great expanse of sea that was to have carried us to our dream.

The impatient clearing of a throat came from behind. "Let's get on with it then," the gruff voice of a sailor demanded.

I bowed my head in grief, as the tears finally ran free, coursing down my cheeks. "*Ich bin so leid*," I sobbed, my arms now empty, "I am so sorry."

My body and spirit spent with sorrow, I collapsed to the deck of the ship, sobs shaking my frail body. Guilt engulfed me. If only I had been content to stay in Switzerland. If only I had left unheeded that beckoning call from across this monster of a sea. The summons which had promised such fulfillment and prosperity now seemed like a cruel joke.

I don't know how I did it, but slowly, I picked myself up from the ship's wooden deck and gathered my two remaining children. Holding them close was the only comfort I could offer. My youngest boy, Jonny, tapped into a reserve of grief and his renewed cries clawed at my heart. Dehydration robbed him of the tears that should have fallen. In contrast, my oldest son Johan Jacob stiffly resisted my embrace as he stared silently over the never-ending sea. The children filled my arms, but my heart was empty.

Chapter 6

After that defining, unthinkably tragic moment of my life, the days passed in a blur. Like water rushing into a sinking ship, I felt engulfed in a deluge of devastation, anger and loneliness. I lost track of time and went through life's motions by habit, until finally one day a dulled, slightly restored sense of anticipation and feeling of relief inched through my wasted body. "Look at that," I murmured.

"Philadelphia," eleven-year-old Johan Jacob said with weakened awe. "Philadelphia ….we are finally here." He glanced at his five-year-old brother, who clung to me as we sat on the upper decks of the Friendship.

"Look up and see it, Jonny. Can you see it?" he repeated with all the exuberance he could find within him for the sake of his little brother. Johan Jacob smiled faintly, and I could tell by the trembling in his voice that his miniscule joy was edged with the pain of remembering all we had lost. "We made it to Pennsylvania."

I turned and watched my youngest son's expression as he meekly surveyed the city situated on the rise far off in the distance. When Jonny finally spoke, his voice was hushed with vulnerable and childish apprehension. He slowly turned his trusting eyes to Johan Jacob, certain that his big brother knew everything. "What's it like?" he asked, his voice trailing off into a spasm of coughs that racked his tiny frame.

"It's the second biggest city in the colonies," said Johan Jacob. "And in Philadelphia they have Indians." This point had caused much exuberance in the young boy at the beginning of the journey. Today, however, a hollow tone prevailed.

Johan Jacob took a deep breath, closed his eyes, and then reopened them to again take in the city view. He grasped that this dream was about to come true, despite the gaping hole torn into his heart by the untimely death of his mother and brothers. Keeping his eyes on the city, I could see the dim glow of desire slowly begin to reignite within him. Although exhausted, he sat a little taller, a little braver, bolstered by a tiny flame of hope and the promise of great escapades yet to come.

Johan Jacob began to tell Jonny details he learned while listening to his relatives and friends discuss the colonies. Back in Switzerland there had been many meetings about the trip. I assumed that my son was picturing a Philadelphia that would boast the pristine streets and orderly shops of Switzerland's neighborhoods, only made so much better by the presence of natives.

"Can we get off the boat right now, Papa?" Johan Jacob looked to me with hopeful and hungry eyes.

"We've waited months, boy," I chided very gently. "Be patient and let the boat drop anchor first. I don't think we have the strength to swim for it." I carefully clapped the boy's shoulder, careful to not injure the hard bones protruding through his thinning shirt. I smiled wanly at my eldest son's slightly improved enthusiasm.

"These clear blue September skies and the mild weather bode well for the journey still ahead," I observed to my sons, trying to sound optimistic, although in fact I had almost forgotten what that felt like. Rising slowly to my feet, and still holding my young son, I attempted to stand solid in my dirty clothes and stinking shoes. Weak with fatigue and extreme hunger, and still shaken to my core by our loss, I again felt overwhelmed.

Nevertheless, I set my jaw with determination and resolved to persevere against the difficulties that were sure to lie ahead. Like my forefathers before me, and for the sake of my children, I would face adversity with steadfast courage. I would endeavor to represent the Kapp family with honor.

I turned toward Johan Jacob, who suddenly had tears glistening in his hazel blue eyes. "You must be strong now," I consoled.

"I know, Papa, but I miss Mamma and Leo and Ben so much. I wish they were standing here beside us."

"I know, son, so do I."

A bit of curiosity began to replace my sluggish countenance as I gazed out over the calm, wide river. A few small boats were steadily making their way toward us, their occupants calling out to us in German, "*Willkommene Freunde!*" "Welcome Friends!"

The men boarded our ship and distributed fresh fruit to the weary passengers as a sign of concern and encouragement. Never had an apple looked so red and tempting since the Garden of Eden. One man, who seemed to be the leader of the group, introduced himself and shook his head with regret.

"We apologize to you folks. Usually more men come out and meet the ships." He continued, "But, because your voyage took so long to arrive, there have been rumors that many of your passengers must be dead or very ill. And so, there's not quite as many of us here to greet you as usual."

The men were very helpful, answering our questions and telling us a little of what to expect in our new homeland. It brought a measure of comfort to hear some particulars and I was very appreciative to the men for having come out to greet the ship.

The leader spoke to us men saying, "You will need to sign an oath of allegiance to the king, report your names, occupations, and the homeland from which you came."

He laughed, "You might have left Switzerland or Germany, but you'll find that you aren't the only settlers here from that part of the world. The Rhineland population has increased so quickly and to such a large number, that it has our Governor Gordon quite concerned. About ten years ago, he decided that the government should keep better track of the number of immigrants. I guess they fear that so many foreigners could become a threat to the crown of England."

After the welcoming committee departed, the captain gathered the passengers, "*Most likely to bid us farewell,*" I thought.

I was impatient to depart the vessel and take the next step toward a future with my sons.

But in his authoritative voice the captain announced, "You will not be let off this ship until the ship master is assured that everyone among the German passengers has paid their debt in full." My plans for a speedy exit evaporated.

I refocused on what the captain was saying. "Some of you have signed yourselves into indenture as payment for your passage. You will keep your promise. Before getting off this ship, you will be sold so that you have no chance to back out on your word and escape into the back country. I've lost money before. It won't happen again."

Then, as if of no consequence, and perfectly acceptable given the nature of the agreed upon bargain, he stated, "There is no guarantee that families will be kept together. If your husband or wife sold themselves into indenture and died on this voyage, we will take a son or daughter to make up for the lost payment. Likewise children, if your parents have died and you find yourself an orphan, you will be expected to replace their debt. You will sell yourself into servitude for the agreed upon amount of time."

Mothers and fathers gathered their sons and daughters close to them, their eyes reflecting the fears they held in their heart. Many more nights passed with the apprehensive passengers sleeping restlessly in the rank ship. Hot and thirsty, our proverbial glass of forbidden water sat just out of reach on the shores of Philadelphia. We viewed the gates of paradise from the throes of hell.

Finally, the paid passengers were given orders to depart. With great relief, but a heavy heart, I handed the ship's master the receipt of my payment. No well-wishing words were involved in the transaction; and with certainty that is what it was. Purely a business matter for the ship masters. Little concern had been shown for the welfare of the passengers other than making sure our payment was collected.

I looked back at those still detained, the ones awaiting a new master or the uncertainty of the auction block. A little boy named Ludwig stood near us, looking forlorn. Both of his parents died from illness during the voyage and now he would be sold to the highest bidder to pay their debts.

"Ludwig," I tried to console the boy. "Child, it will be okay." I fiercely hoped that my words would hold true. After observing the character of men for nearly forty years, I realized that not all masters are kind. The boy stared back at me with tear-filled eyes, wiping his nose with the back of his hand, and sobbing, "I will miss you. Please, take me with you!" Dread ran thick through his words.

"Please, Papa. Can we please take Ludwig with us?" Johan Jacob begged in misery for his friend who would be left behind.

"I wish it were that easy, son. But these people will have no mercy, and his parents' debt must be paid," I replied, casting a hard glance at the ship master to whom I had just given my receipt. I knew that it could have just as easily been my son standing there instead.

After Ludwig's parents died, I tried to show extra concern and kindness to the boy. I thought my heart too full of grief to hold a single ounce more, and yet I still found room to ache with pity for this small child. My sons often played with the boy during the voyage and under their common circumstances, they developed a special bond of friendship.

Taking one last glance at Ludwig, I squared my shoulders and turned back around. I felt like a terrible human being, but I was powerless to help him. Taking my sons by the hand, we walked forward and descended the ship's ladder.

And so we arrived. The stench of garbage and wreaking fish coming from the docks welcomed us. I secured the trunk and bags and headed to the immigrations office. Our appetite had been somewhat curbed by the food brought on board by our German friends, but hunger continued to reign in our bellies.

At the immigration office, we finally reached the head of the line. The clerk looked at us with spiritless eyes. No smile. No warmth in the welcome.

"First and last name," he droned.

"Johannes Kapp."

"Destination," he intoned without interest.

"Lancaster County, Pennsylvania," I said, weariness creeping into my voice.

The clerk informed me that we could arrange for transportation needs, exchange money, and get directions, among other things at the office. I noticed many families huddled together and sleeping around us. The clerk said if we could not afford to rent lodging for the night we could sleep at the office as well. I thanked him for the kindness, but determined to stick with our plan to rest at a local inn.

After completing one last physical exam, the boys and I walked out the door and into the city. We did not have money to waste, but for this one night, after having come so far and having been through so much, my sons would have a warm meal and comfortable bed in respectable lodging. Perhaps we might find more affordable accommodations, but at what cost to my children's innocence I could not imagine. Many of the taverns lacked a good reputation.

Exiting the office and pointing ourselves in the direction of King Street, we headed back down toward the docks. A short way down the road, we were drawn into a bakery by the aroma of fresh baking bread. I paid the storekeeper, and after giving the boys their portion, I forced myself to savor the first bite but then finished it quickly.

We continued on, and I could see that Philadelphia was not quite the immaculate city we had imagined. Some streets were not paved with anything except the garbage of the residents who lived on either side. The stench of rotten food, coupled with a hint of sewage, made it uncomfortable to draw a deep breath. The boys pinched their noses and I was reminded of the weeks aboard the stinking ship. Ahead, a pack of stray dogs growled menacingly over meat scraps and spiked hair rippled down their angry backs. Alarmed, we detoured down a side street.

Finally, as we neared the river, I saw a sign hanging outside of a tavern. Many pieces of wood were hammered together at odd angles, denoting that this was the "Crooked Billet Inn."

As we approached the entrance, a group of men walked briskly out of the tavern doors, deep in discussion. One man in particular caught my attention. He was quite tall and had spectacles resting on his rather long nose. His sense of purpose and confident

58

bearing caught my attention more than anything. I could tell he was a leader of men.

"Good afternoon gentlemen," the man courteously paused, mid-conversation, and doffed his hat to my bedraggled family in passing. Clearly, this man was not a respecter of persons based upon their outward appearances. I was surprised when the man not only acknowledged, but also stopped and turned to us. From behind round metal rims, pleasant remembrances glimmered in his keen eyes.

"Sir, you take me back to my own first day here in Philadelphia back in October of 1723. It was here at this very Inn, those seventeen years ago, that I made my bed that first night."

He pulled a handful of coins from his pocket and pressed them into my hand.

"Oh, no Sir, I couldn't take that. I have a little money put away. That is too kind, I..." I protested, feeling embarrassed, but the man stopped me with a gentle shake of his head.

"No, you take this, and when it is in your power to return good to someone else, take that opportunity."

Humbly, I accepted the money. "Thank you. Your kindness will not be forgotten."

"And may you and your family be blessed," said the man, doffing his cap to us. "Might I ask where you plan to settle?"

"Lancaster County," I replied.

"One of my acquaintances, Peter Etter, has family in that area. Peter's quite a businessman...he makes and sells stockings here in Philadelphia," mused the gentleman. "Well, anyway...I know you boys are tired. Go get some sleep. You deserve it," he said, turning back to his colleagues and resuming his previous conversation.

As we approached the establishment's door, I resisted the urge to show signs of distress at the current state of our condition. Filthy, fetid, famished...yes. Resolute, bold, survivors...yes. It was upon the latter that I would concentrate. Great reward is often brought on by immense sacrifice and sometimes that can look a little dirty.

As we entered the tavern, we were greeted by a neatly dressed man of color. "How may I help you gentlemen?" He asked in a deep, kind voice.

Without waiting for an answer, he continued. "I see you've met Ben Franklin, the pride of our city. It is surely your lucky day!

59

He doesn't come down here to the Crooked Billet much anymore. He's usually up at the Indian King with his friends. But, sometimes he comes down here for a visit. Quite a man. You'll probably run across one of his pamphlets while you are here in the city."

I stored away this information in the back of my mind. For as interesting as this must be, the only thing keeping my eyes open was the loud growl of hunger echoing in my stomach.

"We are looking for a place to rest tonight," I said, stifling a yawn. "And most certainly we need some food as soon as possible. It has been an arduous journey, and my sons and I are extremely tired and hungry." My eyelids felt heavy as they anticipated sleep.

"We were told that this might be a good place to start looking to fill those needs. We can pay you a fair price. Although we are disheveled at the present, we are not without means to compensate you."

I spoke confidently, yet wondered if we would be permitted to lodge here, given our state. If refused, I was unsure of what options would be available. I certainly did not want to go back to the immigrations office.

Mercifully, I heard the man say in a low, mellow voice, "We do have a room available for you and your family sir. The price is 5 pounds per night."

"We will take it," I said in relief as I passed him the coins.

With a solid night of sleep behind us, we felt more hopeful as we descended to the dining room for a hearty breakfast in the morning. Mugs of hot amber cider threw off steam and heat traced through my body as I swallowed the first welcome sip.

Across the table, digging into their warm soft cornmeal mush, the boys paused only long enough to pour excessive amounts of dark molasses on top of the cereal. Ordinarily, I would caution them against such greedy behavior, but I suspected that ordinary was not a circumstance that I would be encountering much anytime soon.

After breakfast, I spoke with the proprietor of the establishment and agreed to leave our trunks there, promising to return again that night. In the morning light of a new day, I stepped out into the street, reassessing our new surroundings. We traveled along a different path than the previous night, and I began to get another idea of what the city was about. Many of the streets were actually quite broad and seemed to be laid out in a well-planned manner. Some were even paved with handsome red bricks and lined with neat, respectable, and orderly homes.

I was no stranger to the bustle of a city, growing up in such close proximity to Basel. However, as I looked around, I saw other, more obviously rural immigrant families milling about the streets and they seemed shocked by the strange and busy atmosphere.

Our very talkative host at the inn mentioned that nearly 13,000 people lived in Philadelphia. Among those thousands of people, English was the prevailing language, as it was of course, a British Colony. Although not entirely fluent in English, I hoped I was knowledgeable enough to get by until I could learn more. In the meantime, there were so many German-speaking folks about that I did not worry.

After some hard bargaining, I finally secured transportation and at last we departed for the more rural parts of Pennsylvania. In my pocket, I held a land warrant for 163 acres of uncut, un-cleared land, west of Lancaster.

After a few days travel, we set out on the last leg of the journey. The trail from Lancaster westward proved arduous, as it was extremely narrow with deep and foreboding ravines and gullies lining the path. It would be easy to get lost or injured in this forest, especially at night.

While in Lancaster, I had purchased supplies that would sustain us in the frontier. The horses were loaded down with bags carrying necessities such as a black iron pot and cornmeal; and included in our entourage was a Devon milk cow and several black, thick-coated pigs. Needless to say, we were not sneaking through the forest. I had heard that hostile Indians should not be much of a concern, but I hoped to make it to our destination without making any new native acquaintances.

Up ahead on the trail, a single traveler jounced toward us. As he neared, I could better see that he was an old man, dressed in a conglomeration of patched dirty linen and well-worn buckskin. I hailed the man who cracked a friendly, toothless smile as he reigned in his nag. In German, he politely asked if he could be of assistance. I described the whereabouts of my land and asked him how long it might take to reach it.

"Just on up the road a few hours, young man," his gruff voice reassured. "You'll need to cross at Wrights Ferry and then head on up a bit north. You can get better directions at the Ferry. Good luck to you." With that he was off, leaving us alone again in the dense forest.

We found the ferry, as the old man said we would, and made the acquaintance of its owner, a Quaker man named John Wright. Paying the small fee, we boarded a contraption of two dugout canoes fastened together with wagon wheels and crossed the wide river. We declined to eat at the tavern, as we were assured our destination was near and set out northward. An hour or so passed and the sun crawled further toward the western sky. I looked down again at the roughly drawn map on the copy of my land purchase application form. If I was reading the markings correctly, we had finally arrived!

I raised my eyes from the map and absorbed my surroundings. My heart raced and for a brief moment, I felt alive again. Never had a place affected me so deeply. In Münchenstein, I loved the landscape for its manicured beauty and I could spend hours gazing with reflection into the river. But this land was different. It was wild, unmarred, untamed… and all 163 acres of it belonged to me.

Veering the animals off the trail and to the right, I commanded them to stop with a loud, "Whoa!" I tethered my newly acquired horses to one of the abundant hardwood trees. Well cared for by their previous owner, I admired my new team. They were strong, healthy, high-quality animals.

Johan Jacob slid down from his horse and then helped his little brother descend as well. My emotions were still labile, and a sense of sadness began to replace my initial sense of elation. Judith and my youngest boys should also be taking their first steps onto this rich and fertile soil of their new home.

"The land of our dreams," I thought, but quickly and correctly adjusted my thinking to, "The land of *my* dreams."

Judith had been supportive of my decision, as any good wife should be, but I knew that had she made the final call, all of us would still be in Switzerland surrounded by friends and family. It had been my ever-restless spirit, not hers, that brought us on this journey. The thoughts haunted me, perhaps they always would, but I desired to give my boys a happy memory of their first day on the land. I made myself smile at them and determined to make this a day for new beginnings.

"Johan Jacob," I called, walking back over toward the children, "pull that satchel from the horse and let's have our sandwiches. We'll have a picnic!"

"I love picnics!" Jonny enthused, his once eager grin emerging from its hiding place.

We all sat down on the ground, our backs resting against the strong, old trees. We were new to this land, but the trees' roots went deep. As the boys intently ate the thick slabs of ham and cheese, I closed my eyes and truly relaxed for the first time in months. The days ahead would be difficult and busy; but for now I soaked in the peaceful setting.

Gradually, heavy thoughts slipped away, and I began to hear the world come alive around me. Squirrels chattered noisily to one another as they scampered through the forest, gathering acorns for the cold winter to come. A bird's sturdy beak knocked out a persistent, hollow rhythm as it searched a walnut tree for supper. Another bird, across the woods, sang a trilling melody. Silence in the undisturbed confines of nature is loud.

"We'll get a fire started. The air is getting a chill to it," I said, after finishing our wilderness picnic. "Boys, gather some fallen logs and brush."

"But papa, I'm so tired," complained Jonny.

"Come on. I'll help you pick up the heavy ones. Besides, it won't take long," offered Johan Jacob.

I was tempted to allow them to rest. After all they had been through, they deserved a break. But, life must go on, and this they must understand. It was important that they learn to work hard, even in difficult circumstances.

And so, with gentle firmness I said, "Go with your brother, Jonny. Stay together. Help each other and the load will be lighter and the job will be done faster."

Johan Jacob was right. Kindling was abundant in the heavily wooded area and soon, the fire blazed and crackled, casting its warmth on the boys as they sat close to each other. I collected a pile of branches that were surprisingly lightweight with beautiful dense, featherlike foliage. Clean and fresh, the scent was invigorating as I broke the twigs and arranged a small shelter. The sky remained clear, but it would be nice to take shelter under the canopy tonight. The children especially might feel more secure with a roof of sorts over their heads while in such an isolated setting. To tell the truth, I might feel better about it too.

"Come on boys," I called to them. "It's time for bed."

Obediently, they came to me and quickly nestled under the blankets. Johan Jacob asked the question I knew he had been thinking ever since he noticed the tall trees casting shadows in the setting sun.

"What about the Indians and bears?"

I wished, as I had on many occasions before, that Johan Jacob could have more discretion in asking such questions in front of Jonny. The little boy might not have even thought to imagine such things on his own, but given the questions of his big brother, Jonny pushed up even harder against my side; his eyes alert and peering out into the darkness, expecting a warlike native or savage beast to materialize at any moment.

Reaching just a few inches from my side, my fingers touched cold metal, and I ran my hand along the long, smooth barrel of my new rifle. The well-polished stock dimmed in comparison to the bright pride I saw gleaming in the eyes of the gunsmith, Martin Mylin, when the boys and I stopped and bought the gun at his shop near Lancaster. Created to embody both perfect accuracy and timeless beauty, each rifle was shaped by the skilled craftsman with utmost care and precision.

"Won't find a better one than this," Mr. Mylin assured, launching into his sales pitch. "Invented and made her myself. Best there is for what you'll need in this country. She's got British rifling, German-styled parts, and you won't find a gun more accurate on account of that nice long barrel. Can't find one of these beauties anywhere else but right here in the colonies."

Thinking back to that conversation and hoping that Martin Mylin did not make empty promises, I reminded the boys, "I've got my gun close by. Don't worry."

This statement did little to ease the concern in Jonny's eyes and I continued. "And like I said before, I was told that the Indians around here are peaceful." I did not directly address the bear question, hoping it would be forgotten. No such luck.

"Well, what about the bears?" Jonny sniffled. "I'm scared! I want mamma!" he demanded, squeezing my arm so tightly that his fingers turned white and his eyes filled with tears. I could also see by the waning firelight that Johan Jacob's eyes began to glisten. Rather than avoid the bear discussion, I decided this was preferable to thinking about the absence of Judith.

"Now, calm down, son. They're just scrawny black bears. If we mind our own business, they will too. They don't like to be around us any more than we like to be close to them. And remember, I've got my gun."

Jonny seemed to take me at my word and relaxed his grip, finally closing his eyes. It had been a long day of traveling on bumpy, treacherous roads and we were all completely exhausted.

"I haven't had a satisfying rest since I stepped on that ship," I thought. I could feel Judith's arm entwined in mine as I remembered standing on the deck that first day, waving goodbye to our home and to our history.

"How can someone be gone and yet still seem so close?" I wondered, swallowing around the hot lump of grief burning my throat. I could see her every time I closed my eyes. Even without closing my eyes. A new thought suddenly struck me and I worried about the day when that clarity would fade. And what of the boys? Would they remember what she looked like at all?

The ground was hard and the air chilly. My discomfort was made complete by contemplating our loss. Yet, in spite of those obstacles and my ever-present grief, I had a feeling I would sleep better than I had in months. As I drifted off beneath the fragrant canopy of hemlock bows, I began to feel a calming sense that better times were ahead as I lie cradled against the sweet brown arms of my new homeland.

Part 2

Katharina

Chapter 1

As a young girl, home became defined not by place but by the people I loved most. My father, Johannes Etter, was an innkeeper and throughout my childhood he leased businesses all throughout Switzerland. Each time he acquired a new property, we moved and the roots of friendships and familiar comforts were stripped away. Only the bond with my parents and brothers and sisters remained.

Though not paramount to my happiness, I did prefer some locations over others and one of the most pleasant places we ever lived was near Niederosch. The inn had large glass-paned kitchen windows which allowed warm sunlight to stream through and bathe the worn pages of my cherished books. My brothers always made fun of me, asking how I could breathe with my nose stuck so far into the pages.

On one of those bright days so long ago, August 23rd, 1728 to be exact, I sat in a rocking chair with my delicate hands wrapped around a treasure. I remember the date, because it was my birthday and having been given a lighter load for the special occasion, I was taking advantage of it.

The particular book I held was a wedding gift to my mother from Lady Katharina von Erlach, Baroness of Spiez and Riggisberg. Just touching it was enough to set my imagination sailing back to the stories mother loved to tell about her days working in the castle as a weaver. Absently, I pushed a dark cirrus of wayward hair behind my ear and then quickly turned another page.

"Today is a special day," my mother Maria said happily, interrupting my reading. She stood at the table briskly mixing cake batter. Stilling her hands, she turned and looked at me, her oldest living daughter.

"Katharina, it seems like just yesterday that you were an infant; a contented bundle of joy. I still remember kissing your soft downy head, inhaling the newness of your life, and looking into your expressive eyes."

"Oh Mamma," I said, brushing her off. I usually enjoyed hearing the memories, but that day I just wanted to concentrate on my reading.

She chose to ignore my hint and continued. "When you learned to smile, it was like sunshine! Your entire face lit up with contagious happiness."

"You're so dramatic," I said, rolling my eyes.

She laughed, but out of habit commented, "Don't roll your eyes at me, young lady!" Mamma continued. "Somehow, twelve years have slipped by, and my little baby will soon be a woman!" She looked out the window. "And I am no longer the twenty-two-year-old woman I was back then," she said, running her hands down the front of her apron and over the generous curves of her hips.

My mother recently celebrated her thirty-forth birthday and I knew she had been thinking a lot about getting older. One day I overheard her talking with my Aunt, commenting that some days could drag on so slowly with washing, cooking, and cleaning; seemingly endless chores of both family and the inn, and yet it seemed that time in general seemed to pass at such a swift pace.

"'Enjoy these days now, Anna Maria Seigrist Etter. They will be gone before you know it!' That's what your grandmother always tells me," said my mother. I could hear the insistent voice of my grandmother as if she were in the room with us. Helena Hofer Siegrist always addressed her daughter by full name when giving a lecture, which it seemed she did more often than not.

I watched as my mother turned back to the cake batter and resumed stirring. She seemed particularly pleased with me this day and it was comforting to know how much she loved me. What a blessing to feel such warmth and kindness.

"You are such a delight to our entire family," mother went on. "And a good example for your little sisters, especially. I know Elizabeth and Susanna are still small, but they look up to you already."

Although inpatient to get back to reading, as a sign of respect I kept quiet and let her continue.

"Katharina, you have earned a reputation in the villages for your gracious and compassionate ways."

I brushed off her compliments with a wave of my hand.

"No really," insisted mother. "I am so proud of you. Just last week Mrs. Staam told me how you stopped to help her carry a basket home from the market. And I heard George's mother telling a friend how you made him smile by singing that silly song after he scuffed up his knee."

My mother, knowing how easily I got lost in a good story, could tell I was eager to get back to my book.

"A dreamer..." I thought I heard Mamma say quietly, a smile playing at the corners of her mouth.

"What's that, Mamma?" I asked.

"Oh, nothing," she said, looking over at me. "I was just thinking that you are such a castle-builder...a romantic at heart. So much like your father."

"Well, I take that as a compliment," I replied, rewarding my mother with one of those sunny smiles she loved to talk about. "As Papa so often says, 'Where there is no vision, the people perish.'"

"Well dear, that is true... all scripture is....but I'm not sure it really applies to visions of adventure and enchantment; such as you find in your reading." She winked at me.

I laughed at her observation. "I know. But do you think that God puts some dreams in our heart? Maybe as a way to help us find our way in life?" I asked this question offhandedly, but I truly did often question within myself how God worked. It was very confusing to me.

"I don't know Katharina, perhaps. I suppose that the trick is to make sure you don't mix up your own desires with those that God plants in your heart," Mamma said and crossed the short distance to where I sat in the chair. She gently laid a flour-dusted hand upon my shoulder.

71

She continued speaking, looking down at me, her soft voice filled with wisdom. "Among your most beloved writers, be sure to include the one who authored the greatest book of all. It is there that you will find the answers to life's most important questions, and it is within those pages that God will give you the direction that you seek. He has great plans for you, my daughter; plans to give you a future filled with hope. I pray daily that he will fulfill the calling that he has for your life."

I took a moment to think about what she said. I wanted to believe in such an attentive God, but I was not sure He had a calling just for me or that He even loved me specifically. He was so far away, and there were so many people for Him to watch over, why would He care about me?

Finally distracted from my reading I looked at my mother pleadingly. "Mamma, can you tell me the story about Lady Katharina?" I implored.

Mamma cast a glance around the kitchen, eying the dirty pots waiting to be scrubbed and surveying the planked floor that needed swept. Making a quick decision, she winked at me and shooed me from the rocking chair. I quickly rearranged myself and sat cross-legged in front of her on the floor, much like when I was a younger child.

"Of course you know I will tell the story. Name one year I've missed telling it on your birthday," she challenged. Mamma then closed her eyes and inhaled deeply as she pictured her birthplace and remembered the crisp, mountain air.

"I was born in the Swiss Community of Vordemwald," she said. I already knew this, but sat patiently, knowing that mother always started the story the same way. It was a comforting ritual to hear her gentle voice repeat the familiar tale. My siblings found it boring, but for me, hearing about the noble Lady held special meaning because of our shared name.

Mamma continued the story, staring out the window with an air of contentment. "The treasured skill of weaving was passed down through the generations in my village. I was no exception to the rule. In fact, I loved it and excelled!"

I silently agreed. My brothers and I had benefitted from mother's able teaching. My younger sisters would also learn when they got older. Though I was becoming quite proficient, I had to admit that my brother Peter was most talented among the children.

"A person should know where they come from. And you, Sweetheart, have weaving in your blood." Pride wrapped around the statement. "From both sides of your family. Your grandfather, Heinrick Etter was a weaver too." Shaking her head, she lamented, "Your poor Papa, losing his father at such a young age. He was only seven years old when it happened….But anyway, now. Back to the point," Mamma got her story back on track. "Weaving. I was an accomplished weaver and was lucky to gain employment at a castle owned by Baron Albrecht von Erlach in Riggisburg. He and his wife, Baroness Lady Katharina, lived mainly at their other grand estate, but they would often come out to their smaller residence where I was employed.

I suppose that the world would not call her beautiful, but Lady Katharina's true appeal was found in her kind and good spirit. She wore her long, dark hair piled high upon her noble head, and although she held the fate of our livelihood in her hands, the staff was always excited when we spotted her coming our way. Though a baroness, she valued us as people, not just servants."

Mother expected me to share not only the name, but those honorable traits as well. The next part of the telling was always bittersweet. Though I loved my name, I knew that I was not the first Etter daughter christened such.

Even though many years had passed, Mamma lovingly recalled Christmas morning 1711. "Your father and I started out to church from the inn that chilly morning. I had walked down the sloping, wooded hill to the church many times before, but it seemed so much steeper as I carried my tiny Anna Katharina that day. But the walk was worth the effort. As we christened our little girl during the service, our friends and her godparents gathered with us. It was a lovely ceremony. We felt so blessed that day to have three noble families as godparents to our daughter. It was an honor."

I realize now how highly regarded my parents must have been among their acquaintances to have been recognized in such a manner. Though remnants of sadness remained, the time for tears had passed long ago, and Mamma spoke with a soft reverence and gentle remembrance. She implored me, much as her own mother had instructed her, to cherish the good days when they come, for surely they will not last forever. Like so many other little ones, baby Anna Katharina did not survive infancy.

Mamma turned to me with a thin reflective smile. "Oh that she would have lived to be your older sister. But that was not meant to be, and now you will carry on the name and good virtue of Lady Katharina."

So as to end the story on a happier note, Mamma continued and told of life in the castle. I envisioned grand balls where genteel ladies were swept off their feet by sophisticated gentlemen as they twirled around the dance floor to the melodic and elegantly plunking tunes of the harpsichord. Once again, as it did every year, my imagination took flight upon the wings of the story.

Later that same day, my father, Johannes "Hans" Etter hurried home to the inn. Although the lifestyle of traveling innkeeper might not have suited everyone, I think he rather enjoyed the change of view from time to time. And what a view it was! The Swiss mountains towered over the canton of Bern, dwarfing all of man's architectural endeavors. And although father had lived in Switzerland for his entire life, he told me that the magnificent grandeur still took his breath away.

Clutched in father's big hand, I could see a small bouquet of flowers, freshly picked from along the path leading up to the inn. He knew the joy they would bring to me, for I have always been able to appreciate and savor the simple things in life. As he got closer, he tried to hide them from me behind his back.

"Papa!" I exclaimed excitedly, racing toward him with open arms and full grin.

Quickly, he kissed my cheek and we embraced. "Happy Birthday, *Kätzchen*! My goodness, I believe that you have grown since yesterday my dear. Where has my little girl gone?"

"Oh don't be silly!" I wrinkled my nose at him as we continued walking toward home, but I delighted in the attention and use of my pet name, Kitten. "You know I'm not any bigger, really," I rushed on, the words rolling off my tongue like a galloping horse. "I am having a wonderful birthday though! Mamma let me take the whole afternoon to read and everybody is coming over for my birthday supper tonight and Mamma made me a lovely cake and…"

74

"Slow down!" my father interrupted with a hearty laugh. "Stop walking for a minute. Close your eyes and hold out your hands," he instructed. As I obeyed, he pulled out the flowers.

"Okay, open up!"

"They're beautiful! I love them!" I accepted the bright array of yellow, orange, and red flowers and brought them to my nose, inhaling deeply of their intoxicating fragrance.

"All of those sunny colors reminded me so much of you that when I saw them, I just had to pick them for your special day."

"You are the best!" I beamed.

"Let's just hope your mamma thinks so too after I get done talking to her tonight," he raised an eyebrow and focused on taking the last few steps up to the door.

"You want to go where? And do what?!" squeaked Mamma in an incredulous voice. She was used to her husband's lofty ambitions, but this was crazy, even for him! Papa sat across the table from her, his jaw set. He was serious about this idea and would not be taken lightly. I knew without a doubt that my father desired for Mamma to see it the way he did.

Just that day, a customer patronizing the inn was full of excitement as he told of his plans to board a ship in Rotterdam and from there sail to the colonies. Father was instantly taken with the idea, but just as quickly, he thought of how my Mamma would respond to such a plan. Her sense of caution always seemed to be at odds with his zeal to forge ahead and try new things. Although it proved to be quite frustrating at times, every once in a while he admitted that her cooler head and measured approach saved him from making a mistake.

I smiled to myself as I anticipated another spirited debate between my father and mother. Though their opinions were sometimes as different as oil and water, they always resolved the conflict by the end of the day and went to bed at night without bitterness stored up in their hearts. Actually, it was usually my mother who made the peace. Sometimes it really bothered me the way she backed down, even when she knew that she was right. Mamma said that it was Biblical to act that way towards your husband, but I wasn't sure if I would be able to be that forgiving to a

75

husband of my own someday. Thankfully, I had no need to worry about that. I was only twelve and had no plans to be married for a long time!

"Think of the opportunity!" my father's tone begged for consideration. "What it could mean for our family."

"What it could mean for our family?!" My mother questioned him, her voice an octave higher than usual. "Do you mean such as the possibility of being shipwrecked or the near certainty of never seeing my mother again?" She sounded sure that her husband had lost his mind for good.

"I think it sounds great," piped up John, my youngest brother. "The boys will go with you Papa, but we might as well leave the girls here if they don't want to go!" he laughed. "What do you think, Gerhard?" he passed the verbal baton to my 11-year-old brother.

"Who needs girls?" The youngster declared, rolling his eyes toward me and my younger sisters.

"Now boys, I won't have you talk about your mother and sisters like that," Papa firmly corrected his sons. "Besides," he said playfully, "we can't clear two-hundred acres of land with no one to cook supper for us at the end of the day!"

"I cook!" My two year old sister, Elizabeth, piped up and everyone laughed.

My mother seemed to soften a bit as Papa joked, but she would not easily dismiss the weight of what he purposed. "It would be too dangerous," She said, biting her lip and shaking her head in worry. "We wouldn't have a place to live. We wouldn't know what to expect," she carefully listed her concerns. "Surely, it is no place to raise a family."

My father decided to let the subject rest for a while. I think he knew that he had already accomplished the hardest part by approaching the topic. They could discuss it at length later.

"Enough talk of such things," said Papa. "Let's have a slice of that birthday cake!" He smiled at me.

I returned my father's smile, and although I relished eating my dessert and was thrilled with the new book that I had received as a gift from my mother; my mind was preoccupied with romantic images of tall ships and crashing waves.

Filled with drive and great vigor, my father was ready to board the next ship to the colonies back in the year 1728. In reality, it took years for him to fulfill the plan. The trip was extremely expensive and it took a long time to convince my mother of the benefits involved in such a risky venture. But, true to father's character, his persistence paid off.

In August of 1735, seven years after the birthday dinner, the heat of summer enveloped Oberried, our family's newest place of residence. However, as nighttime slowly began its approach, the air became cooler and more refreshing. At nineteen years of age, I now carried a full load of responsibility and I was glad to escape the busy inn to relax after a long day.

Leaning back against a soft, grassy knoll, I soaked in the loveliness of the tranquil setting. Sloping, vivid green pastures humbly made way to the lake's edge below, where the majestic mountains' reflection was mirrored in the clear, deep blue water. It was the best time of day to appreciate the subtle shifting of soft sunlight and periwinkle shadows as they played tag along the snow-capped peaks. I went there often to relax and think. The verdant hillside, with its unobstructed sunset view, was then my favorite place in the whole world.

Glancing down at my lap, I smoothed the paper of a well-read letter between my fingers. Contemplating life's changes and looking out again at the mountains, I realized the towering peaks were an ever-present part of my life. The view changed depending on the location of the inn, but they were always there.

I often thought upon the attributes of God when I visited this spot and I remembered how my father once told me that like the Alps, God was an unchanging, rock-solid sentinel of my life. I remembered him saying that God's presence and existence added joy and meaning to each day. But though the years passed, I still did not claim for myself any strong religious convictions. However, the fact that God would create such grandeur and beauty made me consider that maybe He did care about me and desire to give me good things in life.

Turning my attention back to the letter, I looked down to read the scrawled ink in the waning light. Having read it so many times before, it was nearly memorized. That my father packed his belongings early that spring and left us to embark on the journey of a lifetime was sometimes still incomprehensible.

My mother, though a steadfast and resilient woman, struggled with the new course of her life. Having lived contentedly in Switzerland since birth, she did not see the necessity of such a life-altering move. Worry weighed heavily on her mind and tears replaced the laughter which once came to her so easily. None of us admitted it, but we had all worried that perhaps my father drowned at sea, was attacked by natives, or had starved to death. My mind found no limit to the appalling possibilities that could have befallen him.

But at last it came; a letter written in the strong hand of Hans Etter, stating he reached his destination safely. I closed my eyes and pictured what it must have been like for him and the eighteen other families from Berne who lived aboard the ship Oliver from springtime until they arrived mid-summer in South Carolina. The thought of spending so much time on the water made my stomach churn and I fervently hoped that it would be a much faster journey when it was my turn to sail.

My father wrote that many people aboard his ship had to sell themselves into servitude upon arrival and remained in the humidity of South Carolina. Only those with adequate money were able to continue northward to Philadelphia. Papa continued with news that he finally made it to Philadelphia, and after a time, traveled to the interior of Pennsylvania where he purchased two-hundred acres of wooded land in Donegal Township. His letter gushed with the enthusiasm of a young boy and although I missed him very much, I smiled and ventured a guess that he was having the time of his life. He expressed his deep love for us and begged that we join him as soon as possible. I turned my gaze again toward the Alps, wondering if there were any mountains at all in Pennsylvania.

Chapter 2

Pennsylvania

1740

I found that no mountain in Pennsylvania rivaled the height or grandeur of those in Switzerland, but I grew to love the rolling hills, nonetheless. As a twenty-three year old woman, I stood up slowly and gently massaged the small of my back with a calloused hand, stained with Lancaster County soil. Working in the cool earth always brought me joy. I especially loved the month of October, when summertime desperately clung to its glory days. I knew that soon, the icy frost would conquer, and warmth would again await its triumphant return in June.

As I watched my teenage sisters, Susanna and Elizabeth, diligently working in their own patch of garden I was thankful again that it was a good year for our crops and plants; such as it had been for most of the neighboring farmers in our growing community. I turned to my squash plants and took time to analyze them before plucking one that was the perfect shade of butternut yellow. I imagined the burst of mellow flavor it would yield when cooked along the other late season vegetables in the supper stew.

As I withdrew my hand from my pocket, I noticed again the remnants of dark brown dirt caked between my fingers, and I determined to give them a good scrubbing with lye soap when I finished. I tried to ignore the pain in my back. Though the constant bending and hoeing stretched the muscles of my thin frame, the fresh air and hard work made me strong and I found calming power in the act of planting a seed and then nurturing it to its full potential.

"More than pleasure," I thought. "It is a necessity." There were no markets in a nearby town square. It was both rewarding and intimidating to think that survival depended on the results of our own labor. If one did not work, one simply did not eat. Fortunately, the land was incredibly fertile and the forests brimmed with game. My father told me that German and Swiss farmers became eager to settle this area when they saw the large amount of hardwood trees growing in the forests. John, my youngest brother, further explained that hardwood trees grow best when the land is rich in limestone, as this type of soil in turn makes for a very productive crop.

"Well, there are certainly plenty of trees," I said, shaking my head. In fact, sometimes I felt hemmed in by the forest. Slowly, more patches of open land were being cultivated, but it was difficult and time consuming work to clear the land of trees and then plow a field. One technique father used to obtain more planting area was to take a ring of bark off the trees, causing them to die. Once dead, the branches were bare of leaves, allowing sunlight to reach the ground and crops below. Eventually, he would cut down the dead trees and use the wood as needed.

I scanned the winding dirt path that led up to our cabin, hoping to see one of my brothers, either John or Gerhard, coming home from their hunt. Venison, or maybe a few rabbits, would taste good. In the three years since settling, my brothers had become very good shots with their rifles and the Etter family table rarely lacked meat.

As I gently pocketed some freshly harvested carrots next to the squash in the large pocket of my homespun apron, I again anticipated the aromas they would create in our kitchen as they cooked in the big pot over the fire. The kitchen was the heart of our small home, the first room to be entered into when walking through the door. For me, this part of the house always brought back memories of hours spent cooking for guests in our Swiss kitchens.

Taking the vegetables out of my apron and placing them on our roughly hewn kitchen table, I watched as Mamma stacked wood in the large stone fireplace. She stirred the coals, which we endeavored to always keep burning, and as the flames caught the kindling crackled. The smell of smoke lasted a few seconds before catching up into the draft and being sucked out through the chimney.

"I was just thinking about Switzerland," I admitted to my mother, as I carefully wiped a small, unexpected tear from the corner of my eye with the tip of my finger. I had thought my years of moving from village to village would prepare me for this change of living in a new country, but it had been surprisingly difficult. Mamma gave me a sympathetic smile. She understood how I felt, but encouraged and bolster my spirit.

"Katharina. I miss Switzerland too, but this is our home now and we must learn to think of it that way. We are together as a family. I know you understand that is the most important thing. Remember the years of separation from your father? That was no way to live! You know that I, above most people, was scared to leave what I knew and loved, but God has placed His hand of blessing on us. Your father and your brothers are thriving here."

A certain topic had been bothering me of late, and I spoke of it now. "I'm going to become an old maid here." I declare flatly. I seldom sulked, but I had been feeling dejected lately about fulfilling my sentimental desire to fall in love.

"Now listen to me," Mamma sighed. "You know there are many available men here who would take you as their wife in a heartbeat, if only you would give them a second glance. I know that your mind is filled with notions of fanciful passion, but you may have to put that aside. This is not an easy place for a single woman to live. You would do much better to be married to a man who can support and take care of you."

"I've tried to be open to the possibilities, I really have," I responded. Thinking of the rough and hardened older men I encountered, I grimaced. Some were widowed and looking for a mother to care for their children. Some wanted a cook and housekeeper. The younger men were better looking maybe, but none captured my devotion or had the depth of character that I was looking for in a partner. I wanted someone who would understand my heart, share my dreams, appreciate my imagination and cherish my personality.

Mother and I were both silent in our own thoughts when the door opened and my brother, John, ambled into the kitchen. His light brown hair had been tussled by the wind and a crooked grin sat on his face. He stepped toward me and rumpled my hair with his dirty hand.

"Stop that!" I declared, rather sharply. "Go bother Elizabeth! I'm not a child anymore, and look at your hands, they're filthy! Go wash before you come back into the kitchen."

"Oh Kat, you're so bossy! Don't get so upset. No, you're not a child, but you're still my sister. Always will be, so get used to it," he said. And to prove his point, he reached for my hair again.

This time, I expected it and ducked out of the way in time, laughing despite myself. "Did you shoot anything?"

"Of course I did," he retorted. "A nice buck. He's hanging out back."

John became quiet and I noticed that he was biting his lip the way he often did when something was on his mind. With concern and a growing sense of trepidation, I asked, "What's troubling you? You've grown awfully quiet."

"I was going to wait to talk about it until Pa got home, but since you asked, I'll tell you now. I ran into Jacob Banga out on the road and it seems that his wife's nephew and family have arrived from their voyage."

"That's wonderful," my mother enthused! "Anna and Jacob have been waiting so long to see them! Four little boys aren't there?"

John worked hard to swallow before slowly recounting the story of Anna's brother, Johannes, and the tragedy that took place. By the end of its telling, Mamma and I were in tears. My heart ached for this man and his two remaining sons who had lost so much. I also cried for Anna and her family, who had anticipated a happy family reunion. She had spoken of little else after receiving the letter announcing their plans to come to Pennsylvania.

Later that evening I sat in the rigid chair positioned by the spinning wheel, carefully feeding the wool and turning it into thread. The nights were growing brisk with cold, but the fire warmed us.

Father read aloud in our German tongue from the worn Bible, one of the few books we brought with us on our journey. His seasoned voice reassured and calmed, as did the familiar words that spoke of a God who cared for us and loved us; A father who would console us amidst the trials of life. Despite my doubts, my heart seemed to find some comfort in the idea.

My thoughts again turned to Johannes Kapp and his two small sons. I offered a prayer, hoping that if God heard me and if the Bible's words were true, that the Kapp family would find "Peace that passes understanding," as God promised. It would definitely need to *pass understanding*, because how was it possible to apply logic or reason to such a tragedy?

Father finished reading, and then told us his plans to visit with the Banga family the following day. Johannes and his sons were staying at their home until their own cabin was finished, and so it would be a combined condolence and welcome visit. My brothers and sisters planned to stay home while Mamma and I would join Father.

That night, as I lay on the rye ticking of my mattress in the loft, my mind raced with worry about what I should say to Mr. Kapp and the Banga family. Some people seemed blessed with a gift of easily expressing their sympathy. I was not one of those people.

"What if I say the wrong thing?" I anxiously thought. "I don't want to add to their troubles. Maybe I should just stay home. I could write a letter expressing my sympathy. That is usually easier for me. It might be better for everyone." For an instant, the idea of staying home brought relief from my worry, but then I realized it may be perceived as rude and uncaring if I did not go along. Cathy, the Banga's daughter, was one of my best friends and she probably needed a listening ear.

Finally, my fatigue from a long day of hard work overcame me and I drifted off into a restless sleep, resigned to face the difficult day ahead.

The next day, the ride to the Banga's house seemed endless, but despite my misgivings, I enjoyed the beauty of the crisp, autumn weather and the rolling hills beckoned to my nature-loving spirit. Mr. Kapp was a wagon maker, so I had been told, and as the wagon I

83

rode in bumped along, I examined it carefully. It was not fancy, but I suppose it accomplished its purpose.

"That sums up life in Pennsylvania," I thought, thinking of our humble house and the utilitarian nature of so many things in the colonies. But had I given more thought to it, I would have remembered that even the iron stove in our house bore the marks of detailed, creative craftsmanship and had been designed to tell a story, with characters and pictures molded into the sides, depicting Biblical accounts. The same details and care could be seen in the iron works of some of our household goods, such as the waffle maker, and on the pretty paintings applied to earthenware plates and jugs.

At last, we arrived at the Banga's home. Next to the house was a shed filled with the various tools and equipment used by a cooper, the trade practiced by Jacob Banga. The man's skill was admirable. I caught the scent of oak in the air as we drove by the shed.

At the cabin door, we were welcomed into the log home with hugs from Anna Banga and her daughter, my friend, Cathy. Immediately, I noticed the dark haired man standing close to Mrs. Banga, and I knew that this must be her brother, Johannes. A young boy clung to his leg, while an older one stood a bit behind him, trying to blend into the shadows of the room.

The resemblance between Mrs. Banga and Johannes was striking. The man did not appear as forlorn as I had anticipated. His was voice clear and steady; his mannerisms quite charming.

"Perhaps it is for the sake of the children," I guessed to myself. *"Yes, that must be it,"* I thought as I looked into his eyes and saw there a combination of determination and raw grief. His eyes told a completely different story than the one he portrayed with his smile.

"Johannes," Mrs. Banga said, turning to her brother. "Jonny, and Johan Jacob," she continued the introduction. "I'd like to introduce you to our friends, Hans and Maria Etter. And this is their dear daughter, Katharina."

Anna Banga's smile encompassed us all. No doubt she was feeling joyous to be near her brother and nephews. However, I was suddenly alarmed as I looked closer at the older woman. She appeared much thinner than the last time I saw her, and dark circles hung heavy under her eyes. I decided that I needed to ask Cathy about her mother's health as soon as possible. Mrs. Banga had been a friend to our family in the few years we had known each other, and the thought that she may be ill concerned me very much.

Formally trained doctors were scarce in this rural area, and those who did have some type of knowledge usually learned it in the arena of practical experience. Sometimes, we consulted with the Indian women to learn of their traditional remedies. I had recently learned that parts of the Hemlock tree were valued for its medicinal properties, and was warned not to confuse it with a poisonous weed that looks very similar, but could have fatal effects. Chewing the bark of a willow tree was also useful, as it could help relieve a headache. It was very important to speak with someone experienced in the use of such remedies before trying them, for it was critical to make sure they were properly prepared or the results could be deadly. In our own garden, we grew herbs used for simple remedies, but if a person was truly ill, the outcome was often grim.

Pushing those thoughts away, I watched as my father extended a welcoming hand and clasped the newly arrived younger man's upper arm in sincerity. In a fatherly voice he said, "Son, we are truly sorry for your loss. May you find comfort in knowing that your loved ones are in the presence of our good Lord."

At the mention of the tragedy, Johannes looked down and I imagined him blinking back unshed tears, but when he again looked up at the elder man, he sounded confident.

"Thank you for your kind words, Mr. Etter. We miss Judith and Leo and Ben terribly. We are trying our best to keep our focus on the future and not dwell on the past."

My father nodded his head in silent understanding and I knew he was thinking that a man with that kind of attitude would get along well in the frontier.

Mrs. Banga directed us like a mother hen, gently instructing, "Let's all move into the sitting room. There's a little more space in here, and some of you can just have a seat on the bed or sit on a chair around the table there." Her sweeping arms gestured for us to be seated on one of the wooden chairs or upon the low bed to the side of the room that was covered with a red and black plaid woolen blanket. "Cathy, would you and Katharina mind fetching some cider and ale from the kitchen for our guests?" she asked.

I followed my friend around the partition and into the kitchen area. As in our own kitchen, the room was dominated by the large

85

stone fireplace, its raised hearth providing a warm seat on a chilly day. Above it on the mantle rested some candle molds and a red earthenware oil lamp. Cathy poured the cider and ale into the heavy pewter mugs and handed them to me.

"Perhaps the boys could share, as well as the married folks. I'm afraid we don't have enough cups for everyone," she apologized.

"Oh Cathy, don't mind that," I admonished. "You know that hardly anyone would have enough to go around for this many people. Don't worry yourself over it."

"You're right, I guess," she admitted.

Before taking the drinks back to the other guests, I turned to Cathy, asking in a lowered voice, "And how are you? I know how much you were looking forward to Judith being here and to meeting the entire family. This must be very hard for you as well."

Cathy was silent for a moment and then responded quietly, "It was such a shock when Johannes showed up here without them. I knew as soon as I saw him and the boys without the rest of the family that something was not right, but I asked if they were resting overnight at a tavern or somewhere." She continued, "When Johannes shook his head 'no', I broke down into sobs. Later, he told me more about what happened. Katharina," she said with concern, "no man should have to go through that. I know everyone is touched by loss, but he and Judith had already lost so many children before leaving Switzerland. It just seems too much for one person to bear."

"And yet he seems so controlled," I observed. "If it were me, I wouldn't be able to hold myself together at all."

"Yes, he does put on a brave face. For the boys, I assume," responded Cathy, "but also, I suppose doesn't know what else to do but move forward and continue on with life the best way he knows how."

"Will the boys stay with you as he goes about getting settled?"

"Well, I've offered him my help, but lately, Mamma has not been feeling well. I can't seem to put my finger on it, but she is always so tired, and I'm sure you noticed how pale she is. I'm really worried about her. I've been trying my best to do most of the chores, but you know she has a hard time just sitting by watching me work."

I imagined how hard it must be for Mrs. Banga. Her charity was well known, even throughout our sparsely populated community.

"Although I hate to say it so soon after Judith has passed on," Cathy said with a sigh, her eyes begging me to understand, "whether he likes it or not, his best solution would be to find another wife to help care for the children."

I could see that the mention of trying to replace Judith so quickly caused Cathy discomfort, but I too had seen the advantages to both men and women who found themselves in similar situations. And although I still harbored dreams of romance for myself, I knew that many marriages were carried out in a far more practical, business-like fashion.

As we returned to the sitting room, I noticed that Johannes was observing Cathy and me as we served the drinks. He, and anyone that cared to look, could see that we were different as night and day. Cathy had neatly plaited straw colored hair and smoky gray eyes. I, on the other hand, had dark eyes and brunette hair hanging loose about my shoulders. Different, yes, but it was the genuine warmth we shared that made us fast friends.

I leaned down towards the little boy, Jonny, and offered him a drink. He drew close and whispered a secret in my ear. I have always loved children and seem to have a way that sets them at ease. After playfully ruffing up the little boy's hair, I approached Johannes to serve his drink. I shed my comfort and replaced it with nervous hesitancy, silent but smiling.

"You cannot possibly remember a day so long ago when you first served me a drink when you were just a little child," he commented.

I sat the mug before him and bit my lip out of an abundance of shy energy. His eyes followed me and I wondered if he was comparing what he saw to this child he remembered. I felt the effects of a man who sees a woman standing before him, and somehow I knew he thought I was beautiful. But the look was fleeting, and quickly hidden behind other emotions evident in his stormy eyes.

"No, I don't remember," I replied confused.

"You were a cute little thing," he smiled and laughed quietly, recalling. "Very confident and with a particularly wonderful nature. It's not often a child leaves such a lasting impression on a person, but that memory sticks with me for some reason. I recognized your mother as soon as I saw her standing in the doorway today. My father and I were guests at your inn many years ago. She may not remember."

Maybe it came from our meeting so long ago even if I did not remember it… I don't know; but I felt a connection to the man and I was not sure what to think about that.

Chapter 3

Gray sky and chilling drizzle accompanied us, the mourners, as we made our way silently up the meandering path from the house to the graveyard. It was not yet the end of November, 1740. Johannes and his children had been in Pennsylvania for less than two months. I felt the sadness that must weigh anew on his heart as he contemplated the death of his forty-six-year-old sister. I hoped his sorrow was soothed by the fact he had been able to see her once again, if only for a short time.

Cathy walked a few steps in front of me, holding the hand of her father. She was a sweet friend and embodied a good and kind spirit. She felt a responsibility to care for the needs of her father, now that her mother was gone, but I also had a feeling that it would not be long until she found a husband and moved into a home of her own. Many people were a little surprised that she had not done so already, as most of the women our age were already married and tending to children.

Both Cathy and her father slowed and accepted a molasses funeral cookie from a young girl on the right side of the path, and a cup of ale from a young man on the left side. "Another reminder of home," I thought, envisioning funerals of the past and those ever-present cookies. I absently wondered what motif would be stamped upon its middle. Would it be an angel, a skull, an hourglass? I moved ahead and took my hard cookie, noticing the imprinted heart in its center. It was an appropriate symbol with which to honor Mrs. Banga. What a gracious heart she had possessed. Always loving and caring, she was selfless.

Cathy confided to me that Mrs. Banga had taken the time, even in her illness, to talk to her brother Johannes about the importance of trusting God and accepting His perfect will for his life. Mrs. Banga told her daughter that Johannes had done his share of "worldly living." Even though marriage and children had settled him considerably, she sensed the old restlessness that had always been there. She also knew he was angry that God allowed such terrible circumstances to come into his life.

Cathy told me that Johannes had not been ready to deal with such deep issues when her mother talked to him a few weeks ago. But Mrs. Banga thought that soon he would need to take an honest look at himself and resolve the feelings of hurt and anger that churned deep inside of him. I felt like an intruder upon Johannes's personal life when Cathy told me of this, but also found it fascinating to gain a deeper understanding of the man. As the mourners stood at the graveside singing hymns, Johannes looked over at my family and his eyes held mine for a moment. Wordless sorrow passed between us. Dipping my cookie into the ale, I closed my eyes and savored its distinct, sweet flavor. Tenuous was the gift of life and I determined not to waste it.

A few straggling snowflakes sparkled against the sapphire sky and drifted lazily on a soft current. They settled gently atop the already whitened ground outside of our snug cabin. Inside the sturdy log walls, my neighbors joined together around our kitchen table. In the absence of a church building, friends and relatives gathered together in homes to celebrate Sunday service. Johannes was among the congregation. In the months since coming to the colonies, he had spent several hours as a welcome and invited guest in our home.

"Maybe next year we will have a real church building," quietly mused an older woman as she gently eased herself down into the seat at the table. I helped her get settled and smiled at her. The sight of her chapped hands nervously smoothing at her silver hair, tugged at my heart. I wondered what else she had given up in recent years, besides the comfort of a pew and the reassuring words of a regular minister. Not long ago, I overheard some of the other neighbors also discussing their desire to someday have a real church building where we could meet to worship with the Reformed Church congregation. I agreed that it would be a bit more civilized to have an actual building, but I wondered if it would weaken the special bond forged from meeting in a friend's home. The nearby Donegal Presbyterian congregation had started work on construction of a stone church to replace their log structure. Two hundred acres had been deeded to them by William Penn, but I doubted we would be so fortunate to receive such a gift.

"Land is everything in this new country," I thought, recalling the conversation I heard my brother Gerhard having with Johannes when he arrived to the meeting today. Johannes had produced a parchment paper from his shirt pocket and told my brother he had just recently obtained the land warrant for his acreage on December 24, 1740.

I liked the name he chose for his plantation, Safe Retreat. I hoped it would be a self-fulfilling prophecy…a place to call home, where minds and bodies would find refuge from the difficulties and trials of the past and be enabled to focus on a new path. The idea of building a new homestead was exciting, but I could not help thinking it would have been advantageous to start construction earlier in the year, had he been able to do so.

The tract of land would suit his wagon business well, as part of the property was located along the main route running from Lancaster to Harrisburg. If he could build his home and wagon business close enough to the trail, travelers passing by would be able to take full advantage of his services. The rough roads and uneven terrain wreaked havoc on wagons and wheels, and I had no doubt his services would be in high demand. He had spent years apprenticing and honing his skills as a wagon maker in Europe and my father and brothers thought that Johannes would be up to the task of satisfying even the toughest customer.

From what I overheard, Johannes was undecided about exactly where to build. Being near a road would benefit his business, but close proximity to a good water source was more important and usually the determining factor in where people chose to locate their home.

"Would you like more to drink, *Herr* Kapp?" I stopped by his seat at the table. I was helping my mother play hostess to our many guests; a role for which I had been well trained.

"Yes, I would *Fräulein*. Thank you," replied Johannes, a tiny smile tugging up the corner of his mouth. "But please, just call me John. People here have taken to calling me that."

"Very well, *Herr* John." My eyes twinkled, and I knew full well he intended for me to drop the formal "*Herr*" and call him by his familiar name. It gave me pleasure to see the look in his eyes before he dropped his gaze down to his drink.

My attention was drawn to his strong, work-worn hands, as they encircled his cup. As I observed them along with his muscled arms, which were now recovered from his treacherous voyage and bolstered by months of hard work, I was sure he could easily manage with skill and strength to craft iron and wood into a wagon. Taking his mug, my hand brushed his and I caught my breath. I could feel heat rise to my face, and I hoped he did not notice. What would he think of me? The emotions stirring within me were difficult to ignore. The lighthearted jesting, the sensation of our hands meeting…it felt so comforting, and yet totally disconcerting.

Over the last month or two, I had gotten to know Johannes and his boys well. We had much in common. Although I was younger than he, our personalities connected and we talked easily. We shared a love of reading and we often discussed the importance of educating all children, even those far from city limits. From the corner of my eye, I looked over at Johannes's boys and observed them playing with a group of other children. The resilience of youth was slowly returning them to the happy, carefree children they had once been, but they deserved to have a mother. I suddenly had a desire to gather them in my arms and do my best to protect them from further assault of the harsh world.

Winter was really digging its heels into the January morning, and it appeared to be planning on staying in Lancaster County as long as it could. I sat by the fire, trying desperately to get rid of a deep chill that seeped into my bones; the kind I could not seem to shake. My mother was sitting in the far corner of the room, quietly carding wool.

As I worked to embroider a fine, colorful stitch on a white pillowcase, my thoughts wandered to my mother's insistence that I increase my efforts to fill my hope chest. Mamma always seemed to be harping on it, but lately she persisted even more and it annoyed me to no end. I had even recently started on a yellow woolen garment that would make a very nice wedding dress. Hickory tree leaves had turned the material into a splendid shade and it would complement my coloring to perfection. Secretly, I hoped that I would not morph into the shape of an old spinster before I had the chance to wear it. Wrinkling my nose, I chuckled to myself and thought, "Wouldn't Mamma laugh to know that the only person I can't stop thinking about is Johannes!"

I had been vocal with my opinions about young women who chased after prosperous bereaved men and about the callous frontiersmen who married for convenience. Pride inhibited me from admitting to my mother that Johannes, a widower, was stealing my heart. "Isn't that life?" I cringed. "Judge not, lest ye be judged" came to my mind.

A horse snorted loudly just outside the window and startled me from my thoughts. A knock came at the door and I laid aside my embroidery to jump up to answer it. Shivering for an instant, I wondered who would be out on such a day.

Upon opening the door, I forgot the cold. Hoping he could not read my mind, I welcomed the man whom I had been thinking about all morning.

"Johannes!" I exclaimed. I could not get used to calling him John despite his request, perhaps because he shared the name with my brother. My initial elation at seeing him quickly turned to worry. "What brings you over on such a cold day? Are the boys okay?"

"Don't worry. Everyone is fine." He placed a reassuring hand on my shoulder. "I've been working at my cabin, but I had to get something settled, and I just couldn't get any more work done until…" his voice trailed off as he looked to the corner of the house and saw my mother.

"Hello, Mrs. Etter. How are you?" She looked up from her wool and gave Johannes a knowing smile. "I'm fine, thank you Mr. Kapp," she said. "Come in! And my goodness, shut the door! It's freezing!"

"Yes ma'am," he replied, respect edging his voice. There was something else in his tone as well, but I could not place what it was.

"I don't want to be rude, but if you'll excuse me, I do need to go speak with Hans."

I looked at my mother, perplexed at her actions as she grabbed a thick coat, pulled on her leather work boots and exited quickly, trudging to the barn.

"I'm sorry, I don't know what that was about, but you are welcome to sit down. Mother and Father should be back from the barn soon. We just baked some sweets. They're still warm, would you like one?" I glanced at him and offered a soft biscuit.

"No thank you." Johannes paused and took a deep breath.

I sat the cookies back on the table and felt him staring at me. My heart skipped a beat and I looked at him, hoping to see my interest returned in his gaze. I thought I detected what I was looking for, but quickly it was replaced by emotions of only kindness and friendship and possibly a hint of fear. My spirit heaved a sigh of disappointment.

When he reached for my hand, my question must have been plainly written across my face. "What is this about?" I wondered aloud.

"Katharina," Johannes's firm voice faltered a little as he pulled in a deep breath as though to infuse his body with resolve. "Your father approached me with the idea of asking you to be my wife. I could provide for you and you would be a great help to my family. Would you consider marrying me?"

"My *Father* approached you?! I would be a great *help*?!" My world crumbled. Withdrawing my hand as if burned by his touch, I closed my eyes. Stinging tears clung to my dark lashes and threatened to spill down my cheeks. I could not be that woman.

"I'm sorry," I said, biting my lip and shaking my head in disbelief at what transpired. "Please go."

Mamma used to call me a dreamer and I knew she was correct. I dreamed of true love. For as long as I could remember I imagined how this should go; when the perfect man proposed the perfect question in precisely the perfect way. Melting in his secure embrace, all else would recede from my mind as he consumed me with fervent kisses.

As I looked at Johannes's befuddled expression, I knew with certainty that I loved this man, despite the artless delivery of his marriage offer. But no matter how much he meant to me, I would not marry a man who did not return my feelings. With bowed head, Johannes apologized and quietly left the house.

Through my tear-soaked eyes, I saw my mother emerge from the barn and stop to watch Johannes leave. Her breath escaped in a white puff as she let out a sigh and covered her heart with her hand. She felt sorry for him and she was probably mad at me. My sensitive nature was a blessing, but at times a curse. A more pragmatic girl would see the obvious prudence in hastily accepting an offer from such a kind and ambitious man, especially one she loved.

Mamma jogged the short distance back to the house, prodded on by the wind's brutal chill. A few moments later, she entered the warm house and sat down beside me on the bed, embracing me. My eyes were already blood shot and my nose red from crying.

"Sweetheart, what's wrong?" she asked. To my relief, she sounded more concerned than angry.

"I am so mixed up," I admitted, my voice trembling along with the rest of my body.

"He asked me to marry him," another sob escaped, and then my eyes narrowed. "But you already knew," I accused. "That's why you went to the barn, isn't it?"

Mamma wrung her hands as she confessed to as much, and said to me, "I'm so sorry if we went about this in the wrong way, but I was sure that you had feelings for the poor man, and I thought that I detected an interest on his part as well. Otherwise, I would not have encouraged it. I know how you feel about such things, but I thought this could work."

As I buried my head in her supporting shoulder and cried with even greater force, Mamma realized there was more to my reaction than anger or embarrassment. "Tell me?" she made the simple request.

Eventually, I meekly conceded, "I love him."

"Then what is the problem?" she asked, throwing her hands up in the air, exasperated.

"He doesn't care for me." Tears threatened again, but I continued. "He only wants a housekeeper, a mother for his children. He said I would be a *help*! I won't settle for that. I want to be loved for who I am, not wed for the services I can provide."

"Did you ask him if he loves you?"

"What's the point? How can a man so quickly forget the woman he adored most of his life since childhood. You've heard how he speaks of her, mother."

"Don't you think a heart can love more than one person? Do you think that just because he loved his wife he cannot love his children or others?" questioned Mamma.

"That's different, and you know it. And what would people say? They would think I married him only out of convenience."

"Who cares what *people* say? Besides, *people* would probably approve because it *is* convenient. It makes perfect sense for both of you," said Mamma. "But no matter your decision," she continued, "you owe that man an explanation of how you acted today. I saw him leaving and he looked bewildered. I would even venture to say he looked quite sad."

"I would rather die than talk to him!" I panicked.

"Well then, let's proceed with the funeral arrangements!" Mamma crossed her arms over her chest in determination. "Otherwise, get dressed in your warmest clothing because you and your father are going to ride over to his cabin right now."

Arguing with my mother did no good, and I sat shivering in the saddle atop my gentle mare, on my way to confront the most awkward of situations. My father rode out in front of me on the narrow, dirt road leading to Johannes's new place. Neither of us said much to each other, and only the hollow clopping of horse hooves, somewhat dampened by the snowfall, echoed back from the bare trees that lined our snowy path. I could not believe that my mother was making us go out on such a day. She knew that the slippery roads posed a risk to the horses, as well as to us, but she was adamant.

"It's the *least* you owe Mr. Kapp. He deserves an explanation," Mamma had said again to Papa. "You led him to

96

believe he should expect a different answer from Katharina. She needs to talk to him."

My father just saddled the horses and wondered aloud why women had to make things so complicated. Now, as we approached the newly constructed cabin, father must be questioning if this was the best way to handle the matter after all, wondering if he should have come alone, leaving me at home. In my opinion, that would have been easier for everyone involved. But Mamma demanded that I speak with Johannes, and when she was set upon something it was almost impossible to avert her plans.

Father helped me down from my horse and then remounted his, watching as I stood knocking at the sturdy cabin door. He turned his horse toward home as the cabin door opened and I stepped inside. Three glass windows admitted filtered sunshine to the interior of the cabin, but it took a moment for my eyes to adjust. When they refocused, I saw Johannes standing in the middle of the room assessing me silently. His left arm rested on a pile of stones he was fashioning into a fireplace, waiting for me to make the first move. But I could not move, could not speak...I could barely breathe.

After what seemed like eternity, Johannes stepped toward me and took my hand in his for the second time that day. His other hand rested on my shoulder and drew me a step closer to him. His breath warmed the top of my head as I stared down at the new floor boards, apprehensive to look up and see what his eyes would tell me this time; afraid of what he might say...terrified of what he might *not* say.

"I wasn't completely honest with you before," he said.

I continued looking down but heard the sincerity in his voice, the apology.

"But I want to be honest with you now. Katharina, look at me...please." He tipped my chin upward with a gentle, yet steady hand, compelling me to look into his brown eyes.

"When I asked you to marry me...I meant it. It would be beneficial to both of us."

I started to pull away again. He held me firm.

"Look at me, Katharina."

I did.

"But it would mean more to me than that." His demeanor changed, as if a great burden had been lifted from him.

"Katharina, it's true. I still mourn for Judith. It would be false for me to say that I don't." he exhaled slowly, determined to go on. "You *would* be a good mother for my boys. I *would* provide a secure future for you. But what I meant to say the first time, but didn't have the courage to tell you, is that...I," he hesitated. "....I *love* you. I love the way you laugh with your family and friends. I love the way you roll your eyes when you're irritated. I love the gentle scent of lavender that lingers when you walk by me. I love the way you care about others and make everyone feel special. And I do love the way you bring hope and joy to my children. I do. I love you. I didn't plan or even want to feel this way about you and to be completely honest, there is part of me that feels disloyal to Judith. But I think she would want me to be happy and you make me happy," he said.

"I had hoped you might be able to love me too," he said, looking anything but happy. He released my hand. "But, I can see that it may be too soon for you. And I know I'm much older than you. Maybe your heart was set to find someone more your own age."

Tears glistened again in my eyes and I said nothing. It was not like him to be so open, and for the second time that day, he processed feelings of rejection.

"Please forgive me, Miss Etter. I've upset you and said too much." He said respectfully.

As he started to back away, my hand caught his again and I gently pulled him to me. "Johannes." I spoke only his name, but my tone held a thousand words and emotions. He could see now that my tears sprang from joy, not distress.

The guilt, the fear, the trepidation...all melted away as we stood together and I nodded my head "yes."

With a passion resurrected from his youth, he kissed me. Only one thought managed to cross my mind...This was perfect.

Chapter 4

We anticipated the circuit riding preacher's upcoming visit, and planned to hold the wedding when he reached us. Johannes worked diligently on the cabin, his boys helping the best they were able, and the men of the community also assisting. Putting the finishing touches on the contents of my hope chest and planning for the festivities kept me busy.

The day before the wedding, my mother and I baked one of my favorite cakes. I had flour, butter and eggs on hand, but I decided to substitute dried blueberries for currents and black walnuts in place of Jordan Almonds. Fortunately, I learned of a neighbor who was traveling to Philadelphia, and at the last minute I was able to request that he pick up some cloves, cinnamon, nutmeg and ginger along with some lemons and oranges. After the cake finished and cooled I covered it with a sugary white icing. I hoped the end result would justify the expense and taste as good as I remembered.

The wedding was held at my parents' house and relatives and friends crowded into the small space to witness our union. The ceremony was simple, and to me that made it beautiful. Mother earned my thanks for her insistence that I work so diligently on my wedding clothes. I wore the yellow dress and as my dark hair fell about my shoulders it created a lovely contrast to the light hue of the dress, just as I had hoped. In January there were no flowers per say, but I carried a bouquet of fragrant evergreens and crimson berries that my sisters gathered for me from the woods.

I stood before my family and friends to unite destinies with Johannes, and I found that I did not miss Switzerland nearly as much as I had just a few months ago. This country was now my real home and I was eager to forge ahead with new aspirations. Joining hands with my groom, I concentrated intensely upon the minister's words as he recited the ceremony from The Book of Common Prayer. At the conclusion of the minister's reading and after saying our vows to one another, Johannes whispered in my ear, marveling that despite all tragedy, he was so fortunate to find me. I did not want to wait until the end of the service to embrace him, but I found restraint.

Turning to the wedding guests, the minister asked if they would do all in their power to uphold the two of us in our marriage. In resounding affirmation, they respond, "We will."

The minister then led the singing of Psalm 128, one of my favorites for a wedding ceremony. When the hymn concluded, the reverend said to the people, "The Lord be with you."

To which the people responded in automatic unison, "And also with you."

"Let us pray," he instructed.

After the prayer, my brother, Gerhard walked to the front of the house to read another scripture. As I looked at Johannes, I hoped he would embrace the passage, seeing this day as a new beginning and a time to find joy again. Gerhard spoke the Holy words from the King James Bible with respect as he read Song of Solomon, Chapter 2 verses 10-13.

"My beloved spake, and said unto me, Rise up, my love, my fair one, and come away. For, lo, the winter is past, the rain is over and gone; The flowers appear on the earth; the time of the singing of birds is come, and the voice of the turtle is heard in our land; The fig tree putteth forth her green figs, and the vines with the tender grape give a good smell. Arise, my love, my fair one, and come away."

Gerhard returned to his seat and Johannes turned to face me, taking my hands in his. We pledged to take each other for better or worse, for richer for poorer, in sickness and in health, to love and to cherish, until parted by death. Everyone bowed their heads as the reverend asked God's blessing on the ring.

I tried not to think about the fact that this lovely gold ring had graced the hand of many Kapp women before me, including Johannes' grandmother and most recently, that of Judith. No, I must not look back, I reminded myself, only forward. Johannes slid the cool ring onto my finger. In spite of my resolve, I was afraid to look at him, lest I find his thoughts not on the occasion, but perhaps remembering some other ceremony in some other place. But when I did find the courage, what I saw was the devotion of a man solely committed to me in that moment.

My father came forward, nodding at us in smiling approval, and began to read the benediction from the prayer book. When he finished, Johannes and I kneeled as the reverend prayed again. The words of the ceremony were like so many I had heard before, but today the graciousness and power of God was impressed upon me and I felt my heart softening.

We continued to kneel as the reverend added the final blessing, "God the Father, God the Son, God the Holy Spirit, bless, preserve, and keep you; the Lord mercifully with his favor look upon you, and fill you with all spiritual benediction and grace; that you may faithfully live together in this life, and in the age to come have life everlasting. Amen."

The ceremony was complete and Johannes pulled me to him, sealing the vows with a kiss. It was clear to all watching that this union was based on more than convenience. After some good-natured whistles, he pulled away, and I could feel myself blushing. He winked at me and chuckled softly.

We walked back through the group of well-wishers, giving and accepting hugs and kisses. Jonny clung to Johannes's hand, and Johan Jacob sat quietly alongside his cousin, Cathy. Although he seemed to like me, and did not seem to begrudge his father this happiness, I knew that memories of his mother were close. A tear slipped down his cheek and he quickly wiped it away, hoping that no one had seen it. However, the gentle hug that quickly followed from Cathy made him realize that it had not gone undetected. Cathy gave him another reassuring squeeze and walked with him toward Johannes and me. Giving my friend a thankful and knowing look, I embraced Johan Jacob, hoping he could feel how much I loved him already.

The Etter family lavished their famous hospitality upon the wedding guests, with Mamma and Papa's generosity flowing freely. Mamma, a superior cook and baker, flourished as the innkeeper's wife once more. Fresh fruits and vegetables were not available because of the season, but the table was laden with succulent dishes such as sausage and liver pudding, duck and chicken, dried apple pies, and sugar cookies. Fresh breads and biscuits abounded, and everyone, especially me, looked forward to the wedding cake to follow the meal.

The time passed as we enjoyed each other's company and the good food along with a cup of hot tea, coffee, or ale. As the gathering drew to a close, it was time for us to take our leave. Arrangements had been made for the boys to stay with Cathy for the next few days. After making one last round of hugs and kisses, we made our way for the door hand-in-hand and headed toward a new home and a new life.

The months following the wedding proved to be remarkably challenging for everyone in our community. Johannes seemed content in our new marriage, but I think he felt like Mother Nature was punishing him. Not long past, hurricane force storms took his wife and children and now what was being called "The Great Snow" was causing much suffering among our neighbors and friends. At least three feet of snow had fallen, becoming not only an inconvenience, but making daily life dangerous. It took its greatest toll on the newest immigrant arrivals who were not adequately stocked with supplies.

The snow was so deep that the deer struggled and died in its depths. Some households ran out of bread and had to survive on the carcasses of deer they could find. Many cattle and horses also perished in the storm as their grain supply ran out. I heard about a woman who could not to make it any closer to shelter and froze to death within sight of her home. Thus began our married life, but I was hopeful of better times to come.

Eventually another year rolled around and as always, warmer weather appeared. July of 1742 arrived, bringing with it oppressive heat. The promise of rain hung heavy in the air, humidity draping the rolling hills like a wet blanket. A few drops of moisture would materialize throughout the day, bringing hope that the skies would be wiped clean, but still the atmosphere contained its full capacity and refused to empty it. I found myself carrying an ample load of my own. Lovingly, I caressed my protruding belly and laughed as the babe within gave a sharp kick, as if also protesting the conditions of its confined environment.

"Soon now, my love," I whispered down, and smiled again then winced as I was kicked soundly in the ribcage. Of course I was not the first woman in the world to be carrying a child, but I thought I must love this little one more than any mother before me ever loved hers. I was often told by my friends and family that my face held a new joy and a beautiful glow. But as I wiped the sweat from my brow, I felt new worry lines there as well. Concern for the well-being of my baby at times overwhelmed me and turned into an overpowering fear. I had heard that nearly half of the children born in the colonies died. If not in childbirth, then at least before they made it through childhood.

One of the saddest things I ever saw was the day I watched one of my neighbor's young daughters playing dolls. She placed the doll in a casket, designed especially to the size of the toy. I was aghast when I witnessed the child playing, but my neighbor quietly took me aside and explained that because it was such a common thing for children to die young, this was an important way to help the brothers and sisters of the departed learn about what had happened to their sibling.

I still thought it was a horrid thing to play, and determined that I would give my children carved rocking horses or wooden rattles instead. It was bad enough that adults had to constantly deal with such thoughts. Let children be distracted by the innocence of their imagination and interesting toys or by dwelling upon the idea that their brother or sister was dancing in the presence of God and the angels.

The days inched by slowly and the slovenly pigs out in the barn moved fast compared to me. The boys seemed to be almost as excited as I was about the coming baby. Jonny talked constantly about becoming a big brother, and I wondered if he forgot that he had been one before the fateful journey across the sea. Johan Jacob had not forgotten and still carried with him the burden of sadness.

103

He hid it well in front of others, but when he became quiet and sullen at home, I recognized his need for comfort and tried to give it to him.

July was finally coming to a close and I was scouring the blueberry bushes in the woods behind the house. I felt so restless that despite my condition, in a burst of uncharacteristic energy I had decided to get out of the house. Jonny picked berries beside me.

"Now, eat just a few," I instructed him, knowing the temptation that lurked, especially after eating "just one" of the juicy berries. "Save enough for a pie!"

"Yes ma'am," he replied obediently. However, it was not long until dark blue framed his teeth and stained his lips. This evidence, along with the sparse amount of berries rattling in the bottom of his bucket, tattled on him. As I watched Jonny, I thought again of his older brother. Johan Jacob was with his father, out gathering wood to be used for making a new wagon. Business had been good. Philadelphia's demand for crops grown in Lancaster County increased and in return, more extravagant items that were unavailable in the country were shipped back from the city. Lucky for us, most of this shipping was done in wagons.

A fair amount of travelers passed by on their way to either Lancaster or Harrisburg and this was also good for business, as our property was situated halfway between the two destinations. Folks often stopped in the area to rest mid-journey. Since the road went in, our Scotch-Irish neighbor, Thomas Harris, had picked up a lot of customers at his inn. His establishment was only two or three miles up the road from our property. In fact, Johannes told me he spoke to Mr. Harris about that very thing just the other day.

"Business is doing so well, John, I'm thinking of building a larger building," Mr. Harris had said in his thick Scotch-Irish brogue.

"Is that so?" replied Johannes.

"Sure is. Plan to build a place large enough to use as an Inn, tavern, and a store. Even started stacking some field stones at the building sight. Plan to put them to good use when I'm ready. The problem is finding the time. I'm so busy trading with those Indians that I barely have time to think."

"You're an ambitious man, Tom. I'll give you that," Johannes had said with admiration.

Thomas nodded his head in agreement. "That I am," was his solid response.

Johannes had laughed as he told me of the meeting. "Never met a more confident fellow," he said.

Wagon making went hand in hand with farming for Johannes and he spent much of his time harvesting the rye, barley, flax, and oats grown in the small patches of fields. Some of our rye was sold to a neighbor who malted it and sold it for ale to the public houses in the area, like the one that Thomas Harris owned. It could be used to make alcoholic rye whiskey, or used as grain. I made a mental note to make sure Johannes also brought some to the house so I could stuff some into the mattresses. It really helped keep the mice from chewing on them.

I determined to remember to tell Cathy about this useful tip I recently learned. I also decided to make sure that my brother and sister-in-law had a new kitten for their barn. "Another pleasant means of keeping the rats and mice at bay," I thought.

As a newlywed, Cathy would be interested in keeping things as nice as possible for her new husband. I smiled as I thought of the couple, my brother and my friend, now turned sister-in-law. Unlike Johannes and me, they were much closer in age, Cathy being only three months the elder. Each had been twenty-four at the time of their marriage. Of course, Gerhard always teased that he was marrying an "older woman."

As my mind wandered about with these thoughts, the skies began to darken and the wind started to pick up. Apparently, July decided to go out with a bang. Suddenly, the skies let loose with an unaccustomed fury. A trickle of apprehension ran through me, as a forking flash of lightening split the sky and roaring thunder ominously rocked the ground. The wind stung my eyes and took my breath away. The lightning struck again, but this time instead of fear, I felt sharp pain squeeze across my middle. Although not intense, I knew instantly that the time I so anxiously awaited had finally come.

I tried to remain calm, and debated over what to do. It would probably be hours before the baby arrived, but I really wanted to send Jonny immediately to fetch Johannes from the nearby woods. With the storm raging overhead however, I decided it would be best to wait out the weather in the house and then send for Johannes if he did not come in on his own.

"Quickly, Jonny!" I yelled. "Run for the house!"

Without having to be told twice, the little boy raced forward. The house was within sight and it did not take long to reach it, but we were both out of breath and dripping wet when we got inside. After stripping Jonny and wrapping him in a warm blanket and then taking care of my own immediate needs, I settled down on the edge of the bed, bracing myself as I felt another contraction coming on. I committed to wait for Johannes, rather than send for him. "No sense to cause undue alarm," I reasoned.

About an hour later I sighed with relief as the door opened and Johannes and Johan Jacob slopped in the door.

"What a downpour!" laughed Johannes, removing his soaking wet hat and laying his saturated clothing on the cold iron of the black furnace next to the bed. He expected me to join in his good humor, but instead I remained silent.

He smiled at me as I sat quietly on the side of the mattress. My damp hair clung around my face and he told me how beautiful I was, even so far along in carrying our child. My eyes winced from pain and I bit my lip in a stifled whimper.

"Johannes," I gasped softly, sounding like a frightened child. My pleading voice trembled and a look of surprise crossed his handsome features. He lovingly folded me into a comforting embrace. A man with lesser experience might have become rattled, but Johannes quickly took things in stride as he assessed the meaning of the situation. He reassured me, and then asked Johan Jacob to ride the tan mare to fetch my mother.

In the wee hours of the next morning, bright stars splattered the onyx sky and winked their welcome to the newest member of the Kapp family. Johannes kissed the pink cheek of his precious new baby, a daughter we named Anna, a name she would share with each of her grandmothers.

"I feel like Job," Johannes said, recalling the Biblical figure who persevered through much suffering; the loss of his children, the destruction of his property, severe illness and contemptuous friends. God rewarded his faithfulness in the end. "Seven out of my nine children were lost to me in this world. But now, holding this new life, my little number ten, in this land of abundance, I feel that God has once again seen fit to restore His blessing."

Although completely weary, my mind raced ahead to the upcoming days, which would include the baptism of Anna. Conrad Templemann, a tailor and school teacher by trade, was a lay minister to the Reformed Church congregation. I hoped that Anna would be the first in a long line of children that he would baptize for us.

Johannes gently laid Anna down beside me and quietly crossed the room to the blanket chest situated under the small window. Moonlight filtered in, bathing the chest in a pool of pale light. I had used my talents to turn the well-constructed, but rather plain pine box into a work of art. Upon its solid lid I painted two black columned arches, each housing a painted pot of red and black tulips. A larger, dark flower with a red center that reminded me of a graceful windmill towered above the other tulips. This motif was repeated twice on the front of the chest, with red hearts and flowers lining each outer edge of the arch and was painted again on the sides of the furniture. I replicated this pattern from the memory of a favorite piece of furniture I left behind in Switzerland.

As Johannes lifted the painted lid, he closed his eyes for a moment. When he reopened his eyes, he peered into the chest and glimpsed a peek of what he was looking for. Nestled between layers of warm fabrics and a stockpile of winter socks, a small patch of peach colored silk shimmered. He reached down and grasped it, careful not to tear the fragile bundle as he pulled the entire object out of the chest.

I remembered the significance of this object. Johannes once told me how Judith insisted that this be one of the few items brought with them on the trip. "How impractical," he told her. "It's a waste of space!" But now, as I watched him hold that "waste of space" I knew he was glad she won the argument.

"Someday, when we get to Pennsylvania, we will have another daughter," she had said with certainty. Johannes recounted how the hope of bearing healthy children never completely died within her, despite persistent loss. "And when we do," she had smiled softly, "she will have a proper doll."

I wondered if Johannes was now thinking of his other daughters, none of which ever grew old enough to play with the doll. I looked at the peach silk of the doll's head covering. The silk of the head piece and dress bore watermarks from the storm it weathered aboard the ship, but otherwise the doll seemed to be unharmed. The features of her delicately carved face had been painted with meticulous attention to detail, the eyebrows peaked to perfection over dark eyes and red rouge added a spot of brightness to each cheek. Her hair cascaded like soft cinnamon sticks. A golden, lace lined corset framed her bodice and a full skirt was sewn and quilted with strips of peach satin interchanged with a fabric patterned with pink roses, green leaves, and yellow flowers. Hand-knit blue socks filled the delicate red leather shoes that graced her wooden feet.

My heart was full of love for my family as Johannes took the doll and held it out before his daughter. "Anna," he said, as she stared up at him, eyes surprisingly alert, "You my dear, will have many happy days playing with this doll. I know it." She was content and peaceful where she lay, but he just had to pick her up and give her one more kiss.

Chapter 5

September 1742

News of the Friendship's ill-fated journey inhibited many immigrant families from following through on their original travel plans. However, determined to be reunited with our family, my oldest brother Daniel and his wife Rosina bravely persisted with their arrangements and arrived aboard the ship Mary in August of 1742. Philadelphia greeted them with an environment of rising tensions stemming from the upcoming October election.

The Quaker citizens had long dominated the city's government, but the opposing political party of Anglican Church men hoped to gain the upper hand in the next election. Our Swiss and German immigrant communities held the key to victory, as our numbers had increased so rapidly over the past few years, and the Anglican party courted the vote and encouraged participation in elections. We turned out to vote alright, but contrary to the Anglican party's plan, most favored the Quaker's pacifist ways which held the promise of less military service and lower taxes.

Rumors swirled that the Quakers intended to flood the Philadelphia polls with non-naturalized citizens in order to swing the vote in their favor. In retaliation, hearsay alleged that the Anglican party would support ruffian's efforts to suppress the immigrants' ability to cast a ballot. The city held its collective breath, hoping for the best but expecting the worst.

In early September, Daniel and Rosina visited our family in Lancaster County before settling into their new home closer to Philadelphia. They planned to open an inn at Germantown, as the busy city was filled with such a plethora of immigrants who would provide good business. I was disappointed that they could not settle closer, but admitted that it was better than having them live in Switzerland. After all, Philadelphia was not that far away and though it would not be often, visits could be made back and forth. For now, I was thrilled to be able to talk with them after five long years of separation. The Etter family gathered together for a picnic at my mother and father's home.

After eating, Rosina and my youngest sister Elizabeth accompanied me down to the creek to wash the dishes. The unpleasant chore seemed more tolerable when sharing the work, but I will admit to it being one of my least favorite duties. I tried to recall what I could about Germantown, but could not remember much about the area.

"Do you think you will like it there, Rosina?" I asked my sister-in-law as she handed me a dirty dish.

Rosina, petite and graceful, paused to consider and then slowly nodded her head in affirmation. "Yes...Yes. I think so. It's a pretty area. You know, not right in the city, but close enough to be convenient. And the view is very nice looking down across the fields toward Philadelphia."

"Well, that sounds wonderful," I agreed. "I love it out here in the woods, but I sometimes feel a little isolated from the rest of the world. I don't know what I would do if I couldn't see the family like I do. I guess we are lucky that way at least." I affectionately patted the hand of 16-year old Elizabeth, who dried dishes beside me.

Rosina tried to smile, but I could see the tears brimming in her eyes. "I know I'm too old to feel like this," she said, "But, I am so worried about making friends there. Everything will be so unfamiliar. It's hard to know where to start in creating this new life."

I put an arm around Rosina and hugged her. "Oh Rosie, you are one of the sweetest women I know. People love you. You have to know that! You'll have no problem making friends. I'm certain of it," I reassured. "And as for knowing where to start with this

110

different world you've been given..." I chuckled, "Don't worry. You won't have to think about it too hard. The work will come to you...and keep coming! Just take it one day at a time and before you know it, you'll feel right at home!"

"Thank you Katharina. You're so encouraging to me. If only Johannes would let me steal you away to keep me company for a while!" said Rosina, only half joking.

"Peter will be close by," I reminded her. "He probably already knows half of the city. He might be able to introduce you to some of his friends' wives," I offered. "And he's bound to get married sometime soon. I'm sure you will be great friends with our new sister-in-law...whoever she may be."

"You're right of course. I know it won't be so bad. I think I'm still exhausted from the journey," she said and then raised her hand to cover a yawn. "Plus, once we join a church, I will meet women there."

Rosina's outlook seemed to brighten a bit after confessing her fears. We finished cleaning up and joined the rest of the family in the yard where they were visiting in the mild September weather. The trees had begun to turn and I anticipated the deeper oranges, reds, and yellows that would be on display later in the season. Geese honked noisily overhead and looking up to the clear blue sky, I observed a large flock forming a V and heading south.

My attention was drawn back to earth as I admired my family, grateful that we could all be together. Well, almost all. If only Peter had been able to come. But truly dedicated to his work, he was occupied with running his stocking business in Philadelphia.

Even with Peter aside, we still made quite a large group. My youngest brother, nineteen-year-old John Jr. invited a "friend" named Angela over for the meal. I suspected that this friendship would deepen into something more as I observed the way my brother's eyes followed Angela's every move and as I noticed the young woman twirling her light brown curls around a finger while giggling and batting her eyelashes.

"Oh no," I thought, rolling my eyes. Yes, I was pretty sure I knew where this was headed. Angela was three years older than John Jr., but it seemed to me that their maturity levels matched perfectly.

Next I spied my sisters, Elizabeth and Susanna, settling in next to each other, sitting side by side, their backs reclining against the trunk of an old oak tree. Susanna's hand stroked the furry head of the mutt who curled up beside her. The dog seemed to be enjoying the attention and slowly rolled over on his back, hoping for a rub on the belly as well. Susanna obliged him, causing his tail to wag in appreciation. It appeared that my two sisters were already deep in conversation, and I had little doubt that Elizabeth was giving Susanna an earful about her newest infatuation. If not talking about a boy, then it could be sure she was thinking about one.

My sister Susanna, now twenty years old, probably had her share of dreamy reflections as well, especially since she had been spending a lot of time with Rudolph Künzly. Rudolph was from the same hometown as Johannes and he knew the family well. In fact, Rudolph's father, Jacob, was counted amongst my husband's dearest friends. This eased my worries a bit. Marriage is such a serious commitment and I could think of many women who hastily or misguidedly made their choice of partner. Such a matter is not easily undone and one bad decision could last a lifetime.

Cupid was having a busy day. As my gaze traveled to the edge of the woods, I was not surprised to see the newlyweds, Gerhard and Cathy holding hands and smiling, lost in their own world. They made a sweet couple and I was so happy for them. All of my brothers had been taught to have a strong work ethic, and Gerhard was no exception. He had been talking about plans to mine for iron ore and possibly start a forge. A lot of hard work would be required, but I believed he was up to the task.

Over by the sheep pen, my mother had taken it upon herself to entertain Jonny and whatever she was saying to him, he must have thought quite funny for he was giggling hysterically. Mamma also held baby Anna and showed her the sheep and the cows. Although Anna was only a few months old, she appeared to be taking it all in and enjoying the moment as much as her grandmother and brother. I was glad that my mother was looking after Anna for a while. Though I had never loved anyone more, and was loath to admit such, it was relieving to have a break from the constant demands of an infant.

Gathered close to the smokehouse, my father, Daniel, and Johannes were discussing politics and religion as they passed around and shared a pint of my best cherry wine. Johan Jacob stood by his father's side, absorbing the information and enjoying the chance to be included in the company of men. Daniel and Johannes were getting along well, not that I had expected anything less as they were both sincere and amicable people. Johannes was eager to hear about circumstances in Switzerland and Daniel was happy to fill him in on current events. They discussed the deplorable conditions of the immigrants during the ship voyages and agreed that something needed to be done about it.

Warmth and contentment washed over me as I observed my family. I remembered my mother's advice from long ago and savored this perfect moment, storing it away as one of the happy memories of my life.

Part 3

Johannes

Chapter 1

The boys had gone to bed in the loft above the kitchen, and three-month-old Anna was securely tucked into her cradle as Katharina and I sat together at the table in front of the warm hearth. The logs popped and hissed as they burned, sending blue and orange sparks spitting upward and outward. I quickly stamped out a stray ember that landed near my boot.

"Looks like it might be a hard winter," I remarked, staring back into the fire. "If it's this cold in October, imagine what December is going to be like. Maybe that Old Farmer's Almanac is right!"

"It doesn't help that it's rained for three days straight! I can hardly remember what the sun looks like," Katharina complained. Confined to the indoors while caring for a small child and baby was beginning to wear on her. She welcomed any change of routine and her mood picked up as she said, "It was nice to get out a little today though. I really enjoyed hearing the minister preach at my parent's house."

"Yes it was good to see everyone," I agreed. "But it still seems odd to attend church on a Tuesday. I'd really like to see us have a building soon and a regular minister so we can hold services on Sunday mornings. It would be nice for Anna to be married in a proper church!"

"Let's hope we have a building before she gets that old," retorted Katharina. "Or I'll pack up that trunk and head back home!" She raised an eyebrow and smirked at me.

"Sure you would, Kat." She loved it when I called her that and she reached for my hand and gave it a squeeze. "Besides," I said, "you *are* home now."

"I know," she smiled. "I'm just teasing." She raised my hand to her soft lips and kissed it.

"What a week for Minister Templemann to travel around for services," I added. We did not often discuss religion. Our conversations about church always skimmed the surface and never endured long. But now, I saw a glimmer in my wife's eyes and I knew that she too longed to discuss the service. "What he said today, it really made me think about things in a different way than I ever have before." I looked at Katharina. "Do you know what I mean?"

"Yes," she replied. "I think I do, but go on," she encouraged. "I'd like to hear your thoughts."

"Well," I continued, "I guess I treated going to church and talking about God like an obligation. And Katharina, if you had known me when I was young, you would understand that I often shirked that duty. If only you could ask my mother! So often, she would speak to me about it. I think she worried that I would grow up to be a worthless man!"

"Oh Johannes, you are exaggerating," chuckled Katharina. "Surely you weren't that bad. You were just a young man, enjoying the world, exploring new things and places."

"I don't know how I compared to other men, but my life was not as it should have been. For all my days I have been chasing after *something*…Trying to fill this empty part of myself. When I was young, I thought that I could find what was missing in the cities, in new experiences of art or music. But that didn't do it."

"I can understand that," said Katharina, nodding her head. "Even if we change our location and view, we can't run away from ourselves."

Glad for her understanding, I continued. "The traveling didn't satisfy me. My new profession, although I enjoyed it, still left me lacking. And then, I found Judith again and for a brief while, I thought, 'Now, I feel content.' But, life continued. I was still

118

happy, yet I knew I would be happier if only we had a child. We did. I was content again…for a while. More children… now we were a complete family. What more could I want? We went to church. I was fulfilling my responsibilities. But still, I always felt the need to move to that next thing…whatever it might be."

"Katharina," I paused, hesitant to expose my guilt. "It was that restlessness that destroyed my family." I knotted my hands together tightly and my knuckles were white as I confessed to her. "If I had been content with what I had, they would still be alive. Judith didn't really want to travel. My mother worried for the boys on such a journey." Maybe now Katharina would finally and fully understand the shadows that passed over me from time to time.

"Johannes, look at me," she commanded with a force I did not expect. "You did not kill your family. You know that. You only had their best interest in mind. You wanted a better life for them. That terrible storm was not your fault. You cannot control the weather. Only God can do that."

"My logical mind knows that, but my heart tells me differently." My voice broke. It was difficult for me to express the entirety of my thoughts to Katharina. Guilt was my constant companion and doubt and anger walked along with us. What little faith I may have had was weakened by the death of my family and I was finding it even more implausible to trust God…This God who controlled the weather. He could have saved my wife and children, but he did not.

My entire life, I was taught that I should respect God, trust Him and honor Him. I knew verse upon verse about God's authority, His infinite wisdom and goodness, and His rule over the circumstances of life. I had to make a choice. To believe that God was sovereign and good or that he was not. I was tired of the internal struggle I lived with day after day and I desired to find peace. I had to figure it out and try to move on with life. The day's sermon may not have answered all of my questions, but it gave me plenty to think about.

Minister Templemann read to us from a printed copy of a sermon originally written and delivered by George Whitefield, a preacher who traveled about the colonies. Great revivals were taking place wherever he and others like him spread the Word of God. Our preacher told us that George Whitefield attended college at Oxford and participated in a club organized by the Wesley brothers. The club ministered to the sick and poor and members spent hours fasting and praying. George hoped to find harmony through these good works, but they did not quench his yearning. After thinking about how Christ suffered on the cross and cried, "I thirst," George realized that he too thirsted for God. He found that nothing done for personal gain would ever satisfy and only by giving himself fully to God would he ever find the contentment he craved.

"Katharina, when I heard the first part of the sermon, of Templemann's description of Whitefield, I understood how that man felt. I am thirsty. Nothing seems to quench the insatiable thirst in me. Nothing brings the fulfillment that I covet. My questions and resentment eat away at me." It was as if a dam broke and my feelings and emotions were pouring out unchecked. "And then when Templemann started to read Whitefield's sermon, it all started falling into place. It wasn't easy to hear, I'll admit that, but it was like he was talking right to me....like he knew me."

"I felt that way too," agreed Katharina.

"'The 'Almost Christian'...that's what he titled it," I reminded her. "I am that man, Katharina. The 'Almost Christian.' The man who 'wavers between Christ and the World.' I want to have it both ways. Have I considered, 'How will this please God?' Or have I thought, 'How will this please me?'"

"Johannes, don't be so hard on yourself," she comforted me. "You were not the only one to feel the conviction of these words today."

I squeezed her hand in mine. "After he was done speaking, I asked Minister Templemann if I could copy a part of the sermon, so that I could think on it a little more. It took me a while, but I'm glad I did." I reached over to where the family Bible lays. Pulling a piece of paper from it, I read:

The Almost Christian by George Whitefield

"And the first proof I shall give of the folly of such a proceeding is, that it is ineffectual to salvation. It is true, such men are almost good; but almost to hit the mark, is really to miss it. God requires us 'to love him with all our hearts, with all our souls, and with all our strength.' He loves us too well to admit any rival; because, so far as our hearts are empty of God, so far must they be unhappy. The devil, indeed, like the false mother that came before Solomon, would have

120

our hearts divided, as she would have had the child; but God, like the true mother, will have all or none. "My Son, give me thy heart," thy whole heart, is the general call to all: and if this be not done, we never can expect the divine mercy.

...As it is most prejudicial to ourselves and hurtful to others, so it is the greatest instance of ingratitude we can express towards our Lord and Master Jesus Christ. For did he come down from heaven, and shed his precious blood, to purchase these hearts of ours, and shall we only give him half of them? O how can we say we love him, when our hearts are not wholly with him? How can we call him our Savior, when we will not endeavor sincerely to approve ourselves to him, and so let him see the travail of his soul, and be satisfied! ...

....Let us give to God our whole hearts, and no longer halt between two opinions: if the world be God, let us serve that; if pleasure be a God, let us serve that; but if the Lord he be God, let us, O let us serve him alone.

....We must renounce the love of the world; but then it is that we may be filled with the love of God: and when that has once enlarged our hearts, we shall, like Jacob when he served for his beloved Rachel, think nothing too difficult to undergo, no hardships too tedious to endure, because of the love we shall then have for our dear Redeemer.

....be daily endeavoring to give up yourselves more and more unto him; you will be always watching, always praying, always aspiring after farther degrees of purity and love, and consequently always preparing yourselves for a fuller sight and enjoyment of that God, in whose presence there is fullness of joy, and at whose right-hand there are pleasures for ever more. Amen! Amen!"

"Katharina, God can fill me. He will meet my longings that never seem to be satisfied. Even if I don't fully understand why my family experienced such a tragedy, I choose to trust God and surrender it all to Him...My worldly sin, doubt and anger. My entire life. As Whitefield said, I 'must renounce the love of the world, then it is that we may be filled with the love of God!'"

We both bowed our heads to pray. I gave God my life and resolved to follow His way. Katharina followed with her own heartfelt prayer, also committing herself to God and his plan. After we finished praying, Katharina blew her nose and wiped away tears of joy. Though the firelight cast but a dim glow about the room, it reflected a new calm, peace, and purpose in the eyes of my wife and in the depths of my heart.

Chapter 2

1742

𝒞 onrad Templemann stood before our small congregation with a
solemn expression upon his face. "My friends," he started humbly.
"I am but a lay-minister, a tailor by trade, and not a man wishing to
embroil myself in religious politics. However, I feel that it is my
duty to pass along the information that has come to me from the
authority of the Reformed Church." He continued, "As you know,
there have been Moravian missionaries about these parts. And to be
honest, the Reformed leadership is not happy about their
interference." He looked uncomfortable, obviously not enjoying his
role as the bearer of controversy. Nonetheless, he pressed forward.

"Minister John Philip Boemn, as some of you may know, is
considered to be the founder of the Reformed Church here in the
colonies." Nobody seemed impressed, but he went on, determined
to make us understand the importance of this matter. "Minister
Boemn has recently published this 'True Letter of Warning' against
becoming involved with the Moravians." I observed one woman
turn to her husband and whisper something in his ear, the man's
head silently nodding once in agreement. I noticed several other

people either looking down to the floor or casting quick glances in the direction of their spouse.

"You may or may not understand that the Moravian's intent is to bring together all of the surrounding churches, despite theological disagreements, unifying in one cause to preach the gospel of our Lord to everyone. And I mean everyone, including the Indians." Conrad proceeded, "The Reformed Church loves all men as well, but they assert that combining the denominations would be a mistake. Our values are unique and should be preserved." I was not sure Minister Templemann was coming across as too convincing, but to his credit, he was trying.

"Officers of six Reformed congregations have signed the warning letter," he told us. I courteously listened as he spoke, willing to give his words fair consideration. However, my family's worship practices would be decided by the leading of my heart, not based upon directives handed down from the Reformed Church. We came to Pennsylvania for freedom. Freedom from taxes and government, and the freedom to worship in any way in which we chose.

Perceiving the attitude of the room, Minister Templemann tried to press upon us again the seriousness of the situation. "This may not seem like the most important topic out here in the woods," he said soberly, "but just a few months ago in Philadelphia, a Moravian minister was thrown out of his pulpit, dragged into the street, and beaten. *"Schlagt den Hund todt!"* they chanted. "Strike the dog dead!" This bit of information sent up some alarm among the congregation, as some had relatives living in that area. Katharina cast me a look of apprehension, thinking of her brothers Peter and Daniel.

It seemed as if the city was a target for turmoil, which I found somewhat ironic taking into account the large number of self proclaimed peace-loving Quakers who lived there. I thought about Daniel's letter, sent not long after the October elections in which he described the chaos surrounding the event. Folks referred to it as "The Philadelphia Election Riot." Never having reached any kind of agreement on how to proceed with ensuring a fair vote, the anxiety and threats culminated at the courthouse the morning of the election as people gathered. A mob of seventy sailors showed up and started heckling the Quakers and immigrants, shouting out curses along with

124

their pro-Anglican cheers, wielding clubs and throwing bricks. As men can be pushed only so far, pacifist reactions were put aside as immigrants and Quakers fought back and defended themselves. In the end, The Anglicans won the election, but at least we gave them a good fight.

"Brothers and Sisters," implored the preacher, catching my attention once again, "I only ask that you remain aware. Do not be led astray by eccentric men or their teachings."

June 1743

Fashioning a new seat for a wagon ordered by Thomas Harris, I was occupied in my workshop. I could see Katharina sitting on our covered front porch, enjoying the shade. The porch was a recent addition to the house and it was one of Katharina's favorite spots to work on any number of tedious chores. Today, with Cathy's help, she was shelling peas.

As they worked and talked, Anna toddled around in the yard close by. Not quite one year old, she was already walking. Katharina was kept busy, as each of her tasks took twice as long to complete because of the endless interruption and curiosity of our little girl. Katharina would soon deliver another baby, adding to her work and joy. I thanked God every day that Anna and the unborn child seemed to remain healthy. Cathy and Katharina's voices carried across the yard as they chatted.

"Gerhard told me there is a new circuit riding preacher who will be visiting the area," Cathy remarked.

"Has something happened to Minister Templemann?" asked Katharina with concern.

"No, this man is associated with the Moravians."

"Oh. Good," she said with relief. We both liked Conrad immensely and I was glad to hear that he was not unwell.

Cathy sighed. "I'm not sure it's *good*. The preacher is one of those Moravians that we were warned about by the church leadership. His name is Jacob Lischy."

"Johannes says that we are free to worship as we please here," Katharina countered and I smiled to hear my words repeated with

125

such conviction. "We are not going to let stuffy old men miles and miles away tell us who we can and cannot listen to!"

Cathy looked at her and laughed. "Don't hold back. Tell me what you really think!"

"What I think," Katharina replied smiling, her voice calming considerably, "is that if a man is willing to leave his family and subject himself to the hardships of riding a circuit, he deserves to be given at least one chance. Besides, I've heard all of the arguments for and against Moravians." It had been hard not to be aware of the situation, as that had been an endless topic of discussion among our friends and family lately. "And I just don't see the harm in trying to unite people around the one true God. Every denomination has its quirks, but most of that is unimportant compared to the central message of God's love and forgiveness. We are all Christians, right?"

"I don't know," Cathy said uncertainly. "We've been part of the Reformed Church for ages. If the leaders feel so strongly, maybe we should listen to them."

I continued to observe Cathy and Katharina as they sat together. It was rare that I got to be privy to the women's conversation. They were silent for a moment, watching as Anna wobbled after our red-coated hound that we called "Penny." The dog was a gift to us for our wedding. At first, I thought a dog as somewhat of a bizarre present, but I came to appreciate her faithful attention and protection of our home. The woods were full of wild animals and, at times, unexpected guests such as Indians or travelers. Penny's sharp, piercing bark was as good as having a soldier posted at guard duty.

The dog was presently calm, but somewhat fed up with being chased around by the child. Just as the dog would plop herself heavily onto the ground, adjust her head comfortably upon her front paws and close her eyes to rest, Anna would catch up and try to pet her. The dog tolerated the attention for as long as she could stand it, but then jumped up quickly and made a b-line to a different spot in the yard. Anna chased after the dog. The child's journey took much longer than Penny's, as it was interrupted by numerous tumbles onto the ground. Undeterred, Anna picked herself up and pressed on with determination toward her target. When she reached Penny, the process repeated and was likely to do so over and over again...poor dog.

I thought about the variety of pets popular these days. Johan Jacob had been begging for a pet squirrel. Two of his friends had one and he said they were easy to train, would even walk on a leash if you found the squirrel in a nest when it was young. Some of my acquaintances had taken to domesticating wild animals as well. The most useful one I had heard about was a beaver who brought back fish to its owner.

Katharina finished shelling the last pea, snapping off the end of the vegetable, pulling down the tough threadlike string, and then lithely running her finger down the length of the fresh, green pea pod. The peas reverberated against the bucket as they dropped in one after the other. She stood up, smoothed her skirt, and walked out into the yard. Scooping up Anna, she rescued Penny from additional unwanted attention.

She caught me watching her and playfully blew me a kiss. I sent a return one floating through the air. How old am I? Between my soul's lightened burden and Katharina's vigorous youth, I thought I might have actually shed a few years. It was not a bad feeling.

Katharina turned back to the porch and said to Cathy, "Thanks so much for your help. It's always wonderful to visit with you!" She embraced her friend. "Why don't we just give Pastor Lischy a chance? If we don't like him, there is nothing lost."

Cathy shrugged, but still looked doubtful. "I guess you're right," she said. "I really want to do the right thing. I don't want to get caught up in false teachings or anything like that."

Katharina smiled at her friend and reassured her. "I know that if we ask Him, God will lead us. Johannes and I have been praying daily for wisdom in this area. Our lives are His now, and I know that He will guide us."

"You are right," Cathy agreed. "I will start praying more and worrying less!"

The two friends hugged, Anna grabbing Aunt Cathy's skirt and laughing with delight. They walked into the house to have a quick cup of tea before Katharina had to start preparing supper. A woman's work is never done, or so I have heard it said.

Seated on a bench near the back of the chilly barn, we were surrounded by about twenty families that included curious friends,

127

family, and neighbors. Johan Jacob sat to my right and Jonny squirmed to my left as I held Anna on my lap. Katharina was settled next to Jonny and she held our newborn, Margaretha. Bundled up in a heavy blanket, the baby was sure to stay warm.

Looking around the little congregation, I thanked God for the friends and brothers and sisters in Christ that we had here. Just in front of me sat Peter and Anna Ricksecker and Anna's daughter Catharine. Peter and Anna, a former widow, had just recently married. Franz Seib and his family were to the right of them. Franz was known as an intelligent man with a true heart for God. I felt privileged to call him a friend and to serve beside him as a leader of our small church services.

Today there was more of a crowd than usual, as folks came to hear Reverend Jacob Lischy. I admitted that so far, over the last few months of listening to Mr. Lischy, I was impressed with the young man's confidence and his ability in mastering a crowded room. But today, the Reverend's face seemed drawn and deep shadows created semi-circles beneath his usually bright and perceptive eyes. However, with the exuberance of youth on his side and the purpose of his mission foremost, he seemed to overcome the weariness brought on by the tough trail he had travelled, and the Reverend addressed the gathering.

"My brothers and sisters in Christ," he began, his charisma drawing us into his confidence. "Though it has not been long since I too sailed from Germany and set foot in the great city of Philadelphia, God has granted me the privilege of speaking to many good folks such as yourselves here in Pennsylvania. I have traveled to congregations in the counties of Berks, Lebanon, Donegal, Lancaster, and Chester. It has also been my joy to preach to the native Indians as I have traveled."

Again, I noted how weary the young man appeared, but the Reverend continued on with his introduction and then launched into an inspiring and intelligent sermon titled, "The Kingdom of God is within you." As usual, Katharina and I listened and watched the Reverend carefully. Though still a bit wary, we could not find any of the harmful attributes of which we were warned. The words he preached and his teachings were thought-provoking and interesting. I was moved by his passion and conviction, although as the sermon drew to a close, the Reverend's demeanor changed and his energy seemed to visibly fade.

I took a moment to look down at the print of my Bible, and then quickly snapped my head up as I heard a woman gasp. Reverend Lischy had crumpled to the barn floor. Two matronly women rushed toward him in concern, their skirts swishing about them, and they eagerly offered their assistance to the young man. Pulling his weary body and dignity up from the floor, the Reverend rubbed his head.

"I have been pushing myself to the brink of exhaustion. But for the Lord, I gladly give my body as a living sacrifice!" He smiled weakly.

"I don't think I can continue with the sermon, but give me a minute and we will proceed with the baptisms as planned."

"Oh no, Reverend! You ought to rest." protested Abraham Friedrich, one of the men in the congregation whose son was to be baptized.

"Nonsense," Lischy firmly replied. "I don't have much time here with you, and I won't be back any time soon. I had the honor to baptize you, Abraham, and it will be my privilege to do so for your son as well."

Abraham cast a glance toward his wife Elizabeth who held their infant son in her arms. I judged that although Abraham was concerned about the pastor's welfare, he knew how important it was to his wife that their son be baptized. She was brought up in the Reformed faith, while he himself, when asked, would say that he had held to the "Pennsylvania Religion." Some people said that actually meant he had no religion at all.

"Well, all right Reverend. But you need some rest after this is over."

"I do agree with you on that!" Lischy concurred. "The Etter family has offered their hospitality and lunch after the service and I plan to accept." He cast a friendly glance toward Katharina's mother and father. Their kindness and warmth was well known among the traveling preachers who often benefitted from their generosity.

After the baptism concluded, the reverend administered the Lord's Supper and then ended the service by introducing us to a hymn that was new to us.

"These words touch my heart and I think you will like it too. If I fall over...just make up the rest and try to continue on without me!"

129

He laughed at himself. I took that as a good sign of his character. The Reverend continued, "This song is called 'God Himself is With Us' and was written back in 1729 by Gerhard Tersteegen."

He led with a clear, strong voice that belied his earlier episode. The congregation sang along to the lilting tune to the best of our ability, timid at first, but building in confidence and strength as the hymn continued. I liked the last stanza in particular.

"O Thou fount of blessing, purify my spirit;
Trusting only in Thy merit,

Like the holy angels who behold Thy glory,
May I ceaselessly adore Thee,

And in all, great and small, seek to do most nearly
What Thou lovest dearly."

I was struck by the words, 'In all, great and small, seek to do most nearly, what thou lovest dearly.' That was my desire, to please Christ in everything.

Chapter 3

1744

The natives and new settlers made attempts to live peacefully side by side, but as can be imagined when appreciating the differences of the two cultures, it was not easy for either party. In an effort to calm rising tensions between the two, a treaty was signed ordering settlers to bring complaints regarding the Indians to the Assembly of Pennsylvania, rather than taking matters into our own hands. I was told that a man by the name of John Musser already put this ruling to the test by turning in a complaint alleging that the Indians destroyed his walnut trees in order to use the bark over the outside of their homes. Mr. Musser claimed a loss of six pounds, but he was only awarded five pounds by the assembly. We also had to deal with the aftermath of traders supplying rum to our native neighbors. It seemed that after sobering up, the Indians were more inclined to take out their anger not on the traders, but on the residents in our area.

Although dealing with these issues and other struggles of daily life, we did not forget our God or our desire to assemble in a proper church building. Under the guidance of Reverend Lischy, we became the Congregation of Donegal Moravians and determined to build a church. Frantz Seib, Peter Ricksecker, John Etter and I

131

started proceedings to secure acreage for the use of the church. Located in northwest Lancaster County, not far from my plantation, we initially planned to buy one-hundred acres. In the end however, only eleven acres were obtained. Already, work had begun on the new church and much had been accomplished, as the members devoted many hours to the project. Compared to other churches, this building was small. Nonetheless, it was special to me, as the investment of my time and skill made it personal.

In accordance with Moravian design, the church was built with two rows of pews on the lower level, facing a pulpit at the front. The men, or *Brethren*, would occupy one side of the church while the women, or *Sisters*, would sit on the other. Within the Moravian Church, the members were divided into separate groups known as *choirs.* There were choirs for unmarried men, married men, unmarried women, married women, widows and children. I was not sure that we would even have enough members to divide into so many groups, but thought perhaps we could separate into a simple pattern of men and women.

Stairs and a balcony lead to the upper level of the church. The upstairs would be arranged much the same as downstairs and it would be there that special services, such as the Love Feast, Holy Communion and accepting of new church members, would be held. Each level would eventually have an organ. Inspired to pursue excellence, I was honored to work with my fellow church members as we endeavored to give God our best.

Reverend Lischy promised to dedicate the church at its completion. I hoped that the Reverend could sense how sincere I and the others in the congregation were toward our desire for the Gospel. My family, along with others, met weekly in a quiet and orderly fashion to edify each other. Meeting together was a high priority for us. I, along with the other leaders of our small congregation, understood the necessity of taking care of our growing numbers.

I thought of my own growing family. I was pleased that Johan Jacob and Jonny seemed to be adapting to their new lifestyle. I did, however, have concerns over the need for their proper education. I was afforded an education as a child, and could not diminish its importance. Although even the thought of separation from my children caused me great pain, I had been thinking in earnest lately about the prospect of seeking an education for them at the Moravian headquarters in Bethlehem, Pennsylvania. I still held close the memory of my departed family members, but found that I could now remember them with a smile rather than being dragged down to despair. It would be unfair to hold my sons back from an education that they deserved just to keep them nearby; just to keep old memories alive.

I valued Katharina's opinion regarding the boy's education and planned to approach her with my idea on the matter when I got home in the evening. She treated the boys well and I knew that she loved them as if they were her own flesh and blood. Anna, not yet quite three, and Margaretha now a little over a year, gave me great joy; and adding to our happiness was the promise of a brand new addition expected near the beginning of the coming new year of 1745. Everyone was healthy, and I thanked the precious Lamb of God for that every day.

Stepping into our snug house following a day spent working in the unheated church building was a welcome relief. After hanging my coat on the peg by the door, I turned to watch Katharina. Once again large with child, she stood facing the fireplace putting the finishing touches on supper. I stepped behind her and wrapped my arms around her. She knew I desired a little affection, but tried to nonchalantly shrug me off. I had been advised before that hanging on to a woman while she is trying to work, especially when that woman is already exhausted from the demands of caring for a house full of children ranging from teenager to baby, and carrying yet another, does not exactly evoke feelings of intimacy within her. But still, Katharina smiled at me and turned around to give me a quick peck on the lips.

"Now shoo, while I finish up supper!" she instructed and playfully pushed me away with her hands.

"I'll get out of your way," I smiled, "How was your day?"

"Busy as usual. I did get a chance to reread the letter from Peter though," she informed me. "I wish he didn't live so far away, but it is nice that he can keep us informed about what's going on in the city. It makes me feel more connected to the rest of the world."

I agreed with her. "I know what you mean. It's a slower pace out here, but I wouldn't trade it. Did Peter say anything about the Governor?" Resentment grew continually toward the government official according to Peter's last correspondence.

"Peter wrote that Governor Thomas seems to be out of touch with the common people who risked life and limb to come over here and escape the oppressive governments of their homeland. He doesn't seem to understand that they don't take kindly to being ordered around so much."

"Well, maybe Conrad Weiser can talk some sense into him," I said, referring to the respected friend of the Moravian missionaries. Conrad's council was valued by many, including the governor, especially when it came to Indian affairs. He was now in his late forties, but as a young man, Conrad had lived among the Indian tribes and during that time learned the language and formed relationships with the natives. Just recently, Governor Thomas, along with Conrad Weiser, met with the Six Nations of the Iroquois and negotiated the native's support for an alliance with the English against the French. The two countries were currently pitted against each other in a conflict known as King George's War. It was the desire of the British that the French to be driven away from the colonies and even out of Canada.

"There is something else I did want to talk to you about before the boys come in from doing their chores," I said, changing the subject completely.

"What is it?" Katharina questioned.

"I was talking to some of the men at the church today, and we thought it might be a good idea if we went up to Bethlehem ourselves and petitioned for a permanent minister," I said. "Reverend Lischy has never really encouraged us to do that, but we think it will show the church leadership that we are serious, and plus we can then take a look for ourselves and see what it's like up there."

"The thought of such a long trip does concern me a little, but I agree that it might add to our chances of securing a permanent minister. I have actually been expecting this," she said, surprising me.

However, I surprised her more with my next proclamation. "And I've been thinking of taking Johan Jacob and Jonny with me. I've heard excellent reports about the school there, and I think it's the best chance they have for a good education."

"But Johannes, it's so far away!" she protested, and the shock of the idea made her sit down suddenly in the kitchen chair.

"I know, but I've thought and prayed about this a lot. Now is the perfect opportunity to go. We will have other men with us, which will make the trip less dangerous. Besides, the boys deserve to have an education provided by those who will care about their mind and their soul." I paused a moment and then asked, "What do you think?"

She slowly rose from the chair and headed back to the cooking pot, rubbing her hands over her tired eyes. "It's just so far away. I don't know."

"I agree," I said. "And I wish there was another option. But, I think that after a few years we'll be able to organize a better education system around here and maybe then they will be able to come back. For now though, it really seems like the best choice."

"You know I can't lie to you, Johannes. It's going to take me some time to process the idea."

I thought we had finished the discussion, but she went on to say, "We are one family and I'm the only mother the boys have, but I feel I need to say something," she said and paused. "I love the boys," she continued. "But when it comes right down to it, the decision is yours to make. And, I respect that Judith was their mother, so I think it only fair to consider what her wishes might have been as well."

Honor and respect shone through her trusting expression. She did not doubt me. I pulled her to me, grateful for the love of such a kind and supportive woman

Chapter 4

March 1745

It was a balmy March afternoon and Jake Künzly, Katharina's youngest sister Elizabeth, and my family were laboring at the new church building. Jake and I were finishing carving details on the new oak pews. Jake was the youngest son of my friend Jacob Künzly, and though I was more than fifteen years his elder, I was glad for Jake's friendship. My ties to his family persisted over the years. We had weathered many trials, tragedies and triumphs together, including the voyage aboard the *Friendship*.

Our families were working to help ready the church building for the upcoming dedication ceremony. Jake seemed to be having some difficulty concentrating on the task at hand and I noticed him casting sidelong glances at Elizabeth. Jake's brother, Rudolph had married Katharina's sister, Susanna, and I wondered if there may be another Künzly-Etter union in the near future.

The women scrubbed the cherry wood floor to perfection and the six-inch by eight-inch window panes, which were imported from England, were cleaned so that the sun gleamed through with extraordinary brightness. The church was a labor of love and the care taken in its construction could be noted in the details, from the beautifully engraved yellow pine pulpit to the hand dipped tallow candles that graced the candelabras. The children too were doing their part. Johan Jacob and Jonny were out back of the building cleaning up left over scraps and Anna and Margaretha each held a rag in their tender hands as they polished the black stove in the center of the room.

Reverend Christian Henry Rauch, a Moravian minister who at times led our church services, visited with us as we worked. His cheery, hearty demeanor won him many friends and he was well-liked by congregations throughout the area.

"Tell me folks," said the reverend, including us all with his kind, personable manner. "Have you been happy with the services provided by Reverend Brandmiller? I was hoping that having some more permanent ministers assigned to your area would be helpful."

"It has been tremendous, Reverend Rauch. Thank you for your assistance in the matter," I answered. "And, I know that the Scotch-Irish listeners in the area have also appreciated having Reverend Yarell preach to them in English rather than German!"

"I'm sure they do!" replied the reverend.

I added, "The ministers have also been keeping us informed about the Brethren in Bethlehem. The men of the church and I have been thinking about making a trip up there," I paused and caught Katharina's eye, but she quickly looked away. Despite her deference to my decision, she was still working through her emotions about the boys leaving for school. I continued to the reverend, "...to ask about having our very own minister assigned specifically to our congregation."

"That sounds like a good idea," he encouraged. "But, you'll want to keep a watchful eye out for unfriendly Indians in that area as you travel."

Katharina, holding a woven rag in one hand and cradling new baby Elizabeth in the other, addressed the minister. "Tell us, Reverend Rauch, about your travels among the tribes," she requested, interested in learning more about the man before her who had earned the nickname, "Apostle to the Indians." This question was all it took to set him off on his favorite of tales.

"I'll tell you, Mrs. Kapp, many exciting things have happened to me through the years, but I most often remember the time I spent with the Mohican Indians about five years ago when I was sent to preach in New York. It was there that I first met with that Indian tribe."

"Were you able to meet with any of the chiefs?" questioned Johan Jacob, who had just come in the door after completing his chores outside.

"Oh, I sure did," remembered Reverend Rauch, a gleam of excitement twinkling in his eyes. "Two in fact. One was named Tschoop. He was big as a bear," described the minister, reaching his arms out wide and then high. "And just as intimidating. He was powerfully strong. The other's name was Sabash.

I'll admit I was a little scared at first. The Indians were drunk most of the time I was there and I'm not telling stories, that Tschoop was a big man. You just never know what a man will do when he isn't thinking straight." He looked pointedly at the boys, "You two young men remember that," instructed the reverend to the boys. "A man must never allow himself to be taken over by the evils of liquor."

Both nodded quickly, their eyes big as they imagined the gentle preacher surrounded by giant intoxicated Indians.

"I waited until they sobered up and then I talked with those two chiefs. Truth of it is, their drunken state may have been a blessing in disguise, because even they themselves could see what a sorry lot they made out of their proud heritage. They asked me to return to their village of Shekomeko to preach and teach and I said that I would."

"How did you communicate with them?" asked Jake. "Did you know how to speak their language?"

"I had an interpreter in the city when I first met them, but after I moved near their village I was blessed to be taken in by Mr. John Rowe and his wonderful family. They lived close to the Indian settlement and they were able to teach me some of the language. I, in turn, helped educate their children to the best of my ability," he paused and smiled. "They have a daughter named Jaenette. She loves those Indians as much as I do. She never saw the fear or hatred that some have for the tribes. Her parents only showed love and she grew up with that. She sees them as ordinary people and she loves them like the neighbors they are to her." Reverend Rauch's fond remembrance of the girl was followed by silence and then he explained, "Not everyone received me so kindly. Many of the settlers in the area were suspicious of my motives."

"During my time working with the Mohicans," continued the Reverend, "some of the settlers actually accused me of trying to turn the Indians against them. Of course, nothing could have been further from the truth, but the fear and uncertainty of the time did its work in the hearts of some people."

"I'm afraid not much has improved in that regard." I commented. "Wasn't there legislation passed last year forbidding any person from living with a group of Indians with the express purpose of 'Christianizing' them?"

Reverend Rauch nodded his head in agreement. "My fellow missionaries and I have tried to work our way around the law, but we haven't been very successful. The settlers who supported the act do their part to enforce it, and keep watch for missionaries in order to prevent us from contact."

Johan Jacob, eager to steer the story in a more exciting direction, interrupted the reverend's reverie and won a stern look from Katharina in the process. "So what did the Indian village look like?" he asked.

"I'll never forget it," Reverend Rauch reminisced. "I was so excited to be there that before I even properly settled in with the Rowe's, I set off toward the village. It was a hot, humid August day and my horse and I worked up quite a sweat travelling over there. Colonists in the area called the settlement the 'wigwam' and that's what their round little living huts were called. The Indians themselves called this place 'little mountain.' There were about sixteen shelters in the area, and as I approached I could see the Indian homes surrounded by fields prospering with tall corn, beans and herbs. I could hear the running of a stream to one side of the village and rising up from the creek bed there was a beautiful wooded area. It was a pretty and peaceful place at first glance."

My carving tool paused, I looked up at the reverend and asked, "How many Mohicans lived there, do you think?"

"I'd guess about sixty," replied Reverend Rauch. "They were quite an interesting looking bunch, I have to say. Many of them had permanent tattoos on their faces and a lot of the men wore their hair in braids. But some of those men, they had what you call a *mohawk*.

140

That's when they shave all of their hair except a strip down the middle."

"Sounds like a skunk!" piped up Anna, giggling.

"Yes, I guess so," the minister said, agreeing and smiling down at Anna. He then continued. "At the first service, things went quite well. I was really excited and so eager to share the Lord's truth with the village. At first they seemed very open to me and seemed to be listening to what I had to say."

Jake looked at the minister and said, "You're a very honest man, Reverend. Even those heathens..." he paused as the minister cleared his throat and raised an eyebrow. "Mohicans..." he corrected, "could see that."

"Yes, well you would think..." Reverend Rauch responded with a chuckle. "But unfortunately, it did not take long for things to deteriorate and I knew they didn't believe me. They started to taunt and make fun of me. I knew the situation was getting worse and worse, but I didn't give up. I knew that God loved those people as much as he loves you and me. I loved them too and they just needed to see that so badly. I couldn't leave until they understood." Even now, his listeners could hear his affection for the Mohican people in his voice. "And it did take a while for things to turn around. Got a might uncomfortable at times...." He paused, remembering and shaking his head sadly. "They even threatened my life..."

"Oh, Reverend Rauch!" Katharina breathed, her hand lightly covering her mouth with concern. "What happened?"

"For the sake of the little ones here," Reverend Rauch's head tilted in gesture toward the two girls still polishing the stove, "I won't go into detail. Let me just say that another man not long before met an awful fate at the hands of a similar tribe in a nearby settlement and he won't be needing the use of a comb again...if ya catch my meaning," he said, running his fingers through his hair. The girls did not take in the details, but the boy's eyes were wide. "All I can say is that God works in mysterious ways. Only divine timing and the Lord's hand can accomplish His will," he said with certainty.

"I was doing everything I could to make those people understand the love of Jesus and I was tired...just exhausted from the stress of it all. I spent a great deal of energy thinking out my every word and message with great care. It is quite a burden to feel the fate of men's

141

souls resting upon your own weary shoulders." The reverend had been standing since his arrival, but now as if remembering his great fatigue, he sat on one of the new pine benches, reclining to a more comfortable position and continued the story.

"One day I was visiting with the great Chief Tschoop inside his birch bark covered hut. As I said, I was tired and my mind so overwrought that indeed... I fell soundly asleep!" He laughed now, the fateful day removed far enough in the past to allow a chuckle. "When I woke up, I was staring up at the chief's deerskin breechcloth and leggings towering above me. It didn't take me long to remember where I was!" The reverend painted such a picture that his listeners could almost feel the great chief breathing down on them.

"Chief Tschoop was amazed that I could so fully trust him and his tribe, the ones so feared as being savages...as you so aptly put, Mr. Kunzli, as to fall asleep under his roof! I guess he figured I thought he'd ...you know..." and again he gestured to his hair, "or something."

By this time, the girls had ceased their polishing and both they and the boys were sitting at the ministers feet, fully entranced in the tale.

"What happened then?" asked Anna. "Did he hurt you?"

"Actually," replied Reverend Rauch, "Believe it or not...exactly the opposite. The Chief decided that any such man who could be so trusting must be worthy of his time and attention." With a joy undimmed over the years, the reverend still sounded awe-struck as he recounted with great humility, "The chief became one of my first converts. Only God could work in such a way."

"Praise be to the Lamb!" said my sister-in-law Elizabeth, with great enthusiasm.

"Like I said earlier," the reverend reminded, "The chief had not lived a life of moral integrity, so to say, and his people could not help but notice that after his conversion he became like a new person. I heard it said that it was 'like a bear had turned into a lamb!' Through his example, a great revival swept through the village and many souls were saved! At first, even some of the white settlers came and joined in our services. Of course, that didn't last long, but that is a different story."

"That's amazing!" chimed in Elizabeth once more.

"Indeed it is Ma'am," agreed the Reverend. "Our God is surely amazing."

A new day dawned, and I made my way down the rough trail toward the church to put in yet another day of work. I passed Reverend Rauch on my way. The Reverend had tied his horse to a sturdy oak tree, and was situated upon a slightly damp tree stump located a few feet from the side of the trail.

Dainty yellow fig buttercups and small lavender-blue violets dared to peek their heads cautiously from amidst layers of soggy, old leaves, and I savored these first signs of spring. In the distance I could make out the faint roar of a stream swollen from the year's early rains as it competed to be heard above the March wind whistling through the treetops. Patches of bright blue sky were scattered above, interspersed with the budding tree tops.

"How are you this fine morning, Reverend?" I asked in greeting.

"I'm feeling refreshed, Johannes. Thank you for asking. After finishing up my visits yesterday with the church families, I stayed the night at Abraham Friedrich's home. It was wonderful to visit with his family and we were also able to attend to some additional church business. I left early this morning, hoping to get a good start on the day, but I've been sidetracked here at this beautiful spot. I planned to take just a short rest and make a few quick notes in my diary, but I've been here longer than I expected! I really should get started on my journey to see the next congregation."

I watched as he pulled out the worn leather diary from the pocket inside his coat. His rough fingers traced down the smooth spine of the book.

"I've recorded so many memories in other diaries just like this," he said, smiling sheepishly. "It is my hope that someday the records of my extensive journeys and ministries among the Indians and Moravian brethren will provide a historical account of the work we have accomplished."

"It's an important legacy to leave for the next generation," I concurred.

"I do hope so," replied the reverend. "Although I'm an optimist, I sometimes wonder if anyone will ever care about the mundane events I write about in my journal. For example, the story of the

143

Mohican Indians I recounted to you yesterday. My wife Ann becomes exasperated when she hears me telling it again, but I love remembering the excitement of those earlier days."

"I'm glad you told the story," I supported him. "It teaches a good lesson that The Lamb of God is in control of everything."

"Yes, you are right," agreed the Reverend. "Still, not every entry is nearly as exciting. Take this one for instance," he said, turning his attention back to the new page before him in the diary. He read, "*I rode to the church at Donegal to look at it and I was much pleased with it. Then I rode to Abraham Friedrich's where I drew up a statement with regards to the church. It is to be general for everyone who wishes to preach the gospel in it.*"

I laughed. "No, that's not nearly as exciting as the Mohican story, but important just the same!

March 22, 1745

"I'm so glad Spring has finally arrived!" rejoiced Katharina. A robin's song trilled in the distance and the morning air truly held a hint of warmth. The ground was muddy, another sure sign of the season, but it did not impede our black gelding as he and the sturdy mare faithfully pulled the wagon toward our destination. Weaving their way through towering trees, the horses followed the rutted dirt trail that traced the contours of the gently rolling hills and valleys as we headed toward the new church. The children were giddy with excitement and Katharina and I laughed and teased more than usual. Everyone was looking forward to the day.

Although the air had warmed, it was still cool enough that Katharina gathered a blackberry colored cape around her and baby Elizabeth. Underneath the cape she was dressed in one of her favorite garments, a simple lavender gown adorned with colorfully embroidered flowers. Earlier that morning as she was getting ready for church, I heard her fuss that the dress was too tight and causing her some discomfort. Having delivered little Elizabeth only about a month ago, it was still a bit constrictive, but she loved the pretty color and so loosened her stay and squeezed into it for this special day. I could not imagine that I would ever choose fashion over comfort. Katharina smoothed unseen wrinkles from her skirt with the hand not occupied with the baby and then adjusted the bow attached to her new matching lace framed lavender bonnet.

"I hope we can get to church without the children making a mess of their clothing," remarked Katharina.

Glancing to the back of the wagon, I assessed our brood. Remarkably, even the boys were still in order. The girls looked up at me with impish grins, looking adorable in their own bonnets tied with ribbons.

"Settle down, Kat," I said, as she fidgeted beside me on the wagon seat. "Who are you trying to impress?" I joked.

"You're right," she agreed, trying to control her nervous energy. "Although, I see you took some time getting ready yourself today," she quipped, noticing the shine of my knee-buckled breeches and the close shave I gave myself earlier that morning. I gave her a smile.

"Johannes Kapp, I'm telling you, you keep getting better looking with age." She winked at me. "Look how handsome you are in that beaver felt tricorn hat and new coat. Why, with that linen cravat tied around your neck, you don't look a day over forty-one."

I laughed. I was forty-two and admittedly, thanks to the demanding frontier, in the best shape of my life. "Yes, Mrs. Kapp, we make a striking couple, my dear. But I'll keep the hat on so my gray hairs don't show."

She reached over and tipped my hat to the side, brushing at an isolated gray hair. "You only have a few. They make you look distinguished," she declared. Then batting her eyelashes, in a secretly seductive tone she added for my ears only, "And very, very attractive."

"We will surely discuss this more at a later time," I chuckled, as she kissed me lightly on the cheek.

Finally, topping the peak of the hill, the team of horses pulled to the left and onto the church grounds. The undulating terrain was one of the things that had attracted us to this particular piece of land as a place of worship. The church sat slightly elevated on the knoll above the surrounding area, and this seemed fitting, that God should be above all else.

The service was all that we hoped it would be. Reverend Lischy delivered an interesting and inspiring sermon and the music touched my heart as the passionate blending of voices reverberated throughout the sanctuary. To celebrate the occasion, the women prepared their Sunday-best food and we ate together after the service. I was overwhelmed by a strong sense of community as I watched my wife conversing with the other women and our children as they played together with friends.

I watched as Katharina's mother approached her and put a loving arm around her. "How are you feeling, sweetheart?" questioned Mrs. Etter. "You look happy dear, but you're a bit pale and you have dark circles under your eyes."

"Thanks for the compliments Mamma," Katharina said, giving her the customary eye roll and I chuckled to myself. Katharina continued, "I'm doing fine. But I'm kind of worn out. Elizabeth isn't sleeping through the night yet."

"I remember what that's like," commiserated her mother. "Let's just hope she sleeps better than your brother John did," she said, recalling with startling clarity the very long nights and piercing howls of her little one so long ago. "None of you other children had so much trouble. Poor little guy. It didn't seem to matter what I did, he just did not sleep well." She laughed, "I thought we would surely lose a lot of business at the inn that year!"

Katharina smiled at her mother's comment but shook her head saying, "She just needs to wake up and eat so often. Hopefully, she will grow out of it. She goes right back to sleep, but it interrupts my sleep and I don't feel rested. And of course, there is no time for me to nap during the day."

Her mother patted her on the hand and reassured, "This too shall pass, my dear."

"I know," Katharina agreed. "They do grow fast. But by the time she sleeps through the night I'll probably have another one keeping me up!"

"Children are a blessing," admonished Mrs. Etter.

"Oh, I know they are, mother. I'm not complaining. They are my joy," she said, overcome with emotion, a tear sliding down her cheek. She quickly wiped it away. "I'm just so tired that everything makes me cry lately, happy or sad, it doesn't matter." She laughed at herself amidst her tears.

I made my way toward her. She shifted Elizabeth to one side and clutched my offered hand, drawing strength from my presence.

I offered a smile to the grandmother of my children and she returned it.

"Speaking of children," said Katharina, "I do hope that Peter and Margie will have many!" Her brother had finally married the year before in Philadelphia. She often spoke of how much she missed Peter and about how close they had been while growing up in Switzerland.

"Oh, me too!" hoped Mrs. Etter. "I wish you could have gone to the wedding and met Margie. She was lovely. I know they will be very happy." She paused and then carefully voiced a concern, "I just hope your brother remembers that he is married to a *woman* and not his factory. That young man has more ambition than the whole family combined! I pray he keeps his priorities straight."

"I'm sure he will," reassured Katharina. "He's got a good head on his shoulders, mother."

"I certainly hope so," accepted Mrs. Etter. "Now, let's uncover this dessert. I think everyone is probably waiting for it," she instructed, tying on the apron she brought from home, her thoughts never far from how she could best meet the needs of those around her.

Katharina called to our girls to come help prepare the table. As they eagerly ran to her with ribbons flying, excited to help, I thanked God for all of our little blessings.

148

Chapter 5

April 1745

She stood on the front porch, hugging herself tightly to ward off the chill of daybreak and her damp mood. Faint hues of periwinkle and pastel pink sunrise blurred together as tears pooled in her eyes again. I knew she watched us with a heavy heart as the silhouette of her three horseback riders faded out of view.

Bags had been packed and goodbyes said the evening before, but morning brought its share of rustling and jostling in the candle lit cabin as the boys and I prepared to leave for our trip.

"I don't want to leave you!" cried Jonny. The nine-year old boy knew he was too old to act so, but was unable to control his response. "I'm scared and I'll miss you!"

My heart broke, as I'm sure did Katharina's, but she tried to put on a brave face to bring comfort to the child. It seemed unbearable that a boy must be ripped away from a mother not once, but now twice.

"Jonny," she said, pulling him to her and smiling lovingly. "You are a brave and strong young man and you are going to a very nice place. Your brother will be there to watch over you too," Katharina soothed. Jonny continued to sniffle, but tried to hold it back. He loathed crying in front of people, but his feelings were getting the better of him. "You know I will miss you, Jonny. But, think of all the new things you will learn. It will be a marvelous experience!" she encouraged.

The idea of Moravian school had taken awhile for her to fully embrace, but after much prayer she entrusted the children to God's care. She did not want to stand in the way of His plans for the boys. And so, the time passed all too quickly and the goodbyes were now said. Life would continue, I knew that, but it would not be the same without my boys.

The churchmen, my boys and I made our way Northeast to Bethlehem on what were little more than Indian trails. Often blocked or impassible from fallen trees or unmovable boulders, the route was rugged. The rocky streams were swollen beyond their banks with spring rains and more than once I questioned the intelligence of subjecting my youngest son to the harsh conditions. Just a few wrong steps could take us off the path and lead us deep into an unknown area of the wilderness. But most of all, it was the constant need to watch for rattlesnakes that kept me on edge.

Despite the difficulties, we persevered and enjoyed each other's company. We were intrepid men after all; pioneers well acquainted with the challenges of nature. After the rigorous days we relaxed by spinning stories around the fire at nightfall.

At long last, after days on the trail, we reached our destination of Bethlehem, Pennsylvania. The time passed swiftly as we spent hours touring the city and discussing our needs for a minister with the leadership. We participated in church services and became better acquainted with our Moravian brethren and their customs.

Too quickly, the day of my departure arrived and Jonny pressed closely against my left side and Johan Jacob followed closely on the right as we walked down the main street of Bethlehem. A palpable sense of dread weighed me down. Once again I wondered if I was making the right decision.

Despite the demanding journey to this place from Lancaster County, the days on the trail had flown by, each step bringing us closer to our destination which would lead us further from each other. The days we spent in the ever-growing town had passed just as quickly and our final goodbyes would have to be said. Doubts had begun to assail me almost as soon my horses' hooves hit the trail to Bethlehem, and I wrestled with the worry of actually handing over the care of my children to strangers. I tried to draw strength from my new found faith as Katharina had done, and decided to place the welfare of my children into the hands of God and not alone upon the people of this place.

Not that I had been given any reason to doubt the sincerity or good intentions of the humble men and women that I had been privileged to meet here. Indeed, the center of their intentions and devotion rested upon their strong desire to please the Lord and to be servants for his glory. I hoped that even more than a sound education, that my children would acquire the Godly qualities of their teachers.

"What do you think of our town, Mr. Kapp?" Reverend Lischy surprised us by calling in a loud and good natured voice from the doorway of the newly built bookstore. Although Lischy frequently traveled the church circuit, he was often found in the new community.

"It's an agreeable place, Reverend Lischy," I replied, approaching him and stopping to shake his hand. "A very orderly town; Well thought out."

"We've got everything we need, don't we?" questioned Lischy.

"I'd say so," I agreed, thinking of the mill, stables, bookstore, and of course, the church. "We're on our way to pick up some clothing that we ordered from the tailor," I informed the minister.

"I thought your brother-in-law, John, is a tailor," remembered the reverend, recalling having met the young man on several occasions during his time spent in Donegal.

"Yes, he is. But I want to get the boys a new set of clothing, as well as some for myself and Katharina. If I bring back something from Bethlehem, then she can copy the design later to make additional clothing," I explained.

"That sounds like a good idea," assented the minister. "Hey boys," he looked at Johan Jacob and Jonny, who continued to shadow me, "Did you notice the Indians in the church service yesterday?"

"Of course!" exclaimed Johan Jacob, unable to control his enthusiasm. Living in close contact with the Indians was enough to temporarily dispel his melancholy. "Will they be here all the time?" he asked.

151

"They are around quite often," replied Lischy. "We know it's important to share God's love with everyone, right, Jonny?" The Reverend reached out his hand and rested it atop the boys head. Jonny nodded in obedient agreement, but was clearly distracted by thoughts of my impending departure. His lower lip protruded in an uncharacteristic pout.

"I miss my mother and my sisters too," his voice quavered.

Sensing his distress, Reverend Lischy tried to comfort him by saying, "Boys, don't worry. You will be well cared for at this place. You will grow into men." He paused. "Men of God."

"But I don't want to be a man. I just want to be me," said Jonny, defenseless against another life change beyond his control. I pulled him closer in a hug and silently prayed again that I was doing the right thing. At that moment, it surely did not feel like it, but I willed myself to follow through on my plans, believing that future benefit would outweigh the present heartache.

Without the banter of my sons, the trip back home seemed considerably longer than the one to Bethlehem. I missed Jonny's hugs and Johan Jacob's persistent questions. I even missed their childish arguments which irritated me only days ago. It was a lonely feeling, but at least the other men and I had something to discuss and celebrate on the return journey, as the meeting with the church leadership had gone well. We were promised that soon, a pastor of our own would be assigned.

I breathed a sigh of relief as I spotted my log home through the trees. Situated along the creek bank and tucked in amongst the oak and evergreen trees, I admired our new stone addition which complimented the dark wood used on the rest of the house. The smokehouse, springhouse, barn and my workshop were all conveniently arranged neatly around the house. The surrounding pastures were fenced with rough-hewn split logs and the areas of plowed fields were starting to show patches of vivid green winter wheat.

I allowed my horse to stop for a drink at the rippling brook. It was a nice day and the breeze brushed across my cheeks and rustled the sleeves of my homespun shirt. Yes, it was good to be back. Though coupled with a sense of loss at the separation from my sons,

I realized I felt another emotion as I looked at my home; contentment.

Part 4

Katharina

Chapter 1

"Father, please protect Johan Jacob and Jonny and my beloved husband. I pray that great things may be accomplished for your kingdom through the boys' service to you. Please bring Johannes back to me safely, and may it be that you have blessed the men's efforts in securing a minister for our church. I pray these things in the precious blood of your son, the Lamb of God, Amen."

Though many days had passed since they left my arms, sadness still caused my chest to ache with a feeling of helplessness when I dwelt on their departure. I did not know when I would see them again. Their lives were now totally out of my control and I would not be there to comfort Jonny if he had one of his frequent nightmares or be able to offer advice when fifteen-year-old Johan Jacob needed it. I could not help but think this must have been somewhat how Johannes's mother felt as she bid her children goodbye in Switzerland... having no control... fearing the worst...and then eventually learning of the tragedy.

"No, don't let your mind go there," I firmly instructed myself.

It had been a long day and I was especially tired. I needed a few minutes to relax and sat on the porch, rocking Elizabeth on my lap. The dog curled at my feet, sleeping and snoring loudly. Placing my hand gently over my flat abdomen, I sighed. If I had calculated correctly, I was pregnant again. Johannes would be pleased, as was

I, but I wondered how I would handle all of my work and also manage four small children. Of course, many women had large families, and everyone else seemed to get along just fine, so I tried to derive comfort from that thought. As much as I loved my three girls, I found myself hoping that this time it would be a boy. Of course, no one would ever replace the empty places left by Johan Jacob and Jonny, but still, I hoped it would ease the loneliness that I knew Johannes would surely bear with his sons living so far away.

As if hearing my thoughts, Johannes magically came into view. Down along the creek bank, he was watering his black gelding, Snowball. I was sure that the original owner of the horse must have been drunk when he named him. Still, we all found the name amusing, and it stuck. The mare in the barn behind the house nickered out a happy welcome to her friend and I saw the black horse lift his head and reply in kind, obviously happy to be home. The dog, hearing the commotion, roused quickly from her sleep, cocked her head and perked her ears.

Johannes looked up toward the house and raised his hand in greeting, calling out, "I'll be right up. Just give me a minute." Upon hearing her master's voice, the dog jumped up and bolted toward him. With tail wagging, she barked a welcome.

I smiled and raised my voice a little to reply, "Take your time. I'm going to put the baby in her bed and let Anna and Margaretha know you are here. I'll be right back out." I rose up from the chair, placing a kiss atop Elizabeth's head, and went inside to lay her down.

Anna and Margaretha were sitting by the hearth, playing with their treasured doll. I did not allow them play with it outdoors as I was afraid the toy would get ruined. The girls heard me come in the door and looked up.

"You have a visitor!" I said. "Hurry and see who it is."

Immediately Anna was out the door in a flash. Every day she had asked when he would be home. Margaretha came to me with upraised arms.

"Papa!" Anna cried in delight and I saw her run as fast as her legs could carry her toward her father who remained by the water, holding the horse. Snowball had become quite accustomed to Anna's exuberance and the animal was unperturbed as she made a flying leap into Johannes's outstretched arms. He hugged her tightly

158

and placed her in the saddle. She giggled and held on as Johannes led the horse toward the house. When they reached their destination, Johannes reached for Anna.

"I want to stay on!" she pleaded.

"You can take another ride soon, Anna," reassured Johannes.

"I want another one now!" she begged fervently, clinging tightly to the saddle.

"Anna." He corrected her with the tone of his voice, not angry, yet firm and demanding respect. The little girl looked up at him, her eyes round and wide. She surrendered her hold on the saddle and obeyed without further argument. Johannes lowered the child to the ground and she ran to my side, her small arms tangling in the skirts of my simple shift dress.

"Oh come now, Anna." Johannes coaxed, "You know I love you. Don't run to Mamma for safety. Come here and give me a big hug. I missed you!"

Releasing her grip on me, Anna returned to him as he squatted down waiting for her. In an act of pure sweet love, she squeezed him with all her might and planted her lips against his cheek.

"Now, be a good girl and go sit on the porch while I give your mother a proper hello!" he instructed. She did as told immediately, wishing to avoid her father's further displeasure.

Before Johannes got to me, Margaretha wiggled free from my arms and toddled toward her father. He picked her up and twirled her around, bringing a big smile to her face and then sent her toward the porch to wait with her sister. Finally, we took a few steps toward each other, and Johannes folded me into his embrace.

"Ah," he released a satisfied breath against my ear, "I missed you."

"I missed you too," I murmured, savoring the sense of security and peace found in his presence.

Johannes released me and then turned back to the horse. He pulled the heavy saddlebags off with ease and carried them to the porch, depositing them close to Anna and Margaretha. Curiosity made Anna fidget and squirm, her gaze never leaving the bags. She giggled as Johannes sat beside her and guided her tiny fingers to unbuckle the bag.

First, Johannes pulled out a carved, wooden top for the two sisters. They watched intently as he showed them how to spin it around on the smooth hard boards of the porch. Anna tried it by herself and failed, but looked determined to make it work. It appeared that she would be preoccupied for a long time.

Reaching deeper into his bag, Johannes next took out a small leather ball meant for baby Elizabeth. Then a medium sized bundle was offered to me. I sat down on the porch chair and excitedly ripped off the wrapping.

I pulled out plain, black material. I stood up again and shook it out gently in front of me, dislodging a small white bonnet with blue ties onto the floor. There were also two smaller matching bonnets with red ribbons attached. I picked up the cap and admired it and the fine stitching on the black garment, but I felt puzzled. They were nice clothing, but not exactly average attire.

Johannes explained, "This is what all of the Moravian women in Bethlehem wear on Sundays. The white cap is called a *Schnepplehaube*. We thought it might bring a sense of unity to the church here if we all adopted the dress code."

I tried to give away nothing of the disappointment I felt at the gift and he paused and then continued. "Besides, it might help our new pastor and his wife feel more at home in our community."

"Oh, Johannes! They granted our request!" I exclaimed with joy.

"They did! Mr. and Mrs. Jacob Kohn will soon be on their way. They should arrive in time to celebrate Whit-Sunday in May!"

I looked at my husband, admiration shining in my eyes. I was so proud of him and his desire to please God and move our community forward toward a more civilized place for families to live and worship.

I thought about the boys and asked him with concern, "How were they when you left? Are they going to be okay?"

"They're good boys, Kat," he said with a tight-lipped smile and a thoughtful shake of his head. "They'll be okay. Of course they were sad to say goodbye, but Johan Jacob was pretty excited about being able to get to know some Indians, and Jonny will make a lot of friends, I'm sure of it. He's got such a good heart and friendly personality. The school has already got plans to have them help out in the stables. They'll like that."

"Yes, they'll be fine," I reassured us both. I took his hand in mine and gave it a gentle squeeze. Another wave of fatigue and

160

nausea swept over me. I closed my eyes and took a deep breath, trying to keep the bilious feelings under control. Johannes looked at me in a knowing way, and I just smiled weakly and nodded "yes."

"Guess I should have bought you a bigger dress," he teased.

I wrinkled my nose and playfully punched his solidly muscled arm. Just then, baby Elizabeth announced she was awake, her sharp cry echoing from inside the house. I took a step towards the door, ready to tend the infant.

Johannes places a kiss on my head and said, "You just sit down in the chair and rest. Let me go say hello to Elizabeth." I easily agreed and closed my eyes for one more moment of peace. I could hear the silly banter between Anna and Johannes and knew that Margaretha would enjoy being carried into the house high on her father's shoulders. Then the contented coos of Elizabeth floated to my ears as he reached the baby.

I thanked God for the life he had given me in Lancaster County. I might not classify it as "Paradise" as I had heard others call it, but I could say that I really did love it. And if this life required that I wear a boring black dress and a white cap on Sunday mornings, in place of the beautiful colors I preferred, well then, so be it.

Whit Sunday, May 1745

Reverend Jacob Kohn and his wife were permanently appointed to our small church in Donegal with plans to become members of the community and hold regular services at the church. Reverend Kohn gave his first sermon as the official minister on Whit Sunday, in 1745. As the Moravians hoped to attain unity throughout the Christian world, the church was built with the intent that congregations of all denominations could preach the gospel within its walls. Reverend Kohn was actually of the Reformed Church, but worked closely with the Moravians.

The minister delivered a sermon appropriate to the occasion and spoke about the descent of the Holy Spirit on the day of Pentecost. Although I was excited to have our very own reverend, I was a bit disappointed in the pastor's style and admitted that I rather favored Reverend Lischy's approach. Mrs. Kohn seemed quiet and reserved, but understandably so, since she did not know anyone very well. I offered her a seat with us in our pew, but Mrs. Kohn refused and said she would rather sit near to the front, closer to the pulpit.

I've never seen anyone sit up so straight in my life! I thought. Distracted from the sermon, I watched the minister's wife, who seemed to be utterly absorbed in every word spoken by her husband. I was sure that Mrs. Kohn's demeanor would soften after becoming better acquainted with the community. Eager to get to know the minister and his wife, I was glad that my mother and father had invited us all to share a meal together at their house that evening. We would meet after the morning service and afternoon Love Feast.

After a long day at church filled with conversation dominated by Reverend Kohn, we made our way to my parent's house. The children were fed first and then the adults gathered around the table to share in the evening meal. Not taking any pause from his discourse, the minister continued speaking as we were seated.

"A very enthusiastic and intelligent man," is how Reverend Kohn recounted his meetings with Count Zinzendorf as we discussed him over our meal. "And I've never met a more persistent fellow," he said, as he lathered butter onto one of Mamma's homemade rolls. "Not afraid of anything either." The man was clearly impressed, seeming to idolize the famed Moravian church leader.

"About three years ago, soon after Mrs. Kohn and I arrived from Europe, I met up with Count Zinzendorf in the Wyoming Valley," he said, clearly proud to be included in such prestigious company. "I was with David Nitschmann and Anton Seiffert. We went up the Susquehanna along the Indian path to Wyoming Valley. I had some letters from Europe which I delivered to Count Zinzendorf," he said importantly, clearly feeling it was a great honor to be entrusted with such a task.

Just the exertion of eating and talking so much proved to be taxing for Reverend Kohn. I tried, but had a hard time picturing the man nimbly traversing through the forest and trails.

"We made a camp near the village of the Shawnee, and the Count tried his best to communicate our good intentions to those Indians. But they were not very trusting of us... they thought we had ulterior motives," he remembered, narrowing his eyes and thinning his lips as he recollected the chilly reception. "I guess the only white men they ever met before were traders, and they thought we wanted to do business. It did not matter how many presents we gave them to try to dissuade them otherwise. Those Indians were just downright unfriendly! I really thought we might end up being murdered."

During the telling, Mrs. Kohn's face paled. It was not the first time she had heard the story, but I imagined with each retelling her fears of the wild country and unpredictable Indians grew. Perhaps she was trying to be a faithful minister's wife and hardy woman, but it seemed to be a difficult adjustment for her. I would wager that she longed for the past stability of her European home.

Reverend Kohn, ignorant of his wife's pallor, continued. He did not expound more on his own trip with the Count, but started another story. With a great air of authority he announced, "This account was told to me by Count Zinzendorf himself!"

I looked up to find Johannes looking at me from across the table, his eyes smiling as if to say, "He certainly thinks a lot of himself, don't you think?" I took a deep breath, trying to hold back my amusement and set my face in a purposeful, stern expression. I sent a quick, playful kick aimed at his shin under the table.

"Ouch!" exclaimed the minister's wife, shock written on her face.

Everyone looked at Mrs. Kohn in amazement at her loud outburst. I realized immediately that my kick did not meet its intended mark. My cheeks turned crimson and I apologized.

"Please forgive me, ma'am. My foot slipped." *Well it did*, I told my conscience as it prickled at my white lie. I internally whispered a prayer to God for forgiveness, but did not correct my words.

"Well I never!" huffed Mrs. Kohn, her quiet reserve broken by the fit of anger.

"Now, now dear..." comforted her husband, "I'm sure she didn't mean it. Accept her apology."

"Very well," she said, her chin held high as she assessed me while looking down her nose. "I accept your apology. And I expect it will not happen again," she said, her words clipped and precise.

"I *am* sorry, Mrs. Kohn," I said, trying very hard to contain the smile that wanted to form. It was with great difficulty that I tried not to consider under what circumstances a grown woman might repeatedly kick a minister's wife under the table. "It won't happen again," I assured. *She should have been a school teacher*, I thought.

Directing attention back to himself, Reverend Kohn was not deterred from his story about the Count and continued, "Count

Zinzendorf was once again out in the Pennsylvania wilds with some of his brethren and sisters in Christ, and of course they were all on horseback as they travelled through the unforgiving countryside. They were coming up the West Branch of the Susquehanna and were accompanied by Shikellamy."

"Have you ever met Shikellamy?" asked my father, miraculously wedging his question into the ongoing flow of words from the minister.

"Actually, I have," replied the minister. "The Moravians are lucky to know the Oneida Chief and call him an ally and partner. He's been very helpful as an interpreter and guide to our brethren as we travel."

"Has he ever expressed interest in becoming a follower of Christ?" I dared interrupt to ask.

"He's still not willing to become baptized as a believer, but we are praying for that day and his heart seems to be softening toward the truth." Reverend Kohn continued, as his audience showed interest in his knowledge of the Indian Chief. "Yes, certainly a good man to know," he repeated. "He really has a gift when it comes to making peace. He has even smoothed things over with the Shawnee for us at times. Sad though, that the man lost his son in such a way." He paused, dangling the information in hopes to elicit a question to answer.

Johannes cast a glance at me and then asked the minister obligingly, "How did he lose his son, Reverend?"

"It was awful," he responded dramatically, "just awful. Two years ago, his son, they called him 'Unhappy Jake,' was killed by the Catawba Indians. Even Shikellamy couldn't make peace with that tribe. Fierce warriors they are."

Again, a noticeable shudder passed through Mrs. Kohn and I felt a begrudging sympathy for the woman.

Reverend Kohn returned to his original tale as related to him by Count Zinzendorf. "So, Shikellamy, the Count, and the other brethren and sisters were travelling up the West Branch, and stayed in Shamokin for a short time; this is where Shikellamy lives. Then they went to Otstonwakin (Montoursville, PA) and met with Madame Montour."

"Who is Madame Montour?" I questioned, trying to keep track of the names being thrown at us.

"She, my dear, is a formidable, but lovely and polite woman. Her father was a Frenchman and her mother, Algonquin. They were involved in the Indian trade as Madame Montour grew up. As a grown woman, she found herself travelling with her brother in New York, on a trade mission, and during that time, her brother was murdered. She continued to lead the group of travelers to their destination in Albany, New York."

Not one given to condensing the details, Reverend Kohn continued to expound. "Fortunately for her, she was a very intelligent and unique woman. She could speak English, German, Algonquin, Iroquois, and French and this made her a valuable asset to the governor of New York, who hired her as an interpreter. She married an Oneida chief named 'Big Tree' and traveled with him, their children, and Chief Shikellamy, and continued to work as an interpreter."

"What a remarkable woman," I said, impressed. "It would be so interesting to meet her!"

"Indeed," agreed the minister. "Her husband, Chief Big Tree was also killed in an Indian raid, by the Catawbas. I told you they were fierce. But she continued to travel and interpret. She most often traveled back and forth between Shamokin and Otstonwakin, which is where her son Andrew and her niece, 'French Margaret,' lived.

"After meeting with Madame Montour, Count Zinzendorf and his entourage left for the Wyoming Valley and were accompanied by her son, Andrew Montour as a guide. It was of course a very difficult journey and took about five days as they travelled on an Indian path they called the 'Warriors Path.' I remember just how Count Zinzendorf described Andrew Montour, and although I met him as well, I think that the Count described him best." Picturing the minister hanging on Count Zinzendorf's every word, I had no trouble believing him to be accurate and Reverend Kohn continued, as if reciting from a book.

"The Count said that 'Andrew Montour's cast of countenance was decidedly European, and had his face not been encircled with a broad band of paint, applied with bear's fat, he would certainly have taken him for one. He wore a brown broadcloth coat, a scarlet damask lapel waistcoat, breeches over which his shirt hung, a black Cordovan neckerchief decked with silver bangles, shoes and

165

stockings, and a hat. His ears were braided with brass and other wire like a handle on a basket. He was very cordial, but on addressing him in French, he, to the Count's surprise, replied in English.'47

Mr. Kohn continued, "I remember this story so accurately, because I too met Andrew Montour when the party arrived in the Wyoming Valley. It was his ears I remember the most!" Not pausing for breath, the reverend's story flowed seamlessly into the next. "And did I tell you about the elk we saw on our trip down here? ...Big animals. I'd describe the way they look as horses without tails." And on and on he went, continuing his stories long into the night.

Reverend Kohn and his wife were eventually escorted home by my brother, John, no doubt with the reverend chatting all the way. As soon as the minister departed, we took our leave as well. The children immediately fell asleep in the back of the wagon despite the bumps and I peered back at them in the moonlight and smiled. It had been a very long day and I was looking forward to resting my head upon my soft duck down pillow.

I thought of Reverend and Mrs. Kohn and hoped that they would find their place within the hearts of the congregation. The reverend was certainly long winded, but I sensed that he had a good heart and genuine love for people. His wife... well, I would give her some time before making a final conclusion.

The summer days passed swiftly for our family. Life moved on and became increasingly civilized as the seasons changed. One testament to this was the large stone structure called "Sign of the Bear Tavern" that Thomas Harris erected on his property. Busy with his own building project and business ventures early in the year of 1745, he was also an involved member of the Donegal Presbyterian Church. Later in the year, he was part of a group that built a new meeting house on the main road from Lancaster to Harris' Ferry. They called it Mount Joy Presbyterian church. Though religion held an important place in our society, not all in the community counted themselves among the church-going, God-worshiping crowd; and although a more polished way of life was encroaching, at its heart this was still back-country.

Throughout the year of 1745, Peter's letters continued to brim with news from Philadelphia. His latest expounded on the happenings related to King George's War, between the British and French, which seemed to be escalating. In the fall of 1745 French soldiers and their Indian allies attacked and destroyed Fort Saratoga in New York, burning buildings on the Fish Creek and the Hudson River. About thirty families were killed or taken as prisoners.

I could not stop thinking of the recent tragedy which occurred even closer to home, in Conestoga Township, where a woman was executed after being convicted for the murder of her child. I wrestled to sort through my emotions. The mother's heart within me cried out for justice for the innocent child and yet my faith and belief in forgiveness begged for a show of mercy to the woman. It was a question I had asked myself often, for here in the colonies many people pay for their crimes with their life. People had been killed according to the law for much less.

I wanted to speak with the pastor about my feelings, but he was otherwise occupied. Reverend Kohn's appointment to the Donegal Moravian Church proved to be short lived. In November of 1745 he was recalled to Europe. Mrs. Kohn's personality seemed to improve drastically after receiving news of their imminent departure. I smiled as I thought of the stories the minister would accumulate on his return trip home. I sympathized in spirit with the new congregation that would be the helpless captives of the telling.

Perhaps I had judged the Kohn's too harshly. Many people appeared to have genuinely enjoyed their presence and I really did not get to know them well. Maybe my imagination of their feelings and motives had taken on a life of its own. With sincerity, I wished them God's blessing on their future.

The community enjoyed the use of our newly constructed church, but the former camaraderie between the members was missing, as I had so long ago feared would be the case. People were quick to complain and point out the failures of others. The atmosphere was changing.

Another minister was assigned to us and I hoped that with the installment of Reverend Phillip Meurer and his wife Christiana, the mood would change. I did not know much about Reverend Meurer, except that he had been minister of a Lutheran church in Tulpehocken, where there was also a parochial school. I had also heard rumors about dissention in that church. I fervently hoped the stories were false.

Chapter 2

My family was present once again for Sunday morning services in the cold of January 1746. The cast iron church stove was hard pressed to provide adequate warmth for the congregation as we huddled close together, shivering in the pews. However, there was not one person there, minus the children of course, who would rather be home warmed in their bed blankets. Most interested, I believe, was my sister, Elizabeth. Dreams of matrimony foremost in her mind, she sat close to her fiancé Jake Künzly and inspected her ticket to a quick wedding, the newest minister.

Inquisitive eyes followed the man as he made his way to the pulpit. Unfortunately, my first impression was not a good one as the man began his introduction, but I could not really pinpoint the cause of my aversion. There was just something about him that set me on edge, but I tried to be fair, given my past opinion of Reverend Kohn. As he progressed through his introduction, I started to relax and actually began to feel a kinship with Reverend Meurer, remembering Johannes's voyage and my own crossing, as he described his harrowing three-month journey from London to Philadelphia four years prior.

"It was an exciting, but anxious time for me," Reverend Meurer recalled. "Once an unassuming shoemaker, I set out on what became one of the biggest ordeals of my life when I boarded the 'Snow

169

Catharine' in the company of my fellow Moravian missionaries, including Reverend Lischy. We were all determined to push forward on our journey, but it was a concerning time for us," he said. "We worried about the obvious danger of crossing the Atlantic in March, but we also had to realize the possibility of being captured by French or Spanish war ships. After Bishop Spangenburg boarded the ship and prayed for our protection, we were somewhat comforted. Surely, God heard our prayers, but it was a rough journey. The waves were like great frothy mountains and they tossed us about without care. Everyone was seasick. The storm's assault twisted the sails and tackling and the passengers were called upon to assist the captain and crew."

Beside me, Johannes grasped the pew until his knuckles turned white. I knew that his mind replayed his own nightmare. Gently, I squeezed his other hand in reassurance, calling him back to the present.

Reverend Meurer continued. "We were twice almost captured by Spanish war ships, but providentially we were spared, no doubt in order to be able to carry out our Lord's work here." Many hearty "Amens" echoed around the room. Reverend Meurer paused and took time to assess the crowd before him. "Now, let me show you what the Lord has to say about communion."

I refocused on the minister and wilted in dismay. If there was one ritual our church members disagreed upon, this was it. I looked at the minister and wondered if I detected a glimmer of challenge written in his gaze, as if daring anyone to dispute what he was about to say. Suddenly, I almost missed Reverend Kohn's rambling oratories. Once again, a feeling of unease assailed me.

Unfortunately, my skepticism proved well founded. Throughout the year of 1746, a tone of bitter disagreement pervaded the church atmosphere. The debate centered on communion rituals.

My mind churned over events of the last few months as I looked out the house door towards the shed, where Johannes worked on a new project. The dismal weather mirrored my mood perfectly. With a biscuit and drink in hand for Johannes's mid-morning snack, I headed down the porch steps and out to the shed through the drizzle. The workshop door creaked open and I hurried through the entrance, slightly out of breath from my newest pregnancy and from having tried to skirt the spitting rain outside.

Johannes, intent on his work, planed a board which would be used on the side of a wagon. Suddenly his tool slipped and I could see it caused a groove in the wood deeper than he intended. He grimaced and looked as if he wanted to chuck the tool in a corner, but after a second or two he regained his composure and carried on with his job.

Johannes and I had talked much about the unrest within the church and I knew how much it bothered him. He was losing sleep over the matter and his temper was shorter than I had ever seen it. It was unlike him to get so upset, but the church discord weighed heavily on his heart. He had invested a great deal of time and money in the church and more than anything he desired to see it grow and flourish. Finally, Johannes spotted me, set aside the plane, and gratefully accepted the food I brought.

"Thank you, Kat," he said, taking a bite from the biscuit. "I needed a break." Clearing some sawdust from a stack of boards, he sat down wearily and took a drink from the cup of hot tea. "Where are the girls?" he wondered, it being very unusual for me to go anywhere without a cluster of children in tow.

"It's a miracle," I sighed. "They are all taking a nap." Running fingers through my damp hair and casting a glance through the door, I gestured appreciatively at the rain. "It must have lulled them to sleep." I studied Johannes, remembering his actions as he worked, and frowned in concern. "You look as tired as I feel. Are you okay?"

"Yes. …And no. I think I'm making myself sick over this church problem," he admitted. "Initially, I thought it would all work out, but some of the members are unyielding in their positions. I don't understand why they can't calm down and talk about it rationally. I'd think we should be able to have our differences and yet remain civil," he said in a weary voice.

"In essentials, unity; in nonessentials, liberty; and in all things, love," I repeated the Moravian motto. "I remind myself of this often," I said. "The problem is that most people seem to think that communion falls under the 'essential' category."

171

A foundation of the Moravian belief system, present in songs, sermons and daily life, was a strong identification with the blood of Jesus. Even in our private marital bed we were to seek out spiritual symbolism as it related to His sacrifice. Differing beliefs on how the blood of Jesus affected communion was at the heart of this controversy.

"I just can't figure it out, Kat. We all love the same God, want the same things mostly."

"Yes, you would think that would count for something," I agreed, carefully lowering myself down to sit next to Johannes. I put an arm around him and drew him close, hoping to dispel some of his melancholy. He placed a kiss on my hair as I rested my head on his shoulder.

"I honestly think that Satan is trying to break us apart, to prevent us from doing good," he reflected. "It's the only thing that makes sense to me. Even Reverend Lischy is embroiled in the turmoil," he said, raising his shoulders, unbelievingly and in confusion. "You think you know somebody."

I understood what he meant. Reverend Lischy, such a respected leader among us, had always seemed so supportive of our church, but to my mind he had been acting questionably lately. To us he had been such an ardent supporter of the Moravian philosophy, but last year he accepted a position at a Reformed church in York, apparently *forgetting* to fully disclose a few important details, and presenting himself as a Reformed minister. After the Reformed congregation discovered his Moravian leanings, they barred him from preaching in the church for a while.

"For all of their piety, it is very confusing. Controversy surrounds so many of the ministers. Even Andrew Eschenbach has not escaped the scandal and upheaval!" Johannes said unbelievingly. "Andrew prayed with me aboard the *Friendship* as my family passed from this life to the next. He is a good man, Katharina. He was so passionate for God."

"I remember you telling me about him. Maybe he lost focus on what really matters," I surmised. "That is easy to do."

Reverend Eschenbach had been appointed minister of a church in Oley, PA. One of the members had presented a tract of land for the purpose of building a new church. Plans were made to construct a log structure, but as the story went, Reverend Eschenbach had bigger plans in mind. He had his heart set on a large two-story building like the new clergy house in Bethlehem. After his idea was refused, he voiced his disappointment loudly and incorporated his displeasure into the sermons. As one can imagine, the congregation did not approve and soon lost confidence in his ability to lead them. He was recalled back to Bethlehem by Count Zinzendorf and preached sporadically, but his ministry suffered and he left his calling altogether to become a farmer.

"It's a real shame," lamented Johannes. "He was a gifted minister and a kind man." Sighing, Johannes handed his mug back to me. "Well, back to work I suppose," he said, offering a hand to assist me up from the ground.

I kissed the tip of his nose lightly and gave him a hug. "Don't let it pull you down to their level. God is in control," I encouraged as I headed out the door and back into to rain.

"Yes, I know," he agreed as he picked up his plane and began work again. "My burden would be much lighter if I gave my worries to God."

Despite our hopes, throughout the year contention within the Donegal Moravian Church continued to increase. Sometimes I wondered how much more strain the church could withstand. A miracle would be needed to bring the dispute to a happy ending.

The year did end on a joyous note for us however, as we welcomed another daughter to our family on December 26, 1746. We named her Catharina and appointed her Uncle John and Aunt Angela as sponsors.

"Fraternizing with the Moravians!" Johannes declared hotly, reacting to the news that Reverend Lischy had 'repented of his ways' and returned to the Reformed church. "As if we were the French army or something!"

"That man does have some shortcomings," agreed thirty-seven-year-old Peter Schneider, a German immigrant and blacksmith. Johannes and Peter sometimes worked together on wagons and as a fellow brethren, he was a strong supporter of the Donegal Moravian

Church. He and his wife, Louisa, had become real friends to our family and they joined us for a simple dinner. "Although, I have to admit it does feel like we are at war with the Reformed Church sometimes," he conceded this point.

"You know what the problem is, Peter?" Johannes asked. "Lischy has been untrustworthy all along. We should have never relied on him to take care of filing the deed for the church. I can't believe he registered it as a Reformed church when he knew all along what our intentions were."

Peter agreed, but wondered, "How were we to know he would do something like that? He seemed so kind and sincere and so Godly. I don't know why he would have done that to us."

"We're in a mess now because of it," Johannes fumed. "I think we should make everyone sign a promise that whatever happens, they won't expect to get any money back from what they contributed to the building of the church in the beginning. We understood then that it was to be used by *everyone* and *anyone* who wanted to spread the gospel. Not just one denomination! We made that clear!"

"We have to keep a cool head about this," advised Peter. "As upset as I am, I don't want this to reflect poorly on the Lord," he said, and then shook his head in disgust. "Although, I'm afraid it already has."

"You're right," Johannes grudgingly agreed. "But I do think we need to put something in writing."

"That's probably a good idea. Why don't I bring it up after church on Sunday?" suggested Peter.

"I'm sure that will go well."

"It's worth a try," Peter encouraged. "I'll take care of it Sunday."

When Sunday rolled around, Peter was true to his word and after the service took time to explain the document, laying it out before the men. As expected, some stomped out of the building, swearing to never sign such a document. However, there were those who did stay to sign, including Reverend Meurer.

The document read:

*"if at any time I leave the church, I will not attempt to recall what has been
done towards the church either in money or labor."*

It was signed by:

John Philip Meurer
John Gopfert
Francis Seip
Abram Frederick
John Kapp
Peter Ricksecker
Francis Alber
Matthew Baumgartner
Jacob Künzly
Peter (B) Blaser (his mark)
Henry Schneider
Rudolph Künzly
George Gopfort
Peter Schneider
John Etter

Chapter 3

Late October 1748

could scarcely believe my good fortune as I finished carefully folding my best black dress and finest bonnet. I thought again to the letter I received about a month ago from my brother Peter. Peter was now thirty-two-years-old, and both he and Daniel lived in Philadelphia, near Second Street and Race Street. Peter with his stocking factory and Daniel with the Inn. As with all new businesses it took a while for Peter's factory to get its feet off the ground, but now it seemed that the factory was a great success. Peter himself did not brag, but by way of Daniel's letters I learned that Peter was doing quite well for himself and his family, and had developed into quite a respectable businessman in the community.

It had been so long since I last saw Peter. Well educated in the qualities of a good a merchant, he was cultured and articulate. Running an inn required versatility of language, and from a young age, we all learned to speak German, French, and English. This was a great asset now to both Peter and Daniel in their chosen occupations.

In response to my brother's request in his last letter, Johannes and I, along with the children, would be setting out on a journey with our wagon pointed toward Philadelphia. I was so thrilled that my brother would get to meet his namesake, our newest addition, two-month-old baby Peter. The harvest was complete and although it would be no easy task to take four young girls all under the age of seven and a newborn on a trip to the city, it was the only time I could see that it would work at all. We were not able to go earlier during harvest and if we waited too long, snow would be upon us.

Not only was I excited at the prospect of seeing my brothers and their families, I was curious to return to the port city in which I landed eleven years ago. I was sure it would be a shock to my system to replace my current surroundings of unending forest and the peaceful solitude of nature with bustling city streets.

I acknowledged that the trip would not be without risk, but I refused to be held captive by my fear. I reasoned that if we waited until the world was safe to travel, I would remain locked away in our cabin forever. Despite these brave notions, I harbored worries. I was apprehensive that we would somehow become entangled in the military action stemming from King George's War. Philadelphia had not yet experienced any repercussions, but the French and Spanish had been raiding up and down the Delaware River and in my mind, that was too close and concerning when I was about to set out on a journey to the city.

The placating Quakers in the Pennsylvania Assembly refused to pass a militia bill to protect the settlers from the threat of Indian raids that were associated with the conflict. The situation was serious enough that even volunteers in our own community came forward last year and joined together to form what is called The Associated Regiment of the West End of Lancaster County, on the Susquehanna. Our neighbor, Thomas Harris was appointed Captain and commanded one of the companies. I remember hearing somewhere that Ben Franklin wrote "if you want something done, ask a busy person." They asked the right man to command the company.

According to Peter's most recent letter, apparently Ben Franklin also had concerns about his city's defenseless state and organized a company of volunteers to defend the people there. The group was called the Philadelphia Associators. I was somewhat, but not altogether surprised when Peter wrote that he himself had volunteered and his commission as an officer was confirmed. Like Johannes and I, Peter had become a member of the Moravian church.

It was my belief, and apparently Peter shared my view, that although we would wish for peace, it was acceptable to help defend our community if necessary. Although Peter took his turn volunteering with the other men at one of two forts on the Delaware, he assured us that he would be home for our visit.

My thoughts drifted to his wife Margaretta and to their son John, who just turned two in May, and to their daughter, Elizabeth, only ten months old. I was looking forward to meeting them all. Peter first wrote to me about Margie a few years past when he announced he made a request to the minister of the church for a wife. Per church tradition, the lot was cast and he was permitted to marry her. Upon hearing about this, I felt relieved that Johannes and I fell in love *before* joining the Moravian church.

I put aside the letter and returned to tidying up the house. Hearing the door swing open, I cast a quick glance toward it as Johannes came in after completing the evening chores. He hurried through the dimly lit house and embraced me, then let me go so I could continue with my work.

"Why clean the house if no one will be here to see it?" asked Johannes as he watched me scurry around the house by lamplight, wiping down the furniture with a damp cloth.

I shrugged, "I hate to come home to a messy house!"

"Oh, and I forgot, John will be around to take care of the animals. You better warn your brother to clean up if he comes inside."

"Maybe I'll leave him a note," I considered, but then quickly changed my mind. "Better not," I said. "He'll track mud in on purpose if I do that. But I guess I shouldn't be too hard on him," I said. "We wouldn't even be able to go if he hadn't agreed to help out."

"True," Agreed Johannes as he sat down on the bed and began donning his homespun nightclothes and quilted robe.

"I hope the children sleep okay tonight," I worried. "I don't want them to be grouchy tomorrow."

"Quiet yourself Kat, and relax! Everything is going to work out fine. A few days out on the trail, seeing new things and staying in new places…It will be good for us all to have a change of pace."

"I guess you're right," I agreed. However, I did not put down my cleaning rag and my ear slanted toward the loft as I listened for

179

any stray giggles that might float down. It seemed that everyone was asleep and for that I was thankful. Earlier in the day, the girls could barely contain their excitement. I could not blame them, for my own excitement exceeded even theirs.

After making the sandwiches, giving the dog a good-bye pat along with orders to "stay," and packing up the five children, we were finally on our way. Only a half hour of bumping down the trail had passed when four-year-old Elizabeth patted me on the shoulder and put on her sweetest smile.

"I'm hungry," She declared. "May I have a cookie?"

I smiled. Anna, Margaretha, Elizabeth and Catherina had been more excited for these cookies than about anything else. As the soft brown-sugar *leb* cookies baked yesterday, it was torture for the girls when I told them they must wait until the trip to try one. I wished Elizabeth had waited to ask, and I hated to tell her no, but we had just eaten a hearty breakfast and needed to space out the snacks.

"Wait just a little longer Elizabeth," I instructed. With difficulty, the child did as she was told and did not question, but the glistening tears gathering in her eyes revealed her grave disappointment.

As we pressed forward, the autumn foliage of the oak and maple trees blazed around us in varying hues of scarlet, mustard, and burnt orange. Ferns, that just a month before covered the forest floor in lush green, were now turned a brilliant shade of shimmering yellow. The clip-clop of the horse's hooves, the jolting of the small wagon, and the swirling of crisped leaves caught in the wagon wheel current, broke through the stillness. Occasionally a deer startled or a small creature peeked curiously from the woods.

Every now and then, we passed a home or a tavern. As we passed one of the few farm homes along the road, I admired a black stallion in a pasture beside the road. The early morning sunlight glistened in his shining mane as if sparkling jewels had been braided throughout. Apparently inspired by our team of horses, the stallion broke into a powerful gallop, running the length of his field beside the wagon, putting on a show. I thanked God for making such a glorious animal. The girls echoed my thoughts as they clapped their hands and laughed out loud at the sheer magnificence of the stallion.

The morning wore on and Johannes found a suitable area to unhitch the horses for a rest and drink. To the delight of the girls, I finally pulled out the long-awaited cookies, along with a jug of fresh meadow-mint tea. The treats did not disappoint.

"You're a wonderful Mama," Johannes complimented me. "Don't you think so, girls?"

"Mmm hmm!" the girls agreed through smiles wreathed in soft brown cookie crumbs. I painted another mental picture to add to my collection of pleasant memories.

As we loaded back into the wagon to continue on our journey, Johannes looked more peaceful than he had for months and that alone made the trip worth all my trouble and worry. The day went by surprisingly fast, and the sun began to set. Although I appreciated the riot of pink and orange painted in the sky, the weather was turning cold and I hoped the inn would soon appear.

"It should be right up here around the bend," said Johannes. "I think," He added with some uncertainty.

"That's what you said an hour ago," I replied. I tried not to blame him or be angry, but my concern set me on edge.

"I know what I said," bit back my husband.

"Sorry," he apologized immediately. "It's just that I was sure we would be there by now."

"Well, you know we had to make more stops than you're normally used to," I said, glancing back at the girls who were fast asleep already.

"Yes. I know. Maybe we should ease up on the drinks tomorrow," he said, easing the tension with a hint of amusement.

"Probably," I agreed.

The sunlight waned further and finally disappeared, leaving us enclosed and enveloped in the cool, pitch black night. Even the moon hid its face and refused to sprinkle any illumination on the trail. Johannes lit the lantern and hopped down from the wagon seat to walk with and lead the horses. I prayed that we would not veer off the side and worried about the deep ditches known to be along this stretch of road. I was torn, wanting desperately to stop along the trail, yet scared to death to do so. I breathed another prayer for safety when suddenly, a wild scream, like that of a shrieking woman, split the night air. My heart raced in panic and I was sure that attack by a wild animal or unfriendly Native was imminent.

"Johannes!" I screamed. Johannes worked to steady the spooked horses and reassured me.

"Calm down, Katharina," he admonished. "Don't yell. It will just scare the horses more and wake up the girls. It's just a screech owl. It won't hurt us."

I tried to heed his scolding, but my mind and heart continued its frantic pace and I feared for my family. Just as my nerves could take no more, by God's mercy, I spotted candlelight shining from the window of a house not far down the road.

"Thanks be to the Lamb of God!" I breathed.

"Welcome!" greeted a portly woman as we approached the house. In a gruff, loud voice she said, "I'm widow Grubb. Please, hurry and come inside." She placed her arm around me as I stood on the porch, a little too familiar for my liking, as if we were old friends. I broke free and headed back toward the wagon.

"Just give the horses to Nero," she motioned toward a muscular black man, who was already taking the reins from Johannes. The slave gently ran his hand down the flat bridge of the horses' muzzle and steadied the team as Johannes and I unloaded our sleepy children from the wagon bed.

My opinion of Mrs. Grubb dropped even further as I watched Nero lead the horses toward the barn. She did not treat the man unkindly, but I could not imagine how anyone could rationalize owning another human being. It was wrong. People could reason away the evil, but it remained evil nonetheless.

"Now just put your things in that back room," Mrs. Grubb directed. "Your girls can share a bed with my two youngest daughters. I think they will all be able to fit in there and you two and the baby can share the other children's bed while they find themselves a place in the barn."

I arched an eyebrow and cast a skeptical look at the small bed, feeling regret for the Grubb children. Before I could dwell on it long, my thoughts were interrupted by the strident cries of an infant coming from the small kitchen in the back of the house. A hint of annoyance played across Mrs. Grubb's face, but was immediately replaced by what I surmised to be a superficial smile. In a gruff voice, the innkeeper called loudly towards the kitchen.

"Fannie! Keep that baby quiet! We have guests."

"Yes ma'am," a woman timidly replied.

Mrs. Grubb directed us to follow her down the hall towards the small room where Fannie was clearing the remains of an earlier supper. A small infant was balanced in one of Fannie's dark arms while she wiped down the table with the other hand. I smiled at the woman and her child, and then cast a look down at Peter, asleep in my arms. Of course I would always hold to the belief that my own children were the most beautiful ever born, but the infant held in the crook of Fannie's arm held a close second.

As loud as he had been just moments before, the woman's baby was now sleeping, contented by his mother's movement. Black hair curled in perfect flat ringlets tight against his head and his lips pursed as he dreamed of nursing at his mother's breast.

"What a beautiful baby," I remarked, a motherly look softening my gaze.

Fannie looked up from her cleaning and smiled shyly, saying, "Thank you, Ma'am. He's usually a happy child."

"It will be *my* happiness when he's old enough to do more than eat and sleep!" said Mrs. Grubb, snickering in self-perceived cleverness. "He'll be a big boy just like his daddy."

Mrs. Grubb smiled, but her remarks held more than good natured jesting and compliments. It was obvious that she was truly looking forward to the day when her newest slave could be put to good use. Johannes had promptly deposited the sleeping Margaretha, Elizabeth and Catharina in bed, where they now slept without care. Anna, on the other hand, had roused from slumber and stood with us, admiring the baby.

"What's his name?" She asked.

"It's Lark," Fannie replied, lowering her head, anticipating what would happen next.

"Lark!" laughed Mrs. Grubb. "Have you ever heard of such a name for a child? Even for a slave? I'm naming the next one. That's for sure!" Fannie looked away, whether in embarrassment or disgust I could not tell.

Johannes looked at the new mother with compassion. "Lark is an extremely well chosen name in my opinion," he said. Mrs. Grubb's laugh was cut short by the comment.

"How so?" the older woman scoffed and sneered. Then thinking better of her public display of disdain, she smiled.

"Well, look at the little one. Contrary to your comments that he will grow to be a big man like his father, Mrs. Grubb, he appears quite small to me. Almost birdlike. And look at his long fingers and toes. Did you know that larks have especially long claws?"

Mrs. Grubb frowned. Johannes continued. "Lark is also a word used to describe something that is fun, or carefree. I think it's a terrific name, filled with the essence of childhood."

Mrs. Grubb stared at Johannes, all pretense of Christian charity stripped away in a glance, but then artfully replaced by the fake smile once again. "Well sir, you must have read the dictionary this morning," she dripped with sarcastic kindness. "Fannie, see to it that these folks have a bite of left-over supper," she ordered. Then turning to us, she informed us that she would be retiring for the night and instructed us to summon Fannie or Nero from their cabin down the lane should we need anything during the night. She grabbed up a large piece of cake in hand and carried it with her, yelling at her own children to get ready for bed.

"That was an experience," I reflected as we settled into bed for the night.

"Yes. And not a good one," agreed Johannes.

Philadelphia

"Peter!" I exclaimed, jumping from the wagon seat and running up the brick sidewalk toward my brother. He stood waiting in the wide doorway of his three-story row home, a warm smile beckoning to me, the sister he had not seen in so long. When I reached Peter he embraced me in a welcoming brotherly hug.

"You look wonderful - so dignified!" I remarked as I held him at arms-length, surveying him and taking in his clothing. Though they were fashioned in the plain dress of the Moravians that I had become use to, it was easy to see they were finely cut and made of superior dark brown cloth.

"I have a reputation to live up to now." He laughed, smoothing the front of his suit and mocking a stately pose. Extending both hands out in appraisal of his sister, he remarked, "And you are even prettier than when I saw you last. Marriage and motherhood agrees with you!" he complimented.

I beamed happily and looked toward one source of my pride, the children, who waited shyly by the wagon. They crowded around Johannes and watched me with wide eyes as I reunited with a man they had heard much about, but did not know.

"Children, come meet your Uncle Peter."

Anna broke free of the group and ran to my side. She curtsied as she had been rehearsing for the past weeks. "So nice to meet you, Uncle," she said demurely, as practiced.

Acting the part he knew she expected him to play, Peter bent down on one knee and took her delicate hand in his. Placing a kiss on top of it, he smiled at her and replied, "And nice to meet you my dear. You must be Annie."

"Yes sir. My real name is Anna, but people sometimes call me Annie!" she giggled.

"Did you and your mamma come alone?" he asked her.

"No," she laughed. "My papa and sisters and baby brother are right over there!" she turned around and pointed.

Peter squinted and his look followed the line of her finger. "Oh! Now I see them." Peter smiled and lightly mussed the child's hair. "Come over here!" He kindly directed. "I want to meet *all* of you beautiful little girls!"

Johannes gave the girls a light prodding push towards me and their uncle and they shuffled together shyly, each girl gripping the other's dress in front of her. The oldest, four-year-old Margaretha lead the way, three-year-old Elizabeth was sandwiched in the middle, and two-year-old Catharina brought up the rear.

When they reached their destination, Peter folded them all into a big hug. "What a lovely bunch," he said, kissing each on top of their head. Freeing the girls, Peter extended his hand to Johannes, who had made his way to the group and carried baby Peter. Johannes returned the firm handshake and pulled the blanket back from baby Peter to give his Uncle a better view.

"Handsome as I knew he would be!" commented Peter. The baby looked up into the eyes of his namesake and his Uncle beamed down at him. By this time, Peter's wife had joined us on the sidewalk, with two-year-old John in tow and ten-month-old Elizabeth, carried in her arms.

"I'd like you all to meet Margaretta and my two children, John and Elizabeth," Peter said proudly and again, hugs and kisses were passed around the group.

"Please, come inside," entreated Peter's wife. "You must be very tired. And please call me Margie." she said kindly.

Margie stood on the large stone step at the entryway and opened the door, welcoming us into her home. On the outside, only the deeply recessed red door encased by sturdy cream-colored molding and the matching red wood shutters around the windows differentiated this home from the other brick houses connected in rows and lining both sides of the street. But as I stepped inside, it was obvious that a prominent family of some wealth lived here. My eyes swept over the wide pine-planked floors polished to perfection and up to the high ceilings finished with thick crown moldings. There was not a speck of dust or cobweb to be seen anywhere. Mahogany wainscoting lined the stairway, lending a rich, cozy ambiance to the entrance. Though I did not think of myself as a woman easily impressed by money or status, I could not help feeling a measure of pride in my brother and briefly wondered at how he reconciled such extravagance with a faith that embraced finding happiness in simplicity.

"What a beautiful home!" I sighed.

"Thank you," Replied Margie, almost shyly. "We love it, but compared to our friends' homes it is rather simple. Not that I'm complaining, because I know we are blessed. Remind me to show you the courtyard garden out back. It is my favorite part of our home and the children just love to play out there."

"Let's go get the luggage and take it upstairs," Peter said to Johannes, who agreed, handing off the baby to me. He cooed happily and squirmed in my arms.

"He'll be running around with the other children before we know it!" commented Johannes before heading out the door with Peter.

"Just let him remain a baby for a while," I suggested with a tired smile.

Already, my daughters had forgotten their initial shyness and called for a game of tag down the hallway, trying to involve their young cousin John.

"Girls," I admonished. "No tag in the house. I know it's been a long trip, but settle down and show some respect to your Aunt and Uncle. Don't ruin their house in the first five minutes of our visit!"

The children quickly quieted, much to my relief. Grabbing Anna by the hand, Cousin John led her toward the steps and tried to pull on her to go upstairs with him. "My *woom*," he directed insistently in his childish dialect. "Go up to my *woom*."

Anna looked at me for permission. "You may go up with him if it is alright with Aunt Margie." Margie nodded her consent and the two children started up the wooden stairs hand in hand, followed by Margaretha and Elizabeth. It sounded like thunder booming rather than four small children marching up the steps. Two-year-old Catharina decided to stay behind and held fast to my hand.

We resumed our conversation and Margie adjusted baby Elizabeth on her hip as she took me on a brief tour of the house. The long wide hall stretched from the front of the home to the back, where a door was located and I assumed it opened to that idyllic garden I was longing to see. Located to the left near the front of the hall was a parlor and to the right a library. To the back of the house lay a beautifully appointed dining room and a kitchen. The delightful aroma of roasting meat wafted in the air.

"Daniel and Rosina will be joining us for dinner this evening," happily announced Margie.

"Wonderful!" I enthused. "I was hoping they could get away. Mamma said it sounds like they are exceedingly busy."

"They are," Margie agreed. "And it's not just the one inn. Daniel owns three taverns now, you know. The closest one is just down the street and the other two are in Germantown." She continued, "We see them at church every Sunday of course."

I nodded, thinking of the letters I had received from Daniel and Rosina. The First Moravian Church of Philadelphia had been built five years ago, not very far from Peter and Margie's house in fact, but according to what they had last written, it was struggling to grow from the original thirty-four members.

"It's too bad that you weren't here a few weeks ago," lamented Margie. "We had the most interesting visitor at church."

Curious, I tried to guess. "Was it Count Zinzendorf?" I asked.

"No…" smiled Margie. "Guess again."

"Reverend Kohn?" I tried.

Margie laughed. "I said *interesting*! Not…" she cut short and covered her mouth with her hand, embarrassed. I just laughed in knowing agreement.

"It's okay, Margie. No need to say more. I set you up for that one though, didn't I?" I shrugged my shoulders and then continued. "Okay, one more try," I said. "Was it the King of England?"

"No! Now come on," Margie chuckled. "It was Chief Shikellamy."

"Now that *would* have been fascinating!" I agreed.

"He's a compelling man," she remarked and then sobered. "I felt so sorry for him though. His tribe at Shamokin suffered terribly from Malaria last year. He lost his wife and several other members of his family."

"That is heartbreaking," I empathized. "Poor man."

"Yes. It's awful. He was also sick during that time, but the government was able to send Conrad Weiser to him with a remedy and he recovered. But if you ask me, he still didn't look very well. I don't think he should have been traveling that far after having been so ill," remarked Margie.

"It's hard to keep any man down when he desires otherwise," I said, but then praised, "Thank God for his wise counsel. I fear what could happen when he is no longer here to calm the waters between the Indians and the government."

Margie agreed, but then changed the subject to what she hoped would be a lighter topic. "You mentioned your mother and father a few minutes ago. I wish they could have come with you," said Margie.

A faint expression of worry stole across my features as I quietly agreed, "Me too."

"Is everything okay?" asked Margie, concerned for the in-laws that she had only met once.

"To be honest, I'm not sure," I confided. "Mother hasn't been feeling well lately. It started as a cold with a minor cough and I thought it would go away, but it hasn't. In fact it's getting worse. She's been taking every remedy we can think of from Slippery Elm with milk to peppermint tea."

"Peter will be so worried," Margie fretted.

"We all are," I admitted, referring to my other brothers and sisters at home. "But she just brushes our concern aside as if it is no

188

big deal. It isn't in Mamma's nature to attract attention. She prefers giving all the attention to others." Although this was the first time Margie and I had ever met, she hugged me to her in sisterly concern, for we were not only bound as family through the laws of marriage, but we were sisters in our faith as well.

"I will pray for her every day," promised Margie sincerely. "She must get well so my children can meet their grandmother someday."

I wiped the tears from my eyes and nodded in agreement. "She wanted to come along so badly, but we all feared that it would only worsen her health. She wasn't happy, I promise you that!"

"I can imagine," she smiled. "It sounds like she is an opinionated woman. From the stories that Peter tells, she often gets her way."

I laughed and looked at Johannes as he walked back through the door, arms filled with our luggage and chatting amiably with my brother. Thinking back to that freezing cold day so many years ago, when my mother forced me to ride to a certain cabin, I smiled and said, "Thankfully, yes."

Joyfully, late that evening my two brothers and I shared our families with each around Peter's large table and ate from his heavily laden dishes overflowing with turtle soup, roast duck, and several desserts including pies and puddings. Margie explained to us that an abundant variety of goods were available at the market on Wednesdays and Saturdays and having fresh supplies on hand made preparing meals a delight.

"You have to get there early to get the best of the produce and the finest cuts of meat," she said. "But I don't mind. I just love the whole atmosphere and I usually run into a friend or two. I grew up here in the city and my mother would take me to the market. Now I'm taking Elizabeth. I could send the servant I suppose, but it's a good tradition and we enjoy it so much."

I felt the slightest twinge of jealousy, thinking of how easy it would be to walk out the door and buy a fresh peach, rather than having to devote years growing the tree and then spending hours harvesting the fruit. I consoled myself with the fact that my own produce could not get any fresher.

Peter lit the fireplace and the pungent aroma of wood-smoke settled in around us as the celebration lasted late into the October night. Memories of childhood were rehashed and Johannes and I informed my brothers about the latest happenings in the family. We shared with them news that Johan Jacob had traveled with a group of twenty-two other single brethren to establish a new Moravian settlement they called *Albrechtsbrunn*, the Spring of Albrecht. The group had not traveled far, as the land was only ten miles north of Bethlehem. A saw-mill and grist-mill operated at the site and the crops yielded from the land would help supply the Moravian communities. It seemed as though Johan Jacob found pleasure in his calling and for this I rejoiced.

We spoke of politics and religion, of new friends and old. Peter casually mentioned taking tea with Benjamin Franklin's brother and talked of a new acquaintance named John Adams.

"That man is certainly making his mark in the city," commented Johannes of the printer, author and inventor, Benjamin Franklin. "Did I ever tell you about the time I met him? It was my very first day in this country." He sent a look my way. Everyone who had been in Johannes's presence while reading the Old Farmer's Almanac had heard the account. As the conversation continued, each recounted memories of the voyage from Europe, all except Margie of course, who was born this side of the Atlantic.

Peter and Daniel shared with us that they were considering becoming emigration agents. It was their hope that they could help improve the journey for the passengers as they traveled across the sea. By giving their assistance to this cause, my brothers would be giving up any right they would ever have to again reclaim citizenship in Switzerland, but they seemed willing to make this sacrifice. I was proud that they were putting action to their convictions.

I soaked in the culture that oozed from my brothers and relished in their accounts of city life that seemed so foreign to me now. Even as they discussed ordinary every day events such as going to the barber for a hair trimming at five in the morning or gathering with other men for reading and discussion at the local tavern on many an evening, I found myself imagining how life could be so different for me and my family if we ever moved to the city. I quickly dismissed the thought however, as I thought of our snug little cabin in the

190

woods bordered by the sparkling, babbling brook and most of all, I knew that I would never want to leave my Lancaster County friends and family.

As I knew it would, the time spent in the city with my brothers passed swiftly, and before I was ready, I found myself living back amongst the trees. Life returned to its normal routine of mending, cooking and church. But routines are made to be broken.

Chapter 4

1749

I was surprised to see a large gathering of horses and wagons already assembled outside the church as we approached on a freezing cold, February morning. We expected to arrive early to start the fire and for a moment I thought that perhaps I misjudged the time we left home. But that did not make sense. Johannes would have noticed if we had been running behind schedule.

As I looked closer, I noticed that these were not the usual conveyances belonging to the regular Moravian members. I began to feel a rising sense of alarm as I recognized one and then another wagon belonging to families who had decided to return to the Reformed faith. Those friends with whom we tried so hard to reconcile our differences. Glancing at Johannes, he returned my wary look. I felt a deep shiver born of apprehension.

We descended from the wagon and carefully picked our way across the snowy, icy lot as we moved towards the building. Johannes was the first to walk up the front steps and pulled on the door handle. It did not budge. He tried again. Still he was unable to open the door. From inside we heard voices united in song, seemingly oblivious to the outside world.

It was then that I realized the truth. The door was not stuck or frozen shut. We did not oversleep. This was no accident of bad time management. We had been locked out of our own church. Johannes muttered under his breath, trying to keep his tone in check, but his flushed face affirmed his true feelings.

"Just take a deep breath," I advised, but I too struggled to remain calm. "I can't believe they would resort to this," I said, incredulously. Not much more was said between us. What was there to say? We climbed back into the wagon and sat in silence, awaiting the arrival of the other Moravian members.

After waiting in the cold for what seemed an eternity, the other members arrived. Johannes explained the situation and it was decided that further discussion would take place at Peter and Louisa Schneider's home. Packed into the Schneider home, the Moravians were abuzz with an uncommon tone of unrest. Peter Schneider addressed the displaced congregation. His wife, Louisa stood by his side.

"My brethren," he spoke quietly and with a sense of reason. "What has happened today is obviously very unsettling. But let us not lose control of our emotions. It is the Lord's Day and we must honor Him. What others do is not our concern. We will not be judged upon what they have done. However, we are responsible for how we react." A few people quietly responded in agreement. "Louisa and I discussed it on the way back from the church, and we would like to offer our home as a meeting place for worship until this matter can be settled." He looked to his wife and she nodded her head in silent agreement.

One of the men from the congregation had not yet been able to so quickly reconcile his feelings about the incident. "I'm not going to be pushed around like that!" He declared in fierce bitterness.

Another concurred. "I've put a lot of money into that building, and a lot of hard work. We had a deal that it was to be available for the use of any worshipers. Not just one group. When I get my hands on Lischy…"

Again Peter Schneider interjected. "Men," he addressed them sternly to get their attention. "Think before you speak. We are in

194

the presence of women and children, and most importantly our Lord." The room quieted.

"In time," Peter continued, "we will take legal recourse. No one is asking you to give up the property without protest. But nothing will be solved if we don't approach this correctly. It will be difficult, but I'm asking you to put aside your thoughts of anger and frustration and turn your focus to The Lamb in this time of trial. He knows our situation and is the most impartial judge of all."

Johannes stood to his feet and joined in solidarity with his friend Peter. "I am willing," he declared and began singing a hymn in his rich, baritone voice.

I was first to join him, then Peter and Louisa. I noticed also my father giving himself over to song, and soon the home was filled with hymns of praise as attention was turned heavenward, leaving the problems of earth where they belonged. That is, most had turned their attention heavenward. My attention riveted on the space beside my father, unoccupied by my mother. Dread filled my heart.

My worst fears for my mother were realized. The morning that Mamma stayed home from church, bidding my father to find solace in worship despite her condition and claiming that she would be fine- only needing a rest - proved to be her final act of unselfishness. Breathing had become difficult for her over the past few months, with continuous coughing spasms producing blood specked sputum. Grudgingly, Papa had complied with her wishes that cold morning and gone to worship with the Moravian brethren, vowing to bring home an account of the pastor's message and news of friends and family. And what news he had to report. But Mamma would never know of the upheaval that took place that day. Upon his return home, Papa found her at rest, the coughing and wheezing departed along with her generous spirit.

It has been said that time heals all wounds, but I know it must first inflict them. The calendar moved forward, unaware and insensitive to the fact that the world was missing one of its most special inhabitants. Summer passed as I missed my mother. If I had taken more time to look up toward the heavens, I would have seen that God painted yet another masterpiece as the sparse gold and rust colored leaves danced against a cobalt blue November sky. My focus, however, turned inward and obstructed my view.

On the 23rd of the month I tended to the cabin's hearth fire and I thought of Johannes and the few other trustees of the church who were making their way North-East towards Warwick Township to attend the Moravian conference where Johannes would officially be received into the *Gemeine*, or congregation. I knew this was a significant day for Johannes. True, he was already extremely involved in our Donegal congregation, but this would be a more formal statement of his intentions toward the Moravian faith and church and signified his leadership involvement. It would also mean that he would participate in any special events held at the Warwick location and be a representative of our church in Donegal.

I found it hard to even remember what the old Johannes was like. He was now so devoted to the church and to our Savior. He often spoke of spiritual matters and as was preached in church, spent much time contemplating the wounds of Jesus and the significance of the Lamb's sacrifice. His devotion to our Lord brought Johannes to life like never before and his passion was contagious. Always the charming sort, his natural charisma now worked to draw others to Jesus.

As I caught sight of my plain skirt, I remembered that I too had changed, and I did not regret my decision for one moment. Though we lived simply, my life was abundant. However, every day I still felt the empty space created by the passing of my mother. I closed my eyes, gently covering my pregnant belly with my hands, and envisioned how happy my mother would have been to hold this newest baby after his arrival. I remembered anew that the Lord gives and the Lord takes away.

Admittedly, it was easier to trust my Lord when times were favorable and the blessings plentiful than when forced to give up the tight hold on what I claimed as my own. But experience taught me that God's plans work for good even when it was difficult to see how anything valuable could come from the heartache. I remembered back to the pain of leaving my homeland. It was a hard time in my life, but in letting go of the old, I found a new home that exceeded my expectations. I would have never married Johannes or been mother to his children if I had remained in Switzerland.

And then there was Johan Jacob and Jonny. I still missed them and wished they could be closer to the family. The day of their departure was etched in my mind, and their departure left a void. I had physically held on to them until I was forced to let go. However, with each letter, that hollow was filled with the reassurance that Johannes and I had made the right decision. The boys were thriving. Jonny sounded upbeat and comfortable with life in Bethlehem. Johan Jacob was developing a zeal for missions and his love for the Lord was evident in the desires he poured forth in his writing to the family.

I was unsure of what good could come from having to give up the warm embrace of my mother. Perhaps it was still too soon to see it. One thing I did know was that I hugged my children more and determined to give them all the love I had to give, just as my mother did for me. My prayers intermingled with the rising steam of the cooking pot as it bubbled on the hearth. I asked God to bring healing to my injured soul and to replace my grief with joy.

God answered my prayers and I felt His restorative power as I held new life in my arms. Given the spiritual path we had decided to follow, it only seemed fitting that on April 20, 1750, when our new son joined our family we named him Christian. It was a name that spoke to our history as well as to our hopes for the future.

The Donegal congregation awaited a ruling on our complaints of having been disposed from the church property. Meanwhile, we decided to begin construction of another church. This time we also planned to build a school building and parsonage. Peter Schneider generously donated a portion of his land for the structures. We had not expected that our previous hard work of constructing a church would need to be so quickly repeated. The work was well under way on the new church, but remained unfinished.

Johannes and I rejoiced along with the entire congregation when finally, in August of 1750, Thomas and Richard Penn ruled that the eleven-acre tract of land, along with the church, indeed belonged to the Moravian congregation. But the happiness was tempered because the victory came at the cost of lost friendships and broken relationships. In November, Judge Moulton issued an order to "occupy the church" and the congregation decided to move the partially constructed new buildings over to the site as well.

Along with pressures related to the church, Johannes found himself facing another decision. Sadly, his father had passed away six years earlier. Now a sizable inheritance awaited Johannes, but the money remained in Switzerland. My brothers suggested that he enlist the help of a man named Jacob Joner, a fellow with whom they were acquainted through their involvement as emigration agents. Johannes and I were aware of the man even before their suggestion; after all, Jacob Joner was one of the most well-known Swiss emigration agents at that time.

I had never met him personally, but from Peter's description I could just picture the short little man with dark eyes and curly hair, cane held in one hand while the other adjusted his fancy silk, neck scarf. The man did not sit right with us and Johannes hesitated to do business with him. There were rumors floating around accusing the man of being a "soul-seller" and doing anything he could to profit from the misfortune of poor emigrants. It was hard to know if this was true. Perhaps those same rumors circulated about Daniel and Peter, but I knew that their hearts were in the right place when it came to assisting the Swiss emigrants.

So, on one hand those rumors could be just that; possibly circulated by the Swiss government. Johannes heard that just the year before, the city of Basel ordered Jacob Joner out of Switzerland as quickly as possible. He had been involved in helping four shiploads of emigrants leave the country, which after a recent ruling to inhibit all emigrants from departure, had become against the law. With this "robbery" as some called it, Johannes had no problem, as he himself had been involved in secretive meetings so many years ago. It was the possible mistreatment of the emigrants that nagged at Johannes's conscience.

Still, the fact remained that in tandem with being an emigration agent Joner was also a property agent and had the know-how to get Johannes's inheritance out of Switzerland. Joner was scheduled to soon make a trip and Johannes needed to decide quickly. Since Joner was banned from Switzerland, it would be a covert venture this time.

Johannes confided to me that if he did not get the inheritance now, he did not know when he would get another chance. The world

198

was unsettled. In the colonies, there were constant problems related to the British government's dispute with the French over boundary lines. New forts were being built by both sides and I feared that momentum was mounting towards an explosive pinnacle. The British and French had recently met in Paris to try to solve these disputes, but I was doubtful that foreign diplomacy efforts would be effective. The native Indians played both sides to their own advantage, increasing the instability of the situation. And in Switzerland, the Swiss government was making it increasingly difficult for people to collect what rightfully belonged to them.

"Yes, what rightfully belongs to him," I thought. It was his money and he should be allowed to do with it as he pleased. Suddenly, the decision seemed an easy one. I brought it up to Johannes during supper that evening, explaining to him what I had been thinking. He agreed with me and decided to write a letter to my brother Peter, instructing him to strike the bargain with Joner.

"How much money will you receive in the end, after Joner gets his commission?" I asked.

Johannes replied without much expression. "After the deal, I expect to receive about 100 florins, which equals out to about only 10 pounds." It did not take a mathematician to understand that with an inheritance originally worth 330 pounds, he would lose most of the money.

"Is there no other way to obtain the money? You will lose so much!" I lamented.

"Going through Jacob Joner seems to be the only way I will get any of it." Remarkably, Johannes remained fairly calm as he further remarked, "I'm not trying to appear greedy, but between the Swiss government and Mr. Joner I will have lost a large amount of money, Kat."

We had both seen first-hand what greed could do to men and we did not have to think back very far, only to the church property dispute. Men and women we once called friends now harbored bitterness in their souls towards us…all because of a tract of land and a building…possessions.

Johannes's line of thought followed my own. "No, it's not fair, that's for sure, but I won't let myself become obsessed with the money we will lose, but choose to be grateful to receive that which we did not have before."

As the days thereafter passed, we continued to live as devoted members of the Moravian congregation. The lot had been cast in our favor and Johannes and I attained the privilege of participating in the Holy Sacrament. We availed ourselves of the merit of Christ, recognizing that we were indeed, wretched sinners.

We received news that the mills Johan Jacob helped build and operate at *Albrechtsbrunn* were destroyed by fire. They rebuilt only the saw mill, but added a distillery, brewery and milk house. They renamed the town *Christiansbrunn*, Christian's Spring, after the head of the single brothers, Christian Renatus von Zinzendorf.

I was disturbed by this news. Rumors had made their way across the sea and swirled around about the conduct of Count Zinzendorf's son. It was said that he twisted the concepts set forth by his father in regards to Moravian views of a man and woman's marital relationship and used the tenants of our faith to condone inappropriate behavior between the men. I pray that God would show the men His truth and keep our sons from evil.

Chapter 5

On January 6, 1752, baby Abraham joined our family as the world continued on a course towards war. We read in the newspaper that the French Marquis Duquesne was intent on taking over the Ohio River Valley. It did not seem promising for the state of peace when the following year, in 1753, the British Lieutenant Governor of Virginia granted land in this same area to citizens of his colony. In answer, the French built more forts. Both the French and the British continued their efforts to gain favor with the natives. The Six Nations allied themselves with the British, while most of the western Pennsylvania and Ohio tribes affiliated with the French.

On a personal level, in January of 1753, politics of both state and church were far from my mind as my younger sister Susanna and I made final preparations before heading down the aisle of the Quitopehilla Moravian Church sanctuary for the ceremony in which she would wed Daniel Heckendorn. "Mother would have been happy for you," I smiled at Susanna.

It had been a difficult year for Susanna, who was now a widow at only thirty-one years of age after tragically losing her first husband Rudolph. Added to the grief came the enormous responsibility of supporting four children between the ages of three and nine. I hoped that this new relationship with Daniel, a widower, would help sooth her pain.

"What would I do without Johannes?" I wondered. On top of the utter despair at losing my husband, I could not imagine raising and providing for our seven children alone. I had to acknowledge the possibility though, for how many second weddings had I attended since arriving here in the colonies? It was as much a part of life as going to a child's funeral. Johannes and I had actually discussed such matters and he made me promise that if he went to Jesus' side while I was still young, I would remarry. Necessary thoughts, perhaps, but I shook my head to clear them, vowing not to think about such things again on my sister's wedding day.

"Are you ready?" questioned Elizabeth as she popped her head around the corner. "Everybody is in their place and Reverend Rauch said it is time," she reported brightly, coming alongside her big sisters and hugging us both, one per arm.

"I'm so glad that Reverend Rauch could be the one to marry you," I enthused. "I've always liked him."

"I'm glad too," agreed Susanna. "I was worried he might not be able to come because he's been spending so much with the Warwick congregation, trying to organize another settlement similar to Bethlehem. One that is a little less rigid than up there, but somewhere that can provide a little more structure." Susanna caught herself and smiled sheepishly at Elizabeth and me. "I'm rambling, aren't I? It's not like me to be so nervous and ...well it just makes me a little scared to think of living with another man. I was so use to Rudolph's habits and how he likes his meals cooked and when he comes in...came in...for dinner...what if it's hard for the children to get along with Daniel...what if..."

I interrupted Susanna mid-thought. "Susanna, you know we talked about this for a long time at Abraham's birthday celebration last week. What if he's wonderful? What if he's a great father to the children? What if he loves you more than you ever imagined?"

"Yes," emphatically agreed Elizabeth. "Think good thoughts Susanna. It is your wedding day after all!"

"I know. I'm sorry. I just ...." Susanna paused. "You know, I just want to thank both of you for being so helpful to me over the last months. It's been so hard and I don't know how I would have made it without your help. I love you both so much."

"And we love you too, Susanna." I said, daintily wiping at the tears collecting in my eyes. "With the Lord's help I know your future will hold much happiness. God has brought you and Daniel together for a reason. I know that no one can replace Rudolph, but Daniel is a wonderful man."

All three of us brushed away tears; tears for the past remembered and tears for hopes of joy to come. Susanna turned toward the sanctuary, hoping to walk down a path leading to happiness.

"Thank you God for my sisters," Susanna breathed in prayer.

"Amen," Elizabeth and I echoed in agreement.

Seven months had passed since Susanna and Daniel's wedding and I laughed to myself as I thought that things must have gotten off to a good start, as Susanna was due to have a child in two months. This day's weather was a far cry from the cold January day on which they were married. I decided to take a moment to rest after weeding the garden. The hot July sun had beat down upon me relentlessly as I labored, but the work had to be done. A shortage of money, a shortage of time, a shortage of sleep; there were plenty of those to go around, but there was never a shortage of work. Seeking shade under broad, leafy branches of a nearby tree, I pulled out a letter from my apron pocket. I settled down to reread what Johan Jacob had written.

"North Carolina," I thought with a grim expression on my face. A trip to Bethlehem was very inconvenient indeed, but North Carolina…no, it was certain that there would not be a family reunion there anytime soon. Johan Jacob, hard to believe he was already a twenty-five-year-old man, wrote of his plans to set forth on a journey with a group of other single Moravian men that would lead him south to help with setting up a mission there. They were the second group of single Moravian men to go and he planned to arrive sometime in October 1754. Jacob still had not married and seemed focused on the Lord's work. He planned to serve the community there by using his woodworking skills and operating a gristmill. I was excited that Johan Jacob would be able to follow his passion and fulfill his mission, but concern was warranted as well. Tensions between the French and British government and the Indian tribes had escalated even further and real danger would lurk as he traveled.

Johannes and I had been following newspaper articles written by the young officer, George Washington. His journal entries drew attention to the situation with the French and their Indian allies. In the spring, skirmishes broke out in the western part of the state and George Washington had been sent by the British army to deliver a letter to the French. It expressed disapproval over the continued building of French forts. It was no surprise that his letter did no good.

As the French would not cease in building additional forts, the British began to build their own fort and named it Fort Prince George. The name was short lived however, as the French overtook it and renamed it Fort Duquesne, in honor of the Marquis. The French now controlled the entire area west of the Allegheny River. Alarm and fear grew as it was thought by many that the French government may be attempting to take over all of the British colonies. The call went out that more solidarity was needed throughout the colonies in order to present a more consolidated front against the French. One of the most recognized images representing this idea of unity was created by Ben Franklin and published in his and other papers. The picture was that of a wood-cut snake, each section assigned the name of a colony, with the words beneath, "Join or Die."

Philadelphia was still filled with Quakers who were unwilling to aide in the defense of settlers against Indian attacks. It was my opinion that they may have changed their mind if they themselves were subject to the threat of a massacre. I supported the idea of peace, but could not dismiss the importance of having an adequate form of defense for the people living in on the frontier.

My mind was jerked back to the present moment, when suddenly a scream split the air and caused the hair on the back of my neck to stand on end. Without thinking, I shot up, and the letter fell forgotten to the ground as I bolted toward the barn. It was 12-year-old Anna's shriek that curdled my blood and I was terrified at the prospect of what I would find upon reaching her. I was expecting another baby again in three months, but my extra bulk did not slow me down as I raced towards the screaming. When I arrived at the barn, the scene before me robbed me of air and I found it difficult to breathe, not from my panicked run through the fields, but out of fear and shock.

"No, no, no, no…." Anna chanted as she cradled little Abraham against her slight body. Her initial screams had been replaced with sobbing and she pulled the toddler closer to her breast. It was then that I noticed the bright red blood covering the side of Abraham's head and coating Anna's shaking hands. I dropped to my knees beside my son and daughter. I too applied my hands to Abraham's head, trying unsuccessfully to stop the blood from flowing.

"Oh Abraham, Abraham!" I cried.

Peter and Christian, who were not yet in school, heard the commotion and joined us, panic spreading as they looked at their little brother. Johannes arrived from the field, and I felt caught in a tormented dream as I watched him rip off his shirt and apply the linen to the wound, finally curbing the stream of blood.

Anna continued wailing, but I heard her curse the horse and I could now imagine that my son, always exuberant at the sight of the animals, had escaped the careful attention or grasp of his big sister and made his way into the forbidden area behind the stall. All of our children had been repeatedly instructed and warned not to walk behind the horses, but Abraham was only two and a half years old and like the horses, unpredictable.

I clutched him to me, as if expecting him to cry out…to come back to me. But that was not to be. Abraham remained limp and as I lowered my ear to his small chest I heard nothing. No uneven beat; no faint flutter. Just silence. The child's eyes were closed as if in sleep, but he was no longer with us.

Pain ripped through my body, a familiar agony that I now experienced for the eighth time. This time, I welcomed it. It was real and visceral; something at which I could direct the rage and bitterness which I had silently harbored over the last three months. Finally, I could free the pent up emotions held back since the day Abraham died.

I was tempted to allow the pain to consume me, to let it swallow me up and sweep me away to a place where I could hold my son once again. How I missed him. Oh, how I longed to see his perfect sweet face and to hear his bubbling laughter.

But I could not give in to such defeating longings. I had to concentrate on what kept me living when I did not care to go on; the other six children; no, the other *seven* children, for I loved this new one already beyond compare. As another contraction seized me, this time instead of tortured angry screams, tears escaped. They were the first real tears I had cried since Abraham's funeral and I was comforted by their release. After having given birth so many times before, my labor and delivery proceeded quickly. As I held our newest daughter to my breast, I knew that once more I might find healing in nurturing this new life.

Part 5

Johannes

Chapter 1

1755

ADVERTISEMENT.

LANCASTER, April 26, 1755.

"Whereas, one hundred and fifty waggons, with four horses to each waggon, and fifteen hundred saddle or pack horses, are wanted for the service of his majesty's forces now about to rendezvous at Will's Creek, and his excellency General Braddock having been pleased to empower me to contract for the hire of the same, I hereby give notice that I shall attend for that purpose at Lancaster from this day to next Wednesday evening, and at York from next Thursday morning till Friday evening, where I shall be ready to agree for waggons and teams, or single horses, on the following terms, viz.: I. That there shall be paid for each waggon, with four good horses and a driver, fifteen shillings per diem; and for each able horse with a pack-saddle, or other saddle and furniture, two shillings per diem; and for each able horse without a saddle, eighteen pence per diem. 2. That the pay commence from the time of their joining the forces at Will's Creek, which must be on or before the 20th of May ensuing, and that a reasonable allowance be

209

paid over and above for the time necessary for their travelling to Will's Creek and home again after their discharge. 3. Each waggon and team, and every saddle or pack horse, is to be valued by indifferent persons chosen between me and the owner; and in case of the loss of any waggon, team, or other horse in the service, the price according to such valuation is to be allowed and paid. 4. Seven days' pay is to be advanced and paid in hand by me to the owner of each waggon and team, or horse, at the time of contracting, if required, and the remainder to be paid by General Braddock, or by the paymaster of the army, at the time of their discharge, or from time to time, as it shall be demanded. 5. No drivers of waggons, or persons taking care of the hired horses, are on any account to be called upon to do the duty of soldiers, or be otherwise employed than in conducting or taking care of their carriages or horses. 6. All oats, Indian corn, or other forage that waggons or horses bring to the camp, more than is necessary for the subsistence of the horses, is to be taken for the use of the army, and a reasonable price paid for the same."

Note. My son, William Franklin, is empowered to enter into like contracts with any person in Cumberland county.

"B. FRANKLIN."*64

Feeling duty bound and desiring to take part in protecting the good people of Pennsylvania, I watched as my neighbor hitched up a team of horses to one of my wagons. I contributed the wagon, while other neighbors did their part by sending horses or saddles. Some planned to go along on the expedition as team drivers.

Tired of having to look over my shoulder each time I worked in a field, fearing to find the painted face of a warrior staring back, I wished the men success and hoped and prayed that peace would soon prevail. I was heart-sick of hearing stories trickle in from further out on the frontier of innocents being massacred. Each time I unwillingly imagined the frightened face of a victim belonging to one of my loved ones. I desired to have our plantation live up to its name.

Throughout late spring and early summer, we all held our breath in anticipation, eagerly taking in news that came from colonial militia-men on the western front, whose letters continued to be published in the newspapers. It was said that General Braddock's army was well equipped with over a thousand men and that he possessed cannons that could easily destroy a French fort. British "Regulars" were joined by colonial militia-men and wagoners, including one man named Daniel Boone. Twenty-three-year-old officer, George Washington, continued among the ranks.

In July, news came regarding the outcome and fate of General Braddock's attempt to secure Fort Duquesne. I read from the newspaper, George Washington's account which was written to his mother.

"HONORED MADAM: As I doubt not but you have heard of our defeat, and, perhaps, had it represented in a worse light, if possible, than it deserves, I have taken this earliest opportunity to give you some account of the engagement as it happened, within ten miles of the French fort, on Wednesday the 9th instant.

We marched to that place, without any considerable loss, having only now and then a straggler picked up by the French and scouting Indians. When we came there, we were attacked by a party of French and Indians, whose number, I am persuaded, did not exceed three hundred men; while ours consisted of about one thousand three hundred well-armed troops, chiefly regular soldiers, who were struck with such a panic that they behaved with more cowardice than it is possible to conceive. The officers behaved gallantly, in order to encourage their men, for which they suffered greatly, there being near sixty killed and wounded; a large proportion of the number we had.

The Virginia troops showed a good deal of bravery, and were nearly all killed; for I believe, out of three companies that were there, scarcely thirty men are left alive. Captain Peyrouny, and all his officers down to a corporal, were killed. Captain Polson had nearly as hard a fate, for only one of his was left. In short, the dastardly behavior of those they call regulars exposed all others, that were inclined to do their duty, to almost certain death; and, at last, in despite of all the efforts of the officers to the contrary, they ran, as sheep pursued by dogs, and it was impossible to rally them.

The General was wounded, of which he died three days after. Sir Peter Halket was killed in the field, where died many other brave officers. I luckily escaped without a wound, though I had four bullets through my coat, and two horses shot under me. Captains Orme and Morris, two of the aids-de-camp, were wounded early in the engagement, which rendered the duty harder upon me, as I was the only person then left to distribute the General's orders, which I was scarcely able to do, as I was not half recovered from a violent illness, that had confined me to my bed and a wagon for above ten days. I am still in a weak and feeble condition, which induces me to halt here two or three days in the hope of recovering a little strength, to enable me to proceed homewards; from whence, I fear, I shall not be able to stir till toward September; so that I shall not have the pleasure of seeing you till then, unless it be in Fairfax... I am, honored Madam, your most dutiful son."

"Will we be safe, Johannes?" Katharina asked with fear running thick in her voice, her frosty breath of words suspended in frozen cloudy puffs. "Will they come here?"

I looked back at the children, bundled against the cold winter as my family walked quickly into our house after returning from church. "We must do our best to see this as an opportunity to remember that life on earth can be short and perilous. It's just a brief journey on our way to heaven. The Lord can protect us as He wills," I said, trying to bring comfort.

"Why didn't he protect them?" The innocent question came from one of the children.

"We should not question the Lord's ways, child. Sometimes it does not make sense to us," I spoke solemnly. I think they expected me to continue, but I said no more.

It was becoming commonplace to hear reports of Indian massacres upon settlers, from Penn's Creek to the Swatara Creek. Too close. Although the native tribes and immigrants had learned to work together to some degree, each party held such differing views on every aspect of life that it was a volatile relationship. Even the Quakers were finally beginning to realize that something must be done about the Indian attacks. Benjamin Franklin had recently introduced a bill to the legislature, hoping to bring more unity and regulation for the defense of the province. The bill was still in debate, but the war perched at the doorstep of our household.

During the morning service, our pastor delivered sobering news. Indians had murdered many of our brethren at the Moravian Mission settlement at Gnadenhutten on the Mahoney Creek. One man named Peter, escaped to tell the tale of horror and our pastor recounted his tale to us summarizing a letter he had written.

"The missionary's dog barked incessantly and seemed agitated that evening as darkness settled over the community. The missionaries sat down to share their evening meal together, candlelight spreading a warm glow over the table. Martin and Susanna were there, along with Gottlieb and Johanna Christina and their baby, and George and Susanne. Joachim sat alone tonight, his wife being sick upstairs. Several young, single people filled in around them. Everyone seemed tense, but drew comfort from being in the presence of the larger group.

Though our trust lay in the Savior, we couldn't help but feel nervous. The Indian population had been quite unsettled of late and expressed their anger and hostility at the conversion of so many of their tribe to Christianity. Threats had been circulating and the problem was further complicated by the brutal murder of Chief Shikelammy's daughter-in-law and grandchildren by frontiersmen. Shikelammy's son and a formerly converted Indian named Teedyuscung (given the Christian name of Gabriel) were full of rage.

Joachim decided to go outside to make sure that the meeting house door was latched while the others ate. Soon after he departed for the building the quiet evening erupted into chaos as the sound of pounding footsteps and furiously barking dogs clamored together, greatly alarming those inside! One of the young men sitting at the table named Joseph rose to open the door to assess the situation, but as he opened the door he was grazed in the face by a bullet and overcome by painted Indian warriors as they swarmed into the room, firing their guns into the group.

Susanna stared in horror as her husband was cut down by a bullet and three other young men also in quick succession. A biting pain tore through her and she screamed in pain. The other

213

missionaries were fleeing up to the loft, but as Susanna tried to follow she slipped and was dragged outside by her warrior captor. A surreal combination of war whoops, tomahawks, knives and guns swirled around her.

I, one lone man, named Peter, looked on from the single men's house. Fasting that evening, I had not joined the others for supper. I listened as shots were fired repeatedly up through the floor of the loft where the fleeing missionaries had sought refuge. I heard the crackling of burning wood and smelled the acrid smoke moments before I noticed the tall orange flames that quickly illuminated the night sky and licked the structure that imprisoned my friends in a death trap.

Spotting shadowy movement at the upstairs window, I recognized my friend Joseph. Having escaped death once before this night, after being grazed by one of the first bullets, Joseph tried to cheat death once more as he jumped from the second story window. He was closely followed by Susanne and George. Joseph and Susanne picked themselves up the best they could and took off on a run.

It seemed like an eternity to me as shots rang out and people screamed in anguish and terror. The dark shadow of a woman managed to escape the burning building and I silently rooted her on to safety as she ran towards the cellar. Terrible, brutal, ghastly...all of it, but what will haunt me most for the rest of my days is the shrieking cries of Gottlieb and Johanna Christina's baby, the innocent screams rising above the roar of the flames.

It seemed an eternity, but in reality, it only took about 15 minutes to completely destroy our hopes, dreams, and lives of those living there. As the Moravians from the nearby settlement across the river arrived to provide help, they discovered they were too late. All that remained of the missionary's earthly possessions was a cloak and hat draped over a stump and impaled by a sharp, bloody knife."
*Adapted from Moravian accounts of the massacre.

Ben Franklin's defense bill passed on November 26, 1755, one day after the massacre occurred. The day after that, further legislation, named the Supply Act, called for the building of forts throughout Pennsylvania.

We heard reports that Susanna, the captured woman from the Moravian Mission at Mahoney, was taken to Tioga by the Indians and eventually killed there. Her husband Martin, though he did not die immediately after being shot, had been found dead in the woods. George Schweigert's mutilated and bullet riddled body was guarded faithfully by his dog. George and Susanna Partsch, along with Peter Worbass and Joseph Sturgis survived the attack, as did Joachim Senseman. We heard that Susanna Partsch had survived the night by hiding in the hollow of a tree.

The war crept ever closer to home and eventually as we had all feared, claimed one of our own. A Moravian brother in Christ known to our Donegal congregation, Franz Albert, a shoemaker, was savagely murdered and scalped by Indians near the Swatara Creek as he plowed a field in June of 1756. Showing no mercy, the enemy also killed the man who worked beside him, along with two other young men, ages seventeen and eighteen. Their horses were shot as well.

These days, children were becoming orphans before they were even born. Shaking my head in pity, I closed my eyes to the scene before me as Franz Albert's widow held tightly to baby Martha during the baptismal ceremony. Surely this was not how Mrs. Albert had imagined this August day, a day that was to be filled with hope and promise.

As if on cue, Katharina reached for my hand and placed it discretely on her abdomen. The baby within her womb kicked me, a needless reminder of his presence there, a notice that this earthy life was so tenuous, so precious. I thanked the Lamb for the life-giving blood that flowed through Katharina's body to be used in nurturing our unborn child and I thanked the Lamb for spilling His own blood for my sake, to bring me new life in Him.

Our ministers spoke of blood so often. I dreamed of blood. Sometimes it was the blood of Jesus. Sometimes it was the blood of Gnaddenhuten. Sometimes it was the blood of my son Abraham.

Chapter 2

1757

"'m afraid there's nothing I can do," he said, so matter-of-factly. The doctor had finally made it to the cabin, only to deliver the words I felt were inevitable. The Moravian minister had administered bleeding after bleeding, trying to rid me of fever. He told me that he was experienced using this method on countless others and in fact, at one time, the Indian population relied so heavily upon his treatments that he had to limit its use among the tribes. But despite his past success with bleedings, I had only grown increasingly feeble as the weeks passed.

Katharina administered her best care and remedies, but the fever continued and I knew she was frustrated and saddened with my attitude when I explained to her that I sensed my time to meet the Lamb was near. To her, this imminent conclusion of my life seemed so abrupt; so unexpected. Often I heard her pray for God to grant me more time upon the earth. But for me, as the days passed and my suffering persisted, my yearning to meet Jesus became an obsession. When the doctor made the final declaration, I smiled knowingly, already at peace with the future.

"Death is our future, my dear Kat, not the end. I will journey to my heavenly home and wait for you there, near my Savior's side." I consoled her and continued weakly, "Even if the world goes to war, fear not darling, for we find everlasting protection in the Lamb's embrace. He will never let us go…No matter what."

Though I did not regret my wish to enter glory, I did experience grief over the pain it would cause my family. My illness had taken a toll on Katharina as she tended to me. Combined with caring for baby Phillip, who was not yet one year old, she was exhausted. I saw her try to don a happier composure as a light rap came at the door. She opened the entry to Brother Beck who stood with hat in hand, looking rather embarrassed to be visiting at such an early hour.

"Excuse me for the surprise visit, Sister Kapp. I just felt a burden upon my heart to come visit Johannes this morning, and this was the only time I had."

"Oh Brother Beck," she reassured, "You know you are always welcome. Morning, noon or night! I was just getting breakfast around for the children. Would you care for something to eat?"

"Ah, Mrs. Kapp. You remind me of your mother," he smiled but shook his head and continued. "But, no ma'am. I won't be bothering you with that. I'm planning on a full day of harvesting and Mrs. Beck filled me up this morning before I set out. Thank you for the offer though."

Brother Beck made his way to my bedside and pulled up a chair. I shifted and opened my eyes, peering at my friend through gaunt sockets. I always worried that my wasted appearance must be hard for Katharina and the children to handle, but when I told her of my concern she would lovingly hold my face in her hands and assure me that an undeniable spark continued to light my eyes despite the suffering.

"And still you manage to smile, Johannes," she would say to me, with a tone of wonder. "How I love your smile." My love for her arrested my heart, but I turned my attention to the visitor.

"It is good of you to come here, Brother," I said in a debilitated voice, as I slowly reached out to hold the man's hand in welcome.

"You have been close in my prayers, Johannes," consoled the man, concern evident in his demeanor. "How are you, my friend?"

"I would greatly prefer to lie," I responded. Brother Beck looked at me in question, as it was obvious that I was lying upon my bed, and had been there for quite some time. Katharina knew what I meant. It had become my mantra.

218

"I'm sorry. I don't understand," apologized Brother Beck. "Would you like me to help you move to a new position perhaps? Can I try to make you more comfortable?"

I felt the old, easy smile creep back into its rightful place upon my emaciated face. I knew that even after suffering a month of fever, somehow the look of my boyhood charm must be shining through. Now however, I hoped it was tempered with the wisdom of a courageous, confident man. "I wish to lie within the wound of Jesus' side," I responded.

Brother Beck now nodded in understanding. "Yes, Brother Johannes. It is a place of rest and refuge."

I closed my eyes, and I knew that Brother Beck thought I had fallen back to sleep. But instead of slumbering, I quietly began to sing a familiar hymn. "*Ach, mein Lammlein! Komm doch bald und hohle mich.*" (Ah, my lamb, come quickly, do, and fetch me away."

I watched as Katharina opened the door yet again to visitors on October 18, 1757. My dear brother-n-law John and good friend Peter Schneider stood with sober and crestfallen faces. I had sent for them earlier in the day.

"It is time then?" asked John, enveloping my wife in a hug of brotherly concern. Tears streamed down Katharina's face as she nodded her head yes, against his rough coat. The two men walked quietly to my bed and composed themselves the best they could before sitting down.

"I guess this is the best thing to do," said Peter in a hushed tone to John. "But let us pray he doesn't have need of it any time soon. Perhaps he will recover yet," he hoped.

I startled the men, who did not know I was awake and I tried to smile peacefully, though I was in a great deal of pain. "Peter, I will not recover. Do not speak to me about it." My words were not harsh, but matter of fact. More gently, to spare the feelings of my friend and brother-in-law, I said, "I am glad and hope to go quickly to my Savior."

Opening their eyes to the truth of my condition, both men roughly wiped away tears. Tears mingled with ink as each signed their name to the document. John picked up the will and read what was written: *"IN THE NAME OF GOD AMEN. That I John Kapp of*

219

the county of Lancaster in the province of Pennsylvania and township of Donegal yeoman being in good memory and understanding do make and declare this my last Will and Testament first and principally recommending my Immortal Spirit into the hands of my great Creator trusting in the merits of my blessed Saviour for pardon and remission of all my sins and happy admission into the region of immortal bliss and glory and as to such worldly estates wherewith it has pleased God to bless me with, I give and bequeath in manner as following. Imprimis I order that so much of my personal estate be sold by my executors herein after mentioned as will pay all my just debts and funeral expenses and further I order that the remainder of my personal estate with my real estate be given together for the full term of eighteen years for the maintaining of my small children and then to be equally divided amongst my said children and the third part and twenty pound more of all my estate I give to my loving wife Katharina for her maintenance further I order that if my executors and my wife see cause to make any seal or division afore such time of eighteen years thee shall have full power to do it. Lastly I nominate and appoint my loving wife *Katharina (nee Etters) and John Etter of the township of Donegal my executors of this my last Will and Testament in witness wherof I have hereunto set my hand and seal this 18th day of October in the year of 1757."

   As my decline continued over the next two weeks, God mercifully allowed time for me to say goodbye to friends and family. My children gathered around constantly, reading scripture and singing songs. Knowing that our parting would only be temporary brought a sense of comfort.

   As Katharina sat close to me on that November day, wind whipped through the trees outside. Nature was following its set course and did not slow in making her preparations for winter. The seasons would march on without me.

   Two months of illness had caused my once calloused hands to grow soft and weak, but as Katharina held them, she murmured through tears that she would always remember the strength, beauty and kindness they brought to her world. She said they belonged to the man who captivated her love and held it secure. Gently, she

folded those hands over my heart.   Peace enveloped me as she
kissed me one last time, releasing me to heaven, my safe retreat.

November 2, 1757

*"At midday, the dear Savior blessedly granted this wish, when his
soul abandoned its ailing house and passed over to the heart of
Jesus. His age had reached fifty-three years, eight months and one
day."*

Hymn #541:

JESUS. STILL LEAD ON
Text by Nicholas Ludwig von Zinzendorf (1721)[*62]

"1. Jesus! Still lead on,
Till our rest be won;
And although the way be cheerless,
We will follow calm and fearless;
Guide us by Thy hand
To our fatherland.

2. If the way be drear,
If the foe be near,
Let not faithless fears o'ertake us;
Let not faith and hope forsake us;
For through many a foe
To our home we go.

3. When we seek relief
From a long-felt grief,
When temptations come alluring,
Make us patient and enduring,
Show us that bright shore
Where we weep no more.

4. Jesus! Still lead on
Till our rest be won;
Heavenly Leader,
Still direct us,
Still support, console, protect us,
Till we safely stand
In our fatherland."

Johannes Kapp's Memoir

"Johannes Kapp was born in Switzerland at Münchenstein, Basil district, on 18 February 1704. His parents gave him a proper upbringing, requiring him to attend church and school regularly. They adhered to the reformed denomination.

Even in his youth he had reached a conviction that his life must change. He thereafter learned the wheelwright's craft in the city of Basil and later on, traveled in foreign places. During this period he became greatly pre-occupied with living according to the ways of the world.

He married for the first time when in his twenty-fifth year. Nine children were born to him in this marriage, seven of whom have preceded him in passing out of time. The two sons still living now belong to the Gemine in Bethlehem.

In 1740 he became a widower while journeying to Pennsylvania. Thus, his second marriage took place in 1741 in this country, indeed to the present widowed *Catharina, born Etters. Moreover, with her, God again granted him nine children. Two of these have already preceded their father (out of time), but seven are still here below.

He and his wife became spiritually awakened in 1742. Then, in 1745, when visiting in Bethlehem, he became acquainted with the Bruder Gemeine (or Congregation of the Brethren), and the gospel concerning God's power to save was made known to him, as was his condition as a poor sinner.

In the year 1749, during the Brethren's Synod in Warwik (sic), on 23 November, he was received into the Gemeine. He attained the privilege of participating with the Gemeine in the Holy Sacrament in 1751. Since that time of mercy, and even until his death, he has blissfully availed himself of the merit of Christ, indeed, as the Lord's wretched (sinner.)

A good while ago, he had expressed a fervent desire to be at home with the Lord. On 1 September of this year he fell sick with a fever, whereupon he was wholeheartedly glad that he would go quickly to the Saviour. He little wished to hear talk of recovery. Once when Br. Beck visited him during this illness he said that he would greatly prefer to lie. And when asked just where he wished to lie, he said: "I wish to lie within the wound of Jesus' side." He very often quoted the hymn stanza beginning: "Ach, mein Lammlein! Komm doch bald und hohle mich, etc." (Ah, my lamb, come quickly, do and fetch me away, etc.)

The dear Savior blessedly granted this wish on 9 November at midday, when his soul abandoned its ailing house and passed over to the heart of Jesus. His age had reached fifty-three years, eight months and one day."

NOTE: transcribed from German by Frances Cumnock. Memoir housed in the Moravian Archives at Bethlehem, Pa.

*Catharina and Katharina used interchangeably for purposes of this novel. Found documented both ways in records

December 31st, 1757

A summary of an inventory of the goods and chattels of John Kapp

Last of Donegal Township in Lancaster County
Deceased

Cash, Wearing apparel, Five books, Bible, Seven books, Wagon maker tools,….and two chains, Five sickles and two scythes,…Two grubbing hoes and three …hoes,…,…,A tan mare, A black…colt, Two red cows, A red cow and black cow, A heifer, Seven sheep, Twine mill and cutting box, a…mill and two lambs and sheers,…and wetstone, A box and …spoons, Stove, A meal box, A wool wheel and wool cards, Spinning wheels, Four bags,…, A …kettle and tea pot and dishes, Two brass kettles, Two pots, Two pans and two ladles, Seven pails and three kegs, One pewter dish and seven pewter plates, A cutting knife…,One …and half bushel, One bed and bed stead, One bed and bed stead and table, One bed and bed stead, Two bottles and a large tap and two pails, One half gallon and a pint tanckert, The improvement, One fork…

Complete inventory list located at the Lancaster Historical Society. Above translated by Jessica Kapp Green from the written script to the best of her ability

"Were it for the mere pleasure of writing a book, or the evaporative fame of authorship, the contents of this volume would have slept in the unexplored bosom of its fathers; yet there is a motive, a design, and a pleasure in the research, inasmuch as the lights and shades of antiquity may be elicited to refresh the memory of the centenarian, or enlighten the wonderings of the satchelled youth, or the full-fledged collegian.

There, is, however, in this, as there is doubtless in all communities, a portion of our race for whom oblivion would seem to have been permitted, who pass every yesterday of their existence, and that of their ancestors, as though Time had but just marked their being, and the " everlasting now" was the necessary absorbent of all that life holds dear.

'Tis well, however, for our day and its succession, that the germs of antiquity will sprout, from time to time, and bud, blossom, and bloom, under the fructifying influences of its bedewing patronage; and well, too, for history and its cravings, that there are lovers of dusty records, prone to sweep their pages, and present and compare the past with the present, by the autographic details of " the things that were."

My motive, therefore, is to gather, from the dust of oblivion, the atoms of a venerable centre, re-mould the dignity of an ancient pile, and present it, its constituents, and its successors, to the heirs and representatives of their early fathers, as well as to the antiquarian spirit of the present, or the future age.

227

$\mathcal{M}$y design is to call up the spirit of our fathers, to chasten our own waywardness, to simplify our manners, to imbue us with their faith and faithfulness..."

As written by: Abraham Ritter in History of the Moravian Church in Philadelphia*61

Author's Note

This story is based upon the lives of real people. When available, I used language similar to that found in historical records in order to portray events in the most accurate way possible. However, scenarios were added and various quotes adapted using my own wording to craft a narrative.

The feelings, actions and emotions attributed to all characters are of my own imagination, although when I discovered information describing a person I attempted to incorporate this into the story. Some negative traits attributed to characters are for entertainment value only and are not meant to defame their integrity in any way. Though plausible that folks of similar bent existed, some minor, fictitious characters (example: Mrs. Grubb, her slaves, the Philadelphia innkeeper) were invented for the story to add interest.

This book is meant to give a broad overview of what life may have been like for the Kapp family and although I have endeavored to include authentic details related to the times, this work should be classified as a work of fiction. I do not claim to be an expert genealogist, and while my research leads me to believe that the Kapp family written about in this book are very likely to be my direct ancestors, I welcome other family members to verify this for themselves before laying claim to this lineage with one hundred percent certainty. Also, although I have studied it to a great degree, I am self educated regarding the Moravian lifestyle and faith. Please feel free to contact me *at jlynngreen@yahoo.com* with any comments on the material. The Moravian Archives hold many of the original documents referenced throughout the book and primary source material is quoted with permission from the Bethlehem Moravian Archives in Bethlehem, PA.

My appreciation goes to Lauren Freed for her editing assistance. Please note that changes were made to the text after her review and any errors should be attributed to me. Thank you to all those who assisted as I researched at libraries, museums and archives and to those who have done much work before me and published their documents. I also express gratitude to my family. Thank you to my mother, for continuing encouragement as I worked to complete this project. And thank you to my father, who has inspired me with his belief in this book's potential. To Ben, I appreciate that you took time to read it! Chad, thank you for allowing me the opportunity to pursue my dreams and for supporting me in the beliefs I hold dear. I love you. Leigha, thank you for all of your good suggestions, especially about the formatting changes. Ally, thank you for being one of the first people to read my book! Girls, you have been great blessings to me and I love you both. May God fill your lives with much joy and abundant love.

It is my hope that Johannes and Katharina would find satisfaction in knowing that a rendition of their story and an accounting of their faith have been passed along to their descendents and others who may find value in it.

🌼 Please visit:
Pinterest.com/aSafeRetreat
for images and boards related to topics of interest in this novel and
Facebook.com/aSafeRetreat
for further discussion.

Sources:

1.*http://www.usgwarchives.net/pa/1pa/1picts/frontierforts/ff3.html*
(Information related scalping of Franz Albert, Jacob Haendsche,
Frederick Weiser and John George Miess.)

2.*http://freepages.genealogy.rootsweb.ancestry.com/~mickey/1751
betheltaxpg.html ("Two men, Franz Albert and Jacob Haendsche, and two lads,
Frederick Weiser and John George Miess, were ploughing in the field of one
Fischer, were surprised, murdered and scalped by the Indians, as appears, from an
extract taken from the Schwatarer Kirchen Buch: From the same book, it appears
Franz Albert was born at Deux-Ponts, July 20, 1719-he was a shoemaker by
profession, formerly a member of the Reformed Church. J. Haendsche was a
mason by trade, also formerly a member of the Reformed Church. Weiser was
born May 21, 1740, and Miess, September 28, 1739.")

3.* http://www.gw.org/Btl/Btl.pdf (Account of Massacre of
Moravian Missionaries at Gnadenhutten.)

4. http://www.biographi.ca/EN/ShowBio.asp?BioId=35792
(Information related to Swantana, Conrad Weiser and Madam
Montour.)

5.Elizabethtown: The First Three Centuries by Richard K.
MacMaster. The Elizabethtown Historical Society. Elizabethtown,
Pennsylvania. (Information related to Lancaster County, and
especially Thomas Harris.)

6.http://www.archive.org/stream/earlyhistoryofch00reic/earlyhistory
ofch00reic_djvu.txt (Account of Andrew Eschenbach)

7. http://www.usgwarchives.net/pa/1pa/1picts/frontierforts/ff3.html
("In Rupp's History of Berks and Lebanon Counties, p. 364, the following appears:
Peter Heydrich, who emigrated from Germany and located previous to 1738, about
three-fourths of a mile due north from this place it appears, owned the place on
which Fort Smith was erected. My informant says, he knows that a fort had been
erected on his grandfather's farm, to which in great emergencies the neighbors fled
for safety, etc.")

8. http://moravians.org/wordpress/?page ID=490 (Life and Letters of the Rev.
John Philip Boehm, Founder of the reformed church in Pennsylvania, 168-1749

9.
http://archive.org/stream/authentichistory00zieg/authentichistory00zi
eg_djvu.txt

10. www.rcus.olivetree.com (Account of Mr. Schlatter – missionary. He met with Jacot Lischy who had been "Fraternizing with the Moravians.")

11.http://www.donegaltownshipriflemen.org/usa/militiahistory.htm (Information about Donegal Township Militia)

12.* http://www.gw.org/Btl/Btl.pdf (Behold the Lamb: The Story of the Moravian Church by Peter Hoover)

13. "THE VARNADO GENEALOGIST", VOLUME 4, NUMBER 3, FALL 1983
Hutto Family Research by A.D. Hutto (Related to the Journey of the ship Oliver in 1735.)

14. Ushistory.org
15. http://mysite.verizon.net/handworn/water.html (No longer available online)
16. Autobiography of Benjamin Franklin
17. Pennsylvania Germans, A Persistent Minority by William T. Parsons
Collegeville, PA: Chestnut Books, 1985. pp 47-60.]

---

18. foodtimeline.org/foodcolonial.html#colonialmealtimes (A Cooking Legacy, Virginia T. Elverson and Mary Ann McLanahan [Walker & Company:New York] 1975 (p. 14) (Information related to colonial food.)

19. "Passage To America, 1750," EyeWitness to History, www.eyewitnesstohistory.com (2000)
20. Lancaster County Pennsylvania Church Records of the 18th Century: Volume 4 by F. Edward Wright
21. http://dgmweb.net/genealogy/FGS/K/KappJohannes-JudithMassmuenster-KatharinaEtter.shtml
   A. Gerber. 1925. "Lists of Swiss Emigrants from the Canton of Basel, 1734-94." Chap. VII, pp. 89-206 in Albert Bernhardt Faust & Gaius Marcus Brumbaugh, eds. *Lists of Swiss Emigrants in the Eighteenth*

Century to the American Colonies. National Genealogical Soc., Washington, DC (Broderbund CD-267):

B.   Ralph Beaver Strassburger (William John Hinke, ed.). 1934. *Pennsylvania German Pioneers: a Publication of the Original Lists of Arrivals in the Port of Philadelphia from 1727 to 1808.* 2 vols. Norristown, PA (reprinted 1966ff by Genealogical Publ. Co., Baltimore, MD; Broderbund CD-267):

C.   LDS. *Family Search: Internet Genealogy Service: IGI - International Genealogical Index* (online at FamilySearch.org).

22.*http://www.archive.org/stream/earlyhistoryofch00reic/earlyhisto ryofch00reic_djvu.tx (The Early History of the Church of the United Brethren (Unitas Fratrum) Commonly called Moravians in North America A.D. 1734-1748 by the Rev. Levin Theodore Reichel Published by the Moravian Historical Society 1888.

23.Moravian Women's Memoirs: Their Related Lives, 1750-1820 Translated and with and Introduction by Katherine M. Faull

24.http://findarticles.com/p/articles/mi_7051/is_1998_Spring/ai_n28 723999/?tag=content;col1

25.http://www.thefreelibrary.com/The+cultural+significance+of+bre astfeeding+and+infant+care+in+early...-a016350977 (Information about Infant care during the colonial period)

26.http://www.departments.bucknell.edu/environmental_center/sunb ury/website/Shikellamy.shtml(Information related to Shikellamy)

27.http://www.historicwilliamsport.com (Information related to Madame Montour)
28.http://www.kellscraft.com/OldPhiladelphia/OldPhiladelphiaCh01. html (Facing the Stormy Atlantic)
29.History of York County, Illustrated 1886 by John Gibson, Historical Editor

30. freebase.com (information related to *Conrad Weiser)*

31.http://www.founderspatriots.org/articles/louisbourg.htm

32.The Colonial Architecture of Philadelphia by: Frank Cousins, Phil Madison Riley

33. http://www.usgwarchives.org/pa/1pa/paarchivesseries/series2/vol2/pass2-13.html
 (names of men in the volunteer Association in 1747-thomas harris.)

34.http://www.moravianseminary.edu/Freeman/MZTheology/Aspects.pdf
+Vol. 5: Out of the Wilderness

35. A History of the Hamlet of Bethel in the Town of Pine Plains, New York
By: Newton Duel, Elizabeth Klare, James Mara, Helen Netter, Dyan Wapnick 1996

36.http://www.archive.org/stream/attitudeofeurope00brit/attitudeofeurope00brit_djvu.txt THE ATTITUDE OF EUROPEAN STATES TOWARD EMIGRATION TO THE AMERICAN COLONIES AND THE UNITED STATES, 1607-1820

A PART OF A DISSERTATION SUBMITTED TO
THE FACULTY OF THE DIVISION OF THE
SOCIAL SCIENCES IN CANDIDACY FOR THE
DEGREE OF DOCTOR OF PHILOSOPHY

DEPARTMENT OF HISTORY
1937 By
JOHN DUNCAN BRITE

37.Faust, Lists ^ II, 101-02. (Details about Jacob Joner – Swiss agent)

38.http://www.philaprintshop.com/frchintx.html (Information about the French and Indian War.)

39. http://www.earlyamerica.com/review/spring97/ (How Newspapers covered the French and Indian War.)

40. mohicanpress.com

41. http://www.nationalcenter.org/Braddock'sDefeat.html
(Braddock's Defeat by George Washington July 18, 1755)

42. http://www.muttenzdescendants.org/exhibits/adventure/story_01.
htm (Details about the voyage aboard the Friendship)

43. http://www.ephrataministries.org/remnant-2012-11-tschoop.a5w
(Information related to Tschoop and conversion of Indians)

44. http://en.wikipedia.org/wiki/Mahican (Information about the
Mahican/Mohican Indians)

45. http://www.rootsweb.ancestry.com/~nylnphs/V5/5.htm
(Accounts related to the Shekomeko Indians)

46.
http://archive.org/stream/historicalpapersv22lanc/historicalpapersv2
2lanc_djvu.txt (Christian Henry Rauch diary entry)

47. http://www.leveillee.net/ancestry/andrewm.htm (Zinzendorf's
account of Andrew Montour)

48.
http://www.spanishhill.com/whatis/Bressler_Gallery/Bressler_Galler
y.shtml (Information and images related to Madame Montour)

49. PA German Pioneer Life by William T. Parsons 1985.

50. The Evangelical and Reformed Historical Society
(www.erhs.info)

51. Lancaster County Historical Society
    230 North President Avenue
    Lancaster, PA 17603

(Copy of Will of Johannes Kapp 1757, Copy of Memoirs of Margaret Kapp, Copy of Diagram of Donegal Moravian cemetery (original stored at the Moravian Archives in Bethlehem, PA, Copy of Inventory of Johannes Kapp 1757, Inventory of John Etter 1767

52. Elizabethtown Herald Article, January 22, 1908: (Account of Donegal Moravian church and members.)

53. Guide to Genealogical and Historical Research in Pennsylvania by Floyd G. Hoenstine

54. Everyday Life in Colonial American by Louis B. Wright

55. Notebook of a Colonial Clergyman by Henry Melchior Muhlenberg edited by Tappert and Doberstein

56. Full Sail for Philadelphia: The Etter Family Reunited – Lela Hultquist Booth and Joan Magee

57. Seibert Library and Resource Center - Winters Heritage House – Elizabethtown, PA

58. Landis Valley Museum- Lancaster, PA

59. Moravian Archives – Bethlehem, PA

60. At the crossroads: Indians and Empires on a Mid-Atlantic Frontier, by Jane T. Merritt

61. History of the Moravian Church in Philadelphia (Fac Smule) IX Its Foundation in 1742 to the present time. By Abraham Ritter. (http://www.archive.org/stream/historyofmoravia00ritt/historyofmor avia00ritt_djvu.txt)
62. The Liturgy and the Offices of Worship and Hymns of the American Province of the Unitas Fratrum or The Moravian Church. Bethlehem, 1908. (Hymn 541. Jesus. Still Lead On.)

63.http://www.colonialwilliamsburg.org/history/clothing/men/mglos sary.cfm (descriptions of men's colonial attire.)

64. **Credit:** Benjamin Franklin, The Autobiography of Benjamin Franklin, (Chicago: The Lakeside Press, 1915), 207-10.

65. http://military.wikia.com/wiki/Battles_of_Villmergen
66. http://www.zum.de/whkmla/military/17cen/villmergen1656.html

67. http://www.christianity-guide.com/christianity/reformation_in_switzerland.htm

68. http://petrapeters.ch/2014/10/05/on-the-road-discovering-treasures-around-basel-to-the-southeast-vi-castles/

69. http://www.muttenzdescendants.org/exhibits/muttenzhistory/ancient.htm

70. http://www.witheridge-historical-archive.com/wheelwright.htm (Info related to trade of wagon maker)

71. http://www.moench.ch/rebbau/rebbaugeschichte/ (Information about the Münchenstein wine history)

72. http://fish.mongabay.com/data/Switzerland.htm (Freshwater fish of Switzerland)

73. http://www.muenchenstein.ch/de/portrait/portraituebersicht/ (Münchenstein website)

74. http://en.wikipedia.org/wiki/M%C3%BCnch_(family_lineage) (Munch family lineage)

75. http://us.wow.com/wiki/Vogt_(Switzerland) (bailiff's of Switzerland)

76. http://homepages.rootsweb.ancestry.com/~kinofjar/ahnentafel/reports/banga/AT01_001.HTML#P344 (Muttenz link)

77. http://colonialsense.com/Society-Lifestyle/Signs_of_the_Times/Conestoga_Wagon/Wagon_Makers.php
(Lancaster County)

78. *http://www.digplanet.com/wiki/Guild* (Guilds)

79. *http://www.muttenz.ch/de/portrait/fotoalbum/welcome.php?action=showgallery&galid=5475&arcid=0* (Muttenz official website- great pictures)

80. *http://de.academic.ru/dic.nsf/dewiki/990352* (Münchenstein buildings)

81. *http://www.inyourpocket.com/Switzerland/Zurich/Zurichs-guilds:-of-mighty-men-and-merrymaking_73037f* (guilds)

82. *http://www.londonlives.org/static/IA.jsp* (apprenticeship indenture)

83. *http://en.wikipedia.org/wiki/Journeyman* (journeymen)

84. *http://maritime-connector.com/wiki/history/* (18th century ships)

85. *http://en.wikipedia.org/wiki/Arlequin_poli_par_l%27amour* (French Play)

86. *http://en.wikipedia.org/wiki/Parterre_(theater_audience)* (18th Century French theater)

87. *http://www.swissmennonite.org/history/palatinate.html* (Swiss Mennonite)

88. *http://en.wikipedia.org/wiki/Swiss_Mennonite_Conference* (Swiss Mennonite)

89. *http://en.wikipedia.org/wiki/Perkeo_of_Heidelberg* (Perkeo)

90. *http://www.gameo.org/index.php?title=Farming_Among_Mennonites_in_South_Germany* (Mennonite Farming)

91. *http://en.wikipedia.org/wiki/Age_of_Enlightenment*

92. http://www.customwagons.com/wagon_wheels_information/index.html (Wagons)

93. http://lostcrafts.com/Carriage-Building/makingwagonwheels.html (Wagons)

94. http://www.history.org/Almanack/life/trades/tradewhe.cfm (Wagons)

95. http://en.wikipedia.org/wiki/Antonio_Vivaldi

96. http://en.wikipedia.org/wiki/Grand_Tour (Grand Tour)

97. http://en.wikipedia.org/wiki/Uffizi (Florence Museum)

98. http://www.angelfire.com/journal2/zubler/trnsltn.htm (untervogt)

99. http://wc.rootsweb.ancestry.com/cgi-bin/igm.cgi?op=GET&db=ancestralsleuth2&id=I315 (Account of plotting to leave Switzerland)

100. http://wc.rootsweb.ancestry.com/cgi-bin/igm.cgi?op=GET&db=cvar&id=I1451 (Account of plotting to leave Switzerland)

101. http://wc.rootsweb.ancestry.com/cgi-bin/igm.cgi?op=GET&db=mshobe&id=I95 (Account of plotting to leave Switzerland and the journey of Antoni Reiger.)

102. http://timnoonan.com.au/resources/health-and-wellbeing/jasmine-story-aromatherapy/

103. https://suite.io/sharon-falsetto/4cx82e8 (French Perfume)

104. http://thehistoryofthehairsworld.com/hair_18th_century.html (history of hair)

105. http://usslave.blogspot.com/2012/07/gottlieb-mittelberger-journey-to.html (Account of ship journey to Pennsylvania in 1750)

106.
http://nationalhumanitiescenter.org/pds/becomingamer/growth/text9/pennsylvaniaimmigrant.pdf *(Account of Pennsylvania in 1750 and 1756)*

107.
http://hsp.org/sites/default/files/legacy_files/migrated/mittelberger.pdf *Gottlieb Mittelberger's Journey- account of travel down the Rhine River)*

108.
http://books.google.com/books?id=ddwRAAAAIAAJ&printsec=frontcover&source=gbs_ge_summary_r&cad=0#v=onepage&q&f=false *(Abraham Ritter's Account of the Moravian Church in Philadelphia and this books Preface as written word for word by Abraham Ritter.)*

109. http://articles.mcall.com/1988-10-30/news/2666217_1_quaker-faction-william-allen *(Philadelphia elections 1742)*

About the Author

Jessica Kapp Green was born and raised in rural Northeastern Pennsylvania. As a young woman she earned a Bachelor of Science Degree in Nursing from Pensacola Christian College and soon after began working as a Registered Nurse. For several years she resided in Mount Joy, PA, only a short distance from the land once owned by Johannes Kapp. She now makes her home in Chester County, PA with her wonderful husband and two lovely daughters.

www.ingramcontent.com/pod-product-compliance
Lightning Source LLC
Chambersburg PA
CBHW020603180626
46810CB00007B/2627